LOVE
and War
VOLUME ONE

CHARISSE SPIERS

Cover Art © Clarise Tan
Cover Image © FuriousFotog
Interier Title Image © Darren Birks
Edited & Formatted by Nancy Henderson

LOVE IS AN UNTAMED FORCE. WHEN WE TRY TO CONTROL IT, IT DESTROYS US. WHEN WE TRY TO IMPRISON IT, IT ENSLAVES US. WHEN WE TRY TO UNDERSTAND IT, IT LEAVES US FEELING LOST AND CONFUSED.

— Paulo Coelho

PROLOGUE

Detta

JUNE . . .

I pull my old, black, Volkswagen Beetle into the parking lot of *Inked aKross the Skin* and park, killing the engine instantly. To some, this car would be classified as an antique, but to me, not so much. Yeah, this car is nothing fancy and old as shit, but it's paid for and still runs . . . most of the time. It's also all I can afford. I worked my ass off for it senior year of high school, literally, although, it was a lot newer back then—at least to me.

Growing up and paying rent and shit is harder than I wish it was, taking most of what I make; even on weekends I feel like I make bank at the bar. Bartenders are a dime a dozen, especially in a large city like Atlanta, and we all fight for weekend shifts.

City living is much higher than the country, and my one-bedroom apartment isn't exactly budget-friendly, so there definitely isn't money left over for a car note when you count on tips as your main source of income. Truth be told, this old car is on its last leg, or for better terminology, wheel, but unless a miracle happens I'm stuck with it. It's either that or pick up a second job, in which I'm considering if I don't get this gig. I want it so bad that I can taste it. Tattooing is what I'm made for. I know it. I just need someone to give me a shot.

And I'm trying my damnedest not to go back *there*, even though I know he'd hire me back in a heartbeat, but I've lost too much over it; which is why I spent the last of my savings years ago for bartending classes. A girl like me doesn't have opportunities for Harvard or Yale. Even a four-year-university is out of my reach. I'm not going to say I'm dumb, but I was lucky to graduate with a high school diploma. School never was my thing. It's boring. I'll die from hard, laborious work before I go back.

That particular job is hard not to consider, though, because it's damn good money on busy nights, and a hell of a lot easier to stack the cash than this is going to be, should I get the job. I can't deny that. My pride is dreading this more than I ever did with that. Reputation means nothing on having a soft cushion in the bank. I can live with the slutty accusations more so than I can live feeling like a complete failure.

I highly doubt being an apprentice at a tattoo parlor is going to cover even half of the bills, and I'm not sure if I'll be able to work enough at the bar to make what I do currently; or what it takes to pay my bills and survive. Unlike my best friend Lux, I pride myself on my independence. I've never been able to take handouts, no matter where they come from. I understand her need for a *sugar daddy* to acquire what she's never had, but it's a way of life I'll never adopt, no matter how hard it becomes for me. So, here I stand, in the parking lot of the tattoo shop where I received the most recent work of art still healing on my body.

Tattoo . . . Kross.

Out of all the tattoos that I've gotten in my adulthood—and there are many—that was by far the most memorable. His hands on my body; covered in latex . . . The pain of the needle piercing the skin, followed by the smearing of ink. I sigh, following through with a shiver even though it's warm outside, making it even hotter in this car. Every time his biceps and forearms flexed from permanently marking my skin, hunched over my body, the muscles between my legs convulsed in need. It was an experience I've never known. It has to be the lack of sex talking.

I stare at the glass front door, the name embedding into my thoughts, readying my mind to walk inside. Yep. This is most likely financial suicide, but it's a risk I'm willing to take. "Suck it up, buttercup. You'll do what you have to do to make this work."

I take a deep breath, trying to even out my breathing. My hands are shaking. I'm so damn nervous I don't want to get out of this car. I'm not a nervous person. This interview could change my life, though. I just hope I don't fuck it up. So far I've been pretty good at doing just that in my life.

I pinch the bridge of my nose, trying to release some of this nervous energy. Seconds pass. I grab my purse and my keys, before pushing my door open. It makes a sound as it opens: metal against metal. I step out and shove the lock down, shutting it back roughly to ensure it catches. The parking lot looks pretty empty to only be a quarter before twelve.

"Don't be a little girl. You're stalling," I mumble to myself. My Converse shoes start to trudge forward, pulling me toward the same door I entered last night with Lux. I'm reminded, yet again, of that night with each movement of the sensitive, freshly tattooed skin. I do believe this one is my favorite to date. I'm just not sure if it's the design or the artist I favor so much. I can still feel his touch lingering, as if his hand never left. I've never felt like I was on fire by only contact, but every place he touched felt like it was being singed and burning to ash. I kept waiting for that putrid smell of burnt skin to come, but it never did.

I open the door. It looks exactly the same—navy blue walls showcasing the finest framed work under spotlight, and a hell of a lot of pink neon—including the blonde behind the counter that looks completely out of place. I shouldn't dislike her, but for some reason I do. She's beautiful, friendly, and most likely everything I'm not; at least not to the average person. She looks like a happy person. You know, the ones us moody people despise because they're fucking chirpy every waking minute of the day. She has flawless skin to match, in color and texture, a beautiful body, and her hair is the perfect shade of blonde.

I'm staring.

I wonder if he's fucking her . . .

I bite my tongue hard, attempting to inflict as much pain as possible for that thought that is none of my business. Come to think of it, looking at her, I'm not sure I'm even dressed appropriately for an interview. When I got dressed my thought was: *what would Kat Von D wear?* What I never processed was that this is the most unorthodox tattoo shop I've ever seen; yet its reputation is the most immaculate. It's not punk or grunge, not anything that I'm into really. It's—my nose crinkles—professional, and what the fuck is it with all the damn neon? Don't get me wrong. I favor the art of neon lighting myself, and even have a little of it at my apartment, but this is extreme.

I look down at myself. Maybe cut off denim shorts and a crop top wasn't the proper way to dress for a professional interview no matter what the job title. Fuck my life. I'm already starting off on the wrong foot.

"Delta, right?" The blonde pulls me from my thoughts, the place I've been lost in without even knowing. Maybe if she thinks I'm emo it'll never faze her as weird. She looks like a girl that doesn't know what that truly is anyway. A lot of people mistake us dark in nature as 'emo', like we're all one in the same.

I look at her; only this time my brain is working like a normal human being. She has a rather large smile spread across her face, standing and pulling her purse on her shoulder. "Um, yes. I had an appointment with Mr. Brannon at noon. Cassie, wasn't it?"

"That's me." She laughs. "Oh. Word of advice from someone that's already been down that road . . . Don't call him that to his face unless you want an asshole comment in return. He's full of them, and he hates it." *Funny, he didn't seem like an asshole last night . . .* "He's waiting in the studio for you. I'm headed out to lunch. Had to wait on you first to lock up." She pushes her chair underneath the neat and orderly desk and rounds the counter with a set of keys in her hand. "If you're gone when I return at two then maybe I'll see you around."

Two? Damn, that's a long lunch break.

She walks past me without stopping. "Wait . . ." She stops. "Does someone cover you for lunch?"

She winks. "Shop closes from twelve to two for lunch. Longer night hours makes for weird schedules. Last night was just an early night for all of the guys. Some famous artist in town or tattoo event. I'm a little hazy on the details. Not part of my job description, you know. The boss makes them stay up to date on new trends in the inked world. Plus, *Mr. Brannon* never meets with applicants during business hours." She takes a breath. "I'm being a Chatty Cathy. The result of working with all men I guess. Being down here away from the action can do that to you. Limited human contact and all. Good luck, Delta. It'd be nice to have another woman around here. I'm a little outnumbered."

She walks out the door and closes it, before shoving the key into the lock and turning it, locking us in . . . him and me. This isn't awkward at all. Not.

My adrenaline spikes to an all-time high, my nerves shooting off like Roman Candles. I look toward the closed door on the wall, trying to get myself together before I go up there. I need a fucking cigarette or I'm going to hurl. Maybe I should chew a piece of gum. Would that be rude?

Nausea sets in. I start fanning myself with my hand. I stop breathing. "Are you coming or are you going to stand here in the fucking lobby all day?"

Warm air tickles my neck. *Shit . . .*

"I was just trying to prepare myself."

"For what?"

"The interview."

"There isn't anything to prepare for. You either have what it takes or you don't. I'm a cut and dry kind of guy. I do not teach the unteachable. I only give those with wings a place to fly. Got it?"

Oh and that makes me feel so much better . . .

"Sorry," I whisper. "I'm ready, Mr. Brannon."

Fuck.

His hand snakes around my waist, careful not to migrate to or touch the sensitive skin from the fresh tattoo. He flattens his palm against my stomach, causing chill bumps to emerge. The rapid fluctuation of my abdomen from my increased breathing rate is giving my nervousness away. "My name is Kross. Use it." He slams me against his front, the calluses on his hand brushing against my skin. "I'm not a doctor, I'm not a lawyer, and I'm not a businessman. I sure as hell am not old enough in comparison to you to be a mister. Step forward."

He drops his hand, no longer touching me. If I didn't want this job so bad I'd tell him to fuck off. Arrogant asshole. Who the hell does he think he is? Kross fucking Brannon that's who; the God of ink. I don't suppose you get the kind of reputation he has by being a nice guy. He may have me at a disadvantage right now, but he will soon learn who the fuck Delta Rohr is. Right now, though, I need to get my foot in the door. It's not that easy to find someone to mentor you and take on an apprentice.

I do as he says and walk toward the door. "How did you even get down here? I thought you were upstairs."

"I'm everywhere."

I roll my eyes even though he can't see me. What a douche thing to say. It makes me want to gag. I don't care how hot he is. He reaches around me to grab the doorknob and pulls open the door, revealing the staircase to the upper floor. I climb them one by one, quickly, to create some space between us. I hear a dry laugh behind me as I reach the top step and continue into the studio.

I turn around and place my hands on my hips, slightly paranoid. It's not time for my period or anything. I second-guess myself and discretely brush my hands down the back of my shorts as if they are wrinkled or out of place. "What's so funny?"

"Do I make you uncomfortable when we're alone?"

"No. Why would you make me uncomfortable?"

"Because I usually have that effect on people. That and you looked like you were about to trip over your own two feet to get up the stairs before me."

This could be a test for respect. You need this fucking job.

I put on my best Georgia girl smile and dramatically sway from side-to-side. "I'm peachy," I say sarcastically in humor. "Just nervous about this interview, sir, like any normal person would be. Where do you want me?"

He walks toward me slowly, his eyes burning into mine. My skin elevates in temperature. It's getting a little hot in here. The nerves have got to go. He stops when he reaches me. "First question: why do you want to be a tattoo artist?"

His tone is more serious than before, catching me off guard. "Are you serious?"

"Do I look like I'm joking? You have one shot to sell yourself to me for part one—the verbal interview. You pass, you move on to part two—physical. It's pretty simple. My time is limited and valuable. If you don't impress me you're out the door and I move on to someone else. Everyone is replaceable."

"Right. Sorry." I pause, thinking of the best possible answer. I'm at a loss for words here. No one has ever asked me why. The fact that I've always just wanted to with everything that I am has been good enough for me.

Honey brown eyes stare back at me. It's unfortunate that he's so sexy. It's easier to consider working for someone that's unattractive. I don't even know where he's originally from, but I've heard of him, hence why I booked an appointment the second I heard he was opening a shop in Atlanta months ago. I wanted to know if the rumors were true. From what I can tell they are. He's hard, and not in the sense that a girl would normally be referring to a man.

My smart-ass personality is not going to get me this job. There is only one thing that will accurately answer this question, and that is to let my guard down for a few moments and let him see the real me, the one I hide. The girl that would do anything for this opportunity. I straighten my posture and look at him, trying to lay down my pride. I really look at him, in the eyes, unlike last night when he was touching my body while he permanently branded it in black, white, and pink, shading it perfectly where needed.

His hair is the darkest shade of blond, almost brown, and shaved short all over except the top where it falls slightly longer. His face is in the beginning phase of stubble, outlining his plump lips that I can imagine feels amazing against another pair. His earrings only enhance his face, showing his ears are gauged in size, but just barely, and his demeanor remains serious, giving him mystery. I can imagine this broody look he carries is the sexiest one he owns. I'm not sure he'd hold the same sex appeal with a huge, cheesy grin. He's a sexy man. That is a truth I can't deny, and that's what makes this situation harder . . . but this is so much more important than some hot guy I barely know, so I'm shutting down my thoughts or else I'll falter all over my words just from the sight of him.

My eyes travel from his lips back to his eyes, locking into place. I hook my thumbs behind the front waistband of my shorts, giving them a prop to avoid an awkward stance, before going for the introduction I couldn't muster last night. "I'm Delta Rohr, the girl that's going to be one of the best in a man's world. Ink is my life. I wear my portfolio on my body. I'm an artist; only I want my canvas to be skin. I want my artwork to be worn. The thing is, I've wanted an opportunity like this for a long time, and I'll give up anything to get it, but I need the tools to get there. I need the best fucking mentor there is. I need you, Kross."

He remains standing there, staring at me while my intestines start twisting into knots, saying nothing at all. Maybe my answer wasn't adequate enough. I've never been good under pressure. I'm not sure if I should say anything else or leave it at that.

His stance finally breaks and his arms rise and fold over his head, his hands gripping the back collar of his shirt. He pulls it over his head, baring his torso a few inches at a time until it's completely off. "Oh hell."

His body looks better without clothes than with. He obviously works out, his chiseled form confirming it. I would love to know his body fat percentage . . . Let's not forget the normally covered ink spread across his chest and running down both arms. The lower part of his sleeves and the ink that peeks out of his collar, running up part of his neck, is the only thing I've noticed until now. Now that he's standing here shirtless . . . He tosses the shirt over his shoulder, freeing up his hands.

I finally swallow my drool and the words come to me. "What are you doing?"

I immediately notice the silver, square, belt buckle in a dull metal finish, cut out to form a raised skull and crossbones in the center: my favorite emblem, and the masculine opposite to mine. That exact symbol is also what he tattooed on my body last night at my request, complete with a pink hair bow.

The black elastic band of his briefs is peeking out of the waistband of his jeans. I want to rub my hands up and down his body . . . which would be completely inappropriate right now. *Get your shit together, girl.*

He works to unbuckle his belt, letting each end hang, before going back for the button. He pops it through the slit of the faded wash denim and then slides down the zipper, revealing the royal blue underwear hugging his hips. My eyes widen the closer they get to his . . . "Do it, do it."

"What?" His deep, broody voice interrupts my thoughts.

"I didn't say anything."

One single brow peaks. His eyes dip briefly as he stares at me, like he was going to narrow them and then stopped himself. "I'm not deaf. Even whispers can be heard. I could repeat it if you'd like." I don't like his sarcasm. "What is it that you want me to do?"

My mouth falls. I thought I was chanting that in my head. Can I make myself look any more like a Psych patient today? God, but look at him. Would anyone really blame me? Who wouldn't want to lick his tattoos?

I'm doing it again. Maybe I should just walk away and pretend none of this ever happened, go drown myself at the bar, and go sleep for like three days.

"Kross, what are you doing?" I ask again, needing an answer. My heart is beating faster with each movement he makes.

"Starting part two."

"Which is?" I'm becoming nervous again. Is he just using me for sex? Dammit, I feel so stupid; not that he would have been the worst person to use my body. *Stop it.* I actually thought this was a real interview. I should have known someone like him wouldn't take on an amateur. The whole time it was just a setup.

"Letting you tattoo me."

I regain focus. "Say what?"

"I don't repeat myself. Listen the first time." He pushes the band of his underwear down his body, along with his jeans already folded down, leaving them sitting just above his dick.

"It's hard to listen with you stripping naked! You're a guy and I'm a girl. It's human nature to look. Tattoos are a huge turn on for me and you have them covering seventy-five percent of your body. Cut me a damn break."

He grabs me by the arm and pulls me toward his station. "The second part of this interview is to see you give it a shot. To me, tattooing is a natural talent. Those meant to do it generally know how it works before they ever apprentice. It takes more than the ability to trace an object and follow an outline to be a good tattoo artist. Sometimes you have to think on the spot, adjust, freehand, and do cover ups from previous shitty jobs. An *artist* is well rounded in all areas: drawing, tracing, visualizing, shading, design and color, all while having a steady hand. You may be good at drawing with a pencil, but it's a little more difficult with a vibrating gun in your hand puncturing the skin hundreds of times per minute. You're dealing with ink, blood, and three-dimensional mostly soft objects as your canvas. I'm not wasting my time to make shit more pleasant. I'm making great flawless."

He releases my arm and steps over the chair in a straddling stance, drawing my attention to his black, high-top Converse shoes matching my pink ones, before grabbing a thin see-through sheet of paper off the counter space. My nerves are on overdrive now. "I've already drawn you out a design that matches the one I tattooed on your pelvis last night, minus the fucking bow. It's a pretty simple design but a good one. Basic skull and crossbones fit my personality, so I'll deal with it on my body. Wouldn't be the first version anyway and I doubt the last."

We're going to have matching tattoos . . .

"You don't want me to practice on pig skin first since it's the closest to human?"

He's defying everything I thought I knew about learning how to tattoo.

"Do I look like a teaching shop? I don't keep that shit on hand. My artists have years of actual tattooing experience. I don't teach.

It's a choice."

"Then why am I here?"

"Because I want to own you, and so I will. If I'm right I know you have it in you to be a legend. I'm never wrong. In time I will make you like me, so for the first and only time I'm forced to teach. It's a fucking dark road and you'll likely hate me more than you'll like me." He grips my face in his tattoo-covered hand and pulls my lips close to his. "If you choose this, you can't go back. The kiss of death cannot be reversed. I have no soul. You walked into my fucking shop and now I want you. You will be mine . . . in every fucking way."

I have no fucking idea what any of that shit means. He's a little scary, and maybe even borderline weird; most definitely controlling, but the first and last line are the only two that have seared themselves onto my brain. My heart is pounding. My stomach is twisted in about forty knots. Death is a scary word no matter the context, but for some reason, with him, it's also appealing. I know one thing to be true: this, no matter what I have to do, is what I want. "Where do you want it?"

He smirks, but it's so brief it'd be easy to miss if I wasn't paying attention. He's hot and cold. I noticed that last night. You only get a glimpse of personality before he's back to the emotion-lacking guy he seems like at first glance. "Since this is your first it's going somewhere I can cover up if you fuck it up. My sleeves are sacred: my masterpieces. Only the best adds to it. You earn the right to leave your mark as an artist there."

He pushes his pants down some more, until the top half of his firm ass is bare. If he pushes them down any further I'll be able to see his dick. Without breaking he applies the transfer of ink from paper to skin below his waistline, and low enough he can cover it by simply buttoning his pants. He cannot possibly expect me to give him a tattoo that close to his dick, especially my first. That important phrase 'lack of experience' means a lot in this situation. Come on . . .

He grabs a pair of black, latex gloves off the tray, handing them to me. It looks like everything is already setup. "If you want to be the best in a man's world, so you say, then you better be serious as fuck about learning and perfecting. It takes practice. Even when it looks perfect, in your head it's shit, and you start all over again. There are some that have made it and done well, but tattooing has always been primarily a man's art. The women that have made their mark will never be forgotten. Most would say you have big shoes to fill, but I say that's bullshit. Only the real artists strive to be better, to be more memorable. I'm not showing you how to setup or prep today. You'll be able to do that with your eyes closed should you get the job. I saw your ability to draw when I looked at your body last night. A large percentage of the population can draw; that doesn't mean they could tattoo for shit. I want to see technique. I'm a hands-on learner, so that's how I teach. Your current window is about two hours. All of my artists will be back at three today. I gave them an extra hour for you. Don't abuse it. It's a rare occurrence. That gives me time to clean up after you're done."

I pull the gloves on my hands until they form a tight fit. "Is this how you choose all of your artists? How do you have any blank skin left?"

His face remains serious. "Nope. You're the first."

My nerves were at a good five. They were just bumped to ten. "Uh, then why do you want me to do it this way?"

"You lack a client portfolio. That's why. I'm going to see if you can work under an uncomfortable pressure." He sits down on the chair, leans back, and slightly bucks his hips forward as if trying to get comfortable. "Since you're a girl and I'm a guy, tattoos may turn me on too." Then he laces his hands behind his head. "Tattoo me."

I am totally and inevitably fucked . . .

CHAPTER ONE

Delta

FOUR MONTHS LATER . . .

I run through the employee entrance of the bar at half past twelve, buttoning my black, sleeveless crop top as I come to a halt at the time clock. I grab my time card from the grip of my mouth and swipe it, before shoving it into the pocket of my short cutoff denims and rush toward the bar, hoping like hell Abel isn't here.

I'm late. My shift started at ten and I've had excuse after excuse since I started at *Inked aKross the Skin*, but the truth is Cassie wasn't kidding about having late night hours. Kross is a fucking workaholic and I can't leave until he does . . . since he's mentoring me and all. I assumed being the boss he would do less work than the rest. I was wrong. I don't think I've gotten out of there before nine thirty since I started, and that was maybe a handful of times

In the beginning I tried to sneak away early if I could, especially if Kross had to leave for his mysterious second life I hear nothing about—apparently no one does. The man is like a ghost. But being the maid, errand runner and bitch girl for the world's biggest asshole makes it hard to leave early. That moment I thought we had during the back and forth conversation the day of the interview was squandered quickly the second I became his employee. Him barking orders is about the only conversation I've gotten from him since—one way.

I knew it was going to be hard starting at the bottom, and most everything that I've been doing I was prepared for, but what I didn't know was the first time I picked up a tattoo gun that day would also be the last. The perfect tease . . .

I haven't held one since, except to change out a part or clean up to give the artist a break due to a client running past the time allotment, which happens often, especially with the little whiny girls that cry and scream over a little pain. If only they knew how much they were made fun of when they left . . . It's a fucking needle. Of course it's going to hurt. If you can't handle the pain then you shouldn't be getting a tattoo. It's a waste of the artist's time to have to babysit when they should be concentrating on what's going to be on the client's body for the rest of their life.

Even being a slave, I love the life of a tattoo shop. It's exactly what I anticipated in regards to the mood and environment, and the staff I love. I also know right now I need the extra income of a second job until I work my way up past the shitty pay of an apprentice. I'm pretty sure I've never worked for minimum wage a day in my life before this. Not even in high school. A certain person in my life made it very easy to make money.

I want this to work; however, nightlife bartending is competitive and I couldn't get a permanent late shift. Apparently everyone would love to come in at rush and make all the good tips when the average American is drunk, especially the highly coveted weekends, but that wouldn't be fair, so it's a shift rotation among all bartenders with no option for changes to the schedule unless you're pretty much dying. We know our schedule months in advance and your body never gets used to the constantly changing schedule. We conform to it, not the other way around.

Here I am, walking toward the bar with yet another tardy against my record. Before I can even make my way behind the bar Abel targets me in his sight and points toward the office. Fuck!

I file into the small room behind him and he shuts the door. "I'm really sorry I'm late," I state.

"Save it, Delta," he says as he walks to the seat at his desk and sits. "Sit down." Abel is the co-owner of the bar. He and Kane are brothers, mid-thirties, and sexy as fuck. I wouldn't mind riding on that train, if for no reason other than the scenic view—as I'm sure so many already have—had I not deemed sex with men completely lame at this point. Years with no orgasm manmade will do that to you. They can be greedy fucks and competitive as shit when it comes to coming; yet it's not in me to switch to the other side and become a lesbian. I may dabble from time to time, but it's all in young fun. Sure, the old hide and seek still feels good, but hell, I can make myself feel good for all of five minutes. Even get myself off by way of clit. But the missing part is that inner orgasm that makes you feel like a fucking Rockstar.

Abel is the one that looks more like he belongs on my side of the tracks— tattoos, unshaven jawline, dark features and untamed clothing. Kane, well, he looks like he belongs to a prep school— clean, neat, and stale. Lighter hair and eyes. I think on their names often. Makes me wonder if their mother was some bible freak on drugs to name her sons after a duo where one killed the other. I'm not as knowledgeable in the good book as I should be, but I'm pretty sure everyone knows that tale. And just because she spells one different doesn't mean people don't notice.

I stare at him from inside the door, not moving. Both are extremely buff and sexy, yet completely opposite of the other in everything but build, and also the reason for their take-no-shit attitude they always have as well as hot, young trophy girls hanging on their arms. He glances down my body as I stare at him shamelessly. He sighs. "Delta, sit down." His voice comes out a tad bit less frustrated than before.

I do as told and sit on the opposite side of him. "You've been one of my best bartenders since you started, but this isn't going to work anymore. You've obviously got other priorities or you're into shit that's bad for you. Either way, it's shit I don't have time for in my club. I don't know what is going on in your life, but this is a business. On a slow night we still turn over revenue in the high thousands. We're talking six figures on the weekends. I can't be short a bartender for even thirty minutes."

"Please don't fire me."

"I'm not firing you, but I am demoting you to a fill-in. When I need an extra body I'll call you, and if you prove to me you can be here at every needed allotment then I'll give you your job back in a few months' time. You'll learn I'm not a pushover."

"Abel, I can't lose this gig. I need the income. I could be homeless by then."

"Then I suggest you find something else in the meantime that can work around your new schedule. No one did this to you, Delta. You did it to yourself. I've been a damn good boss to you. You get more late night weekend shifts than most of my full time bartenders. The only reason I'm not cutting you all together to make an example out of you is because the regulars fucking love you, and regulars keep this place going. They bring in new people. You're the hot girl with the tattoos that serves as every man's darkest fantasy. Fantasy is what keeps me from going bankrupt. You also keep up with a max capacity bar full of drunk, demanding customers better than anyone else on my payroll. It's a damn shame to lose you, but if I continue overlooking the way you've been doing I lose my respect as an owner. And I can't have that, can I? This is the best I can do."

By the sudden rise in my body temp it's clear that I'm starting to stress. I don't need this shit. My income has already dipped significantly only working half my shift on most days. I should just tell him I picked up a second job with a very demanding boss. *One that I want to defile me on most days . . .* But I wasn't raised to make excuses when shit hits the fan, so I'll sit here and take the ass whooping bent over with a bare ass. "Are you at least going to let me finish my shift tonight?"

"No. I had to call in someone to fill your spot when I realized you weren't going to show on time and it's fucking Friday night. We're at max capacity and the line outside is wrapped around the building. I need all hands on deck and it's not fair to send her home when you're the one at fault. In the real world, remember there is always someone waiting to take your spot if you fuck up." *Which is why I will live in my car before I give up working for Kross.* "You're an adult, Delta. Act like one if you want a full-time income. This is me forcing you to take responsibility."

I huff, knowing he's right even if I don't want to admit it. My pride won't acknowledge it though. I've been on my own pretty much my entire life. It's no different now. The only difference is there isn't a neglectful mother paying the bills that put a roof over my head should I fail at it.

He sits back in his chair, the silence lingering between us. My hands are trembling in my lap, but I try to mask the stress as I hold my chin up and stand to leave. "I'm sorry. I may seem like an irresponsible young adult to you, but I'm trying. Just because I look the part doesn't mean I'm part of the club. Things aren't always the way they seem, Abel." I turn and walk out, slamming the door shut behind me as I hear my name coming from his lips. Doesn't look like I'm going to be catching up on rent today . . .

I make my way into my car and grab my pack of cigarettes, pulling one out and instantly placing it between my lips. Upon lighting, I suck hard, inhaling the toxic goodness into my lungs. I know it's bad for me, but it's something I found long ago to cope with an abnormal lifestyle. Bad girls do bad things. That's all I've ever been, and that's never going to change.

I glance at my phone for the first time since I left the shop in a hurry. The only one that catches my attention is a text from Lux.

Lux: Miss you, bitch. Retail therapy soon? You're dodging me . . .

I toss my phone aside. Dodging? Have I been dodging her? I figured I was just giving her space since she's so new in culinary school and orgasm deep on a nightly basis with her hot fiancé that's head over heels for her. Any man that can keep her from running is a damn good one if you ask me. I've known her for a long time. Lux can be the most conniving woman for luxury, and she's never hidden that fact. She knows what she wants and she'll do whatever she has to in order to get it. You can't fault her for that if you know her history and what life she came from, but she'll run in the face of her demons without thought.

Who am I to interfere in their newfound love bubble? I've had years by her side. I know when it's time to let her go. Kaston is good for her. Lux is happy. Something she's never been. Content maybe. But happy—never. We've been best friends since we were kids. You know what they say. Broken souls tend to migrate together. Lux didn't ask for her shitty hand like me. She didn't have a part in the evil she was exposed to. Mine came with open arms. She was a victim. I was a player.

So dodging? Maybe I am. It's best for her. She's on her way to healing in the arms of someone who loves her. I'm still suffering alone. For the first time I believe that she's better off without my sad, miserable life holding her back. I knew she was destined for greatness. I love her. I want to see her fly. It's why I sent in her application for culinary school all those months ago. Me—I'm just a traveler down a dark road. Those roads are meant to be traveled alone.

I start the engine, ready to go home. It sounds like a bubble bath and metal music kind of night, so I shall.

"*Eviction notice? What the fuck! I'm not* even that far behind. I don't think..."

I grab the bright orange professionally printed sticky note off the door and walk inside. My body automatically navigates to the small, high-end kitchen and I lay it down along with my purse, still staring at it, and reading the writing in the black printer ink on the front. It's signed by my leasing manager. "Three days! That's impossible. Who could come up with that kind of money to pay a balance in that short amount of time? If I had it I wouldn't be late. Dammit. And who the fuck pays for eviction notices to be printed?"

I turn and reach for the liquor cabinet, pulling one of my beloved men from his shelf, along with my skull and crossbones shot glass. I pour until it's full and bring it just before my lips. "Don't let me down, Jack."

Then I turn it back, allowing him to burn me as I consume the entire glass in one swallow—the way my mother taught me. The most desirable pain. The warmth of the liquid stings its way down my throat, yet a velvety embrace is left behind. I pour another, repeating the same steps, my thoughts already going there. A place they're forbidden. "Show me there's another way," I whisper.

I pour it down my throat, letting my head fall back as the poison lines my esophagus on the way down, leaving the heated bite behind. My black heart knows there is no other way to come up with that amount of money in a weekend's time. I have to have a place to live and I refuse to ask Lux for a loan. I never have and I never will.

She's finally living her dream and she's . . . settled. God knows most of us run into the Hell we're lost in. That girl was pushed in fucking barefoot, and besides, she's not working anymore. I sure as hell am not taking Kaston's money. My pride would never let me, even if it came to sleeping in my car under some graffiti-covered bridge. And there is no one else. All I've ever had in this world besides her is my mother, and that's probably not saying much. I'm not sure there was ever a point that she wanted me. I certainly wasn't planned. It was no secret that my chosen physical appearance embarrassed her. In ways, I think what happened that day was her out for motherhood. After all, it was so easy for her to wash her hands of me.

The comments over the years try their best to surface—*I was not cutout to be a mother, nothing about you makes me proud, you're a financial burden, I never asked for this*—but I shove them away with a long swig from the bottle. It doesn't matter. Nothing matters. Now, I'm a chosen orphan. I'm not convinced it's any better than abuse, regardless of the method. Loneliness welcomes madness. I sometimes think misery with someone is better than peaceful solitude.

I place my hands on the counter and stare at the small piece of paper once again. I said when I left I would never go back there. It cost me too much; but the truth is I have no choice. Some people have easy lives while others have it hard from the start. Some people get second chances to light the darkened way they've been walking for what seems like forever, and then there are people like me. I was bred into a single parent household to a woman that just wanted to party. I lacked a glittery childhood. I was starving for some small speck of attention, preferably male—female wasn't what people made it out to be and I had no experience with the other. The biggest truth of them all: I was forced to grow up faster than most from making countless bad decisions that will forever haunt me. I'm always going to struggle.

Some of us are just meant to be lost in the dark . . .

I pull my phone out of my purse and search for the contact I haven't used since I graduated high school; the day I walked away from one person and lost another, all in the same day. I just hope the number hasn't changed. There are no other options for me. After a deep breath I press the call option and hold it to my ear. Three rings and he picks up. "Delta?"

"Hey, Chuck. Can we talk?"

"About?"

"Money."

"You finally coming back to me?"

"In some ways."

"Meet me in an hour. My office. I'll leave your name at the door."

"Okay."

The call disconnects. A nervous tick is brewing in my stomach. I look at my outfit. "I'm going to need different threads for this. It's time to break out the old suitcase."

I walk into my room and search through my closet until I find the dark purple duffle bag on the top shelf, buried under a pile of purses that come crashing down as I try to pull it free without messing anything up. I leave the mess, hauling the bag to my bed.

With every item of clothing I go through memories return; a life I sometimes wish I could forget. Getting what I want takes sacrifice, and this is one I'm willing to make. My hope is that one day I'll be able to leave all of this behind and never look back. It'll become a faded memory of my past that I'll rarely think of.

My hands settle on the short, black dress, pulling it from the bag. I shake it out, releasing some of the wrinkles from it being stowed away. The rest stays where it is and I zip the bag back. It's going to have to come with me.

I quickly change, pulling on the shredded material that is way too revealing for wear in public. Ink peeks through every gash. It's what made me purchase something that looks like it's been mutilated by a lion. There are parts of me that I cannot change, no matter what type of job I'm in.

I walk to my mirror and change out my earrings for a pair a little bigger. I've been slowly gauging them out for months until I get to the size I want, which isn't really all that much bigger than normal earrings; the hole taking up a little less than the circumference of my existing lobe and no more.

I change the ring in my nose to a diamond stud for a more feminine effect, and then reach for my gloss, painting it on my lips but dabbing around the ring that sits snug against my skin in the center of my full bottom lip. Luckily, the rest of me is already made up with smoky eyes and thick liner—the usual standard when I wear makeup. Black and dark are just my colors. Color pop gets thrown in from time to time. My long, black hair reflects the color of my heart; silky smooth and still holding the large barrel rolls done from a curling iron this morning.

I pull my high tops on my feet, the shoes I'll need later already in the bag with everything else. I take one final glance at myself in the mirror. "Maybe it's like riding a bike; something you never forget."

If everything works out I'll be running on no sleep come tomorrow morning at the tattoo shop. I just hope and pray Cassie has some strong coffee made and I can make it through without making any mistakes. Pissing off the sexiest fucking asshole alive is not something I want to add to my record, because he's been ice cold since the day I started . . .

"You wanted to see me?"

I adjust my cleavage, bringing it into full focus, before walking in his office where I drop my duffle bag beside the chair, relieving myself of the weight. "Things haven't changed much around here," I state.

His hungry eyes skim over my body, making me slightly uncomfortable. Even for his age he's a good-looking man, still, but it's an attraction you outgrow with time. It's funny how often someone we once saw as everything, as beautiful, can suddenly have lost their luster upon seeing them again years later. It makes you wonder what you really saw in them the first time. We grow up, we mature, and just like taste buds over the years our likes and dislikes change.

"Business is good enough I don't need to change things." The desire may no longer be there, but the need is. Even fat and happy, metaphorically speaking, the starving girl I once was tries to emerge with the sound of his voice. The girl that wants to please him. That wants him to want her. The girl that needs him to love her. The girl that seeks his attention more than she seeks her next breath. The girl I thought I ended long ago.

He shuts the door and locks it, before walking toward me, wasting no time. He's never been scared of this. He's never been hesitant. At least not since the day it all started. Once he broke the ice, he's never held back. It's happened again and again and again. He's always been the big bad lion, yet appealing all the same . . .

I stand in front of my mirror in a pair of black, lace panties and a matching camisole, the barrel of my curling iron wrapped in a section of my long, dark hair, the steam rolling off of it with every second I leave it held to the metal. I release it, letting the large, loose spiral fall free, before picking up another straight section and wrapping it, repeating the steps over and over until my entire head is done.

My makeup is already done, waiting on Lux to come over.

There is a house party tonight at Derek Knight's parents'. They've run off to their vacation home this weekend, like they do at least once a month except in winter, and every time they do his house on the lake is full. He throws the best parties, his older brother scoring the alcohol, and as long as cops are left out of the equation and everything is cleaned up with no evidence of his behavior upon their return, he can do whatever he wants—a free hotel for those incapable of driving.

The front door opens and closes. "Lux, back here!" I shout. "I'm almost ready."

I don't hear her heels tapping against the lackluster hardwood floors that need sanding and refinishing. Maybe she wore flats tonight. Out of the ordinary, but not impossible. Less hazardous when alcohol is involved for sure. My right arm remains in the air, holding my curling iron, the beginning of a tattoo sleeve running down my shoulder and upper arm, against my mother's wishes. It's 'trashy' she said, but it's a good thing I don't give a fuck what she thinks anymore. At least that's what I tell myself. She still can't figure out how I'm getting them done. I'm underage without an adult's consent, but that's the beauty of knowing a tattoo artist and looking like a carbon copy of my mother, only a younger version. Stealing her ID for a day or so at a time is easy, as long as I put it back at the end of each day. She never needs it till night.

A figure in my doorway pulls my attention from my reflection in the mirror. My nerves kick into overdrive as I watch him through the mirror, staring at my backside from his propped position inside the doorframe. He's been in the picture for a while, as so many before him, and this look is now familiar since I've hit puberty and developed a chest size—from him and many others, but he's the only one that has a reason to look at me this way.

He's . . . different. He's stuck around the longest, and he's always around, even when it's just me—a little in the beginning when it was forced upon him, but more often as time goes by, it seems to be voluntarily. It's usually always just me. But he gives me company. It makes my belly feel warm—something I've never felt before.

Our eyes lock, as they do often when he's around now, waiting to see who initiates it first. It sends a volt of excitement down my spine to a center only I have explored before him. "Where's—"

"Still at work," he replies.

"Doesn't surprise me."

"It shouldn't."

"Is she meeting you here?"

"No. She wants to go out. She doesn't even know I'm here."

Another small piece of my heart falls away. A part of me was hoping, just once, that she . . . I sigh. I know better. This is why I don't care. Over and over again I chant it to myself. "Then why are you here?"

I shouldn't ask. I know why he's here. But I still want to hear it. I 'need' to hear it. He walks forward. The last section of hair leaves the metal as I press the release on the curling wand. I set it on my old dresser I've painted to match my particular taste, along with everything else in my room. She won't even come in here anymore. "Because unlike her, I want to be."

He stops behind me, placing his hands on my hips; the tension I'm carrying is already fading. He's looked more times than I can count, but the touches feel so much better. Last week he sat on the couch and watched a movie with me while she locked herself in her room with her wine. Never even acknowledged me when she came home. He noticed as I was putting the dishes away from a *dinner set for three she didn't show up for. We watched in silence, the occasional word or phrase being exchanged. It was harmless, even though I found myself wishing it wasn't, but it was . . . nice, nonetheless.*

His fingers caress up my sides, not making an attempt to move my undergarments. "She ignores you," he states.

"Yes," I whisper.

"But you still try?"

Embarrassment rises. "Yes," I admit.

"You shouldn't try so hard on someone that isn't worthy of the effort put forth. If I didn't know any better I'd say she doesn't want—"

"She doesn't," I finish, his eyes falling to my lips, "want me. She never has."

But I still love her I want to say, even though I wish I didn't.

"I want you," he says simply.

And there it is . . .

Three words.

Words that apart mean nothing, but together mean everything.

Words I've never heard.

A sentence I've wanted to feel.

A phrase that leaves me bare.

I turn in his arms, placing my palm on the back of his hand. I move it slowly to my front, and push his fingertips under the waistband of my panties until they graze a part of me that's never been touched by a masculine hand other than his. And I do something I've been doing for a while. Something I'll never be able to take back. "Then have me."

His hand ghosts up my arm, pulling me out of my head. I lock my feet to the ground below me, mentally preparing myself to do this if I need to. I've done it plenty of times before. Some of those times I truly wanted it. A very small part of me is curious what it would be like to rekindle something I left behind so long ago. With someone that awakened a part of me I never knew existed. Someone that I gave so much to.

My first isn't worthy of storybooks, unless you were telling a tale of a darker someone, like the villain in the princess fairytales perhaps. Imagine if the story had ended with the bad succeeding. It would lose all of its magical goodness to a theme of darkness. No one likes those stories; at least not out loud. It may be more dramatic of a story, but happiness lies nowhere in the pages. No one would like me if they knew the person I was deep down.

He grabs my chin between his fingers and rubs his thumb over my lip ring. "You've changed."

"Most people do."

"Why are you here, Delta? You walked out on me seven years ago."

"I need my job back."

"I have enough girls. What's in it for me?"

I internally cringe. "What do you want?"

"You know what I want. The same thing I wanted then. I want you."

"Do you still talk to Mom?" The question flew out before I could even stop it.

"No. I haven't since then. It was never about her."

We stare at each other. The memories are assaulting me, clouding my judgment and making me weak. That person is hard to totally rid of, no matter how long it's been: the person you gave your virginity to. They take a part of you with them that you can never get back. It's a void that you can't cover or replace with someone else. At one point in time I loved him, regardless of how wrong it was.

But a long time has passed. I've grown up. I've changed. I've moved on; but also, there is still that part of me that remembers the way he made me feel when I needed it the most, and maybe that means something. There is one fact I can't escape: I need the money and he's the only one that can provide me with it. "I can't guarantee anything, Chuck. We're two different people now. But if you give me my job back we can try and see if things are still like they were. It has to be slow. That's all I can agree to."

I can already see his face change. He's happy with my answer. "I didn't think you'd ever come back. I've missed you," he says, and closes in to kiss me. I let him, because, well, I don't have much of a choice at this point. Our lips don't have the right rhythm. It doesn't give me the rush of emotions that it used to. It used to make me feel wanted, needed, and loved. Now, it just feels familiar.

He breaks the kiss, his hands settling on my waist. Slowly they start to descend. They always did when he wanted to take things further. "When do you want to start?"

"Tonight."

"I'm going to need you to sign a contract, Delta. Six-month intervals and then we reassess. I do it with all my girls now to protect my business and my customers. You're no different. I want you to give this time to see if it'll work; not just tell me shit to get your way. No running away this time. I loved you and risked everything for us and then you left me high and dry. You fucked my heart up. No companion has lasted long since, because no woman has left a mark on me like you. None of them are *you*."

My heart is racing. Six months? Shit. That's a long ass time. I was hoping I wouldn't need two jobs in six months. "Will you work around my day job's schedule? Guaranteed? I don't need any shit because the hours vary and it's not flexible. This isn't something I can make a career out of, that is."

"Can you guarantee you'll work five nights a week if I work with you on the lineup, even if you take the late slots?"

"Yes."

"Okay."

The time period repeats over and over in my head, screaming at me not to do it. "Let me work this weekend just to make sure you still want me here. I haven't done this in years. I may be bad at it. Then, if everything goes well, Monday morning I'll make it legally binding."

He stares into my eyes as he grabs the bottom of my dress and pulls it up my body, removing it. "Only if you put up collateral. I need to know you're serious. And I need you. It's been too long."

My bra is next to leave my body, my chest heaving up and down. I'm faced with a choice. In life a lot of times we are. Nothing is ever simple. There is no right or wrong answer. There simply is the requirement to make a decision. We have to prioritize and bargain to survive. We have to do things that sometimes make us feel dirty, or bought, so I allow my soul to tarnish a little more. "Do you have a condom?"

Without saying another word he kisses me like a dying man, pushing items off his desk to make room for me, and for the first time in two years I allow a man to have me. The worst part is . . . I was hoping someone different would be the one.

CHAPTER TWO

Kross

"Meet me at the loading dock in twenty minutes."

I set the burner phone down on my desk and check the security cameras once more, ensuring no one is around or near the building. Business is starting to get too heavy, so I had to come up with a different shipping strategy to keep attention away from my shop. Everything is about perception.

The key to being a successful criminal is a cover-up. Kaston's is his P.I. firm and mine are my tattoo shops. At the rate I'm going I'll have at least one in all major cities throughout the U.S. soon. I invest some of the money from arms dealing back into growing my businesses to make it more believable. It's about outsmarting those trained to catch the very criminal activity you're making a living doing.

My shops serve two purposes: tattoos by day and shipping

warehouses at night. With more trucks coming in and out I've had to add warehouses in sketchy places through the city to intercept some of my shipments. On top of that, I'm getting closer to launching a tattoo supply company I've had in the works in Spain for several years now. Kaston's dad, Phillip, has been my investor to make it legit. Well, he was, but now that chip falls on Kaston's shoulder.

Production on the first line started last year and will hit all of my shops within the next year. The goal is to eliminate as many outside vendors as possible so that my own trucks are coming and going from my shops, making it easier to mix shipments instead of wasting time disguising trucks. If I take on enough clients and become a global vendor for tattoo businesses I could very easily have access to all major highways, water, and air within a short amount of time.

It all started small—just a kid on the street trying to make enough to survive on his own. Any kid in the system knows it's a hell worth escaping, whether criminal activity or honest work is the way out. Being placed in home after home was my life, each one becoming worse than the last. Becoming an easy monthly paycheck for some worthless piece of shit was all I was valued for. It's also the only thing I remember about my childhood aside from the occasional slice of a flashback I get.

Nightfall was the easiest time to get away, and the time least likely to get caught since representatives of the state didn't pop in. Once the sun went down and she disappeared to her room I was free. No one ever comes looking for you when they don't want you there in the first place. I realized quickly the dark was where I like to be. It's where I belong, and in a short period of time I learned why. Recreational drug use was something I experienced at a young age. It's the easiest way to forget shit you don't want to remember.

That was my gateway into a world I've been in for over half of my life span thus far.

A runner for a large operation drug ring is where it began. It gave me contacts, it gave me allies, and it opened a door for me to grow and become bigger. Loyalty is the only thing that will guarantee success in an underworld, because everyone has the same common goals: to make money, to avoid the law, and to move up to a place where you hire out for the small-time jobs. Disloyalty in this life doesn't get you fired; it gets you put in the ground. You have to watch your back. And I've had a plan since the beginning. Every man has a weakness except me, whether bad or good.

I stand and grab my keys, shutting everything off as I walk to the door. If I know Kaston he'll be early. Everything is locked up in minimal time and the alarm set on the building before I walk to my truck. I check my surroundings, as I do every time I leave. No car is out of place and nothing looks abnormal.

Fifteen minutes of driving and I pull in, his truck already backed up to the old loading dock. When my headlights shine on the front, I shut them off and stop, waiting for him to get in. It doesn't take him long. "This the shipment from New York?"

I nod and pull my truck around to the side door that sits in a narrow alley, killing it. "Fresh out of the shipping containers."

"What's in this one?"

"Your investment."

"And . . ."

"Something you'll want. Let's go."

We both get out at the same time and make our way to the door. I quickly unlock it and we walk inside, locking it back behind us, before making our way toward the bay. The large warehouse sits outside of town off several back roads. It used to be a warehouse for a huge feed and seed company that went bankrupt. It's been abandoned for decades. Years with no activity keeps the cops away and paying the owner with no use for it cash that doesn't have to be reported to the government makes for an easy and private sale. I wanted something far enough outside of town that it's obvious when people are lurking.

I pull the small flashlight from the pocket of my jeans and turn it on as we walk further into the dark, the large wooden crate becoming visible. When I remove the top he looks inside. "Looks like a chair."

The beam of light bounces throughout the room, showing every large crate. "I designed them. They're going in the shop. More positions, a more comfortable experience, and better for the artist to work with. That's not yours. Here. Give me a hand." Together we remove the chair from the crate, setting it down out of the way. "Hold this."

He takes the light from my hand and I grab the ax standing head down against the column not far from where we are. Grabbing it in one hand, I swing it up until both hands grip it like a baseball bat. He backs up when I take stance and begin swinging it, driving the blade into the bottom of the crate. Each new lick creates a cut.

Over and over I swing, wood pieces flying and already sweating, until the hole is big enough to see inside the lower half of the crate. "This is yours," I say, out of breath as I replace the ax to its point of origin. Handkerchief now in hand, I grab the rifle lying on its side and carefully navigate it through the large opening, handing it to him. "You wanted a sniper rifle; here is an Armalite AR-50 single-shot bolt-action rifle."

He grabs it with latex-covered hands and inspects it carefully, like he always does. "This will work. For now anyway."

A thick envelope makes its way into my hand when he pulls it from his back pocket. "Where's your next job?"

"I'm not taking any right now and I'm not sure Chevy is ready to fly solo yet. I don't know what fucked up shit lives in his head, but I can sense something isn't right up there. This is actually a gift."

I nod. "Going clean?"

"No, even though I've considered it; just enjoying a break for now. There are parts of that life I need. Right now the cravings are silent, but it's only a matter of time before they come calling. When you're raised up in something it becomes normal."

"How's that whole relationship thing going for you?"

He shines the flashlight in my eyes. I don't blink. "Why? Are you finally deciding to take what you've been wanting for months?"

"I have everything I want."

"Bullshit. Lie to someone else, Kross. I've been there. You seem to keep forgetting we found them at the same time. I've also seen you two around each other and it's awkward as fuck. Even Lux asks me about it. I guess she wants to know what's up with the two of you and is sick of getting nothing out of Delta."

"She's just an artist with the potential to be of value to me. Nothing more."

"When's the last time you got laid?"

"What the fuck does that matter?"

"Just answer the question."

"It's none of your business."

He props the barrel of the gun on his shoulder, the butt sitting in his hand. He's still got the fucking bright light in my eyes. "If it's nothing then answer the question. We're two grown-ass men here. Secrets are kind of our thing. It's why we trust each other." An arrogant smirk follows. "Unless it's something . . ."

"Four and a half months. I'm a busy man and I don't trust many people. I don't need it like you."

He lowers the light and flips it around; handing it to me, handle first. I grab it. As soon as his hand is free he smacks the back of my shoulder, causing every muscle to tense. I growl. "Watch it."

"It happens to the best of us. You'll figure it out eventually. I'm out, bro. My uninterrupted time with Lux is pretty narrow lately. Holler at me when you head to the gym; otherwise, I'm going to get fucking fat from all the food."

I shine the light at him this time, watching his retreating form. "What the fuck is that supposed to mean?"

"When you remember how long it's been since you hired her, you'll know. Better hurry your ass up, though, before you miss your chance. Later."

He walks away, and shortly after I hear the door open and close. What's he trying to say; I can't go fuck someone else? That's coincidence. My entire life is private. Trust is earned. Not many have it, and even the ones that do is limited on how much. I have too much to lose if my shit gets out, and twenty minutes of a wet dick isn't worth it to me.

Has it already been four months?

"Are you sure you want me to do this?"

"I don't revoke my decisions, Delta. Just do the damn tattoo. You're wasting time."

She scoots closer to me on the rolling stool and finds a comfortable position with her arms. She stares at the transfer on my skin as she holds the gun in her hand. Her lip ring starts scraping against her top teeth in a nervous way. "You can just outline it today. We'll work on shading techniques later. I want to see how steady your hand is even when you're uncomfortable.

There will be times you'll have to tattoo someone in a more personal area than this . . . Males and females."

She looks at me, her eyes focused on my lips, similar to the way she was watching me last night when I was tattooing her pelvis. Her eyes were on my face, not the tattoo. "I've even had to tattoo a female's name on a dick before. Also, Prince Albert—just one among the masses of areas to pierce a dick—and clit piercings have gotten popular on top of nipple rings. This is a business. I need to know you can do anything asked of you without acting like a shy teenager. Professionalism is my one and only fucking rule here. Break it and you're gone, no questions asked. Reputation takes years to build and can be destroyed instantly."

Her breathing quickens and her eyes veer to mine. "Are you going to make me practice a Prince Albert on you too?"

I quickly glance at her now shaking hand. A smirk slowly appears when our eyes meet again. "I may let you practice a lot of things, even with my dick, but a needle going through it won't be one of them."

Her eyes widen just a hare, and then she clears her throat before the buzzing sound begins and the needle touches down on my skin. There is something about her that piques my interest, and maybe even reminds me of myself starting out, except for the buried shyness. Shy is something that's never lived within me. The weird part is . . . in all of my years of tattooing, I've never been attracted to another artist, and I've worked alongside a few females prior to starting my own business.

I personally don't hire females aside from the receptionists because I don't want fraternization in my studio. The cattiness that occurs between opposite sexes usually just pisses me off. I watch her as she slowly reloads the gun, ink slinging on the first *try. She's trying to get a feel for the gun. On the second attempt she gets it and starts again. If you were to ask me why I'm changing everything now . . . I have no fucking idea. But as I watch her, I already know I'm going to give her the job.*

I walk to my truck and get in. Maybe I should go get some pussy just to prove a point. Several of the dealers I do work for always have girls on hand. That's usually where I go. Girls already trained in crime know to shut their fucking mouth. They're rewarded well for offering their body out to anyone that wants it. They're also tolerant of all forms of sex. Rough and slightly abusive are nothing for them. I start the engine and the rock music immediately begins; still Godsmack that was playing on the way here. Instead of deciding on the topic at hand, my thoughts go back to that fucking tattoo I've yet to let her finish.

Fuck it.

I grab my phone and filter through the contacts, holding it up to my ear as it connects. Straight to voicemail. *"Hey, it's Delta. I probably won't call you back."*

I hang it up when I hear the beep, glancing at my dash clock as I back out of the gravel. Why would her phone be off? We went over my expectations long ago, and one of them were that I need to be able to get in touch with her at all times. What the fuck could she possibly be doing? She has to be at work early in the morning to open.

Better hurry up, though, before you miss your chance.

"Motherfucker."

My tires spin a little as I shift into drive and take off. Shit planted in my head is the last thing I need right now. It's time to take my ass to the house.

CHAPTER THREE

Delta

I pull into the employee parking lot and kill the engine to my car, tired as hell. By the time I got to my apartment and showered off the filth of the night, I only had an hour to sleep before I had to be up again to get ready. Now that I'm here Kross has split opening and closing shifts between Cassie and me, and the one that opens is responsible for making coffee for the rest of staff here at open with appointments.

In my state of panic as I jumped out of bed, realizing I hit snooze too many times, all I had time for was Starbucks drive thru, arriving promptly two minutes before the doors are supposed to be open with the sign on. I still have to have the computer booted up and ready to go, and unless I'm going to go up and down stairs I have to walk around the building.

I get out and reach in to get the drink holder full of cups off my passenger floorboard. I walk as quickly as I can to the front door and unlock it, turning on the open sign as I walk inside. Luckily, it only looks like Wesson is here so far. Thank you, God. Maybe I don't have to deal with the wrath of Kross running on minimal sleep, because I was supposed to be here thirty minutes ago. To be so hot he's scary as fuck. All of the artists are uptight when he's here. You'd think it was a totally different staff compared to when he's gone.

As I round the desk and hit the button to startup the computer, the door leading to the studio opens, Wesson stepping off the bottom step. "Someone's late," he says with a smile smeared across his face.

I hand him the tall medium roast—what he always orders. "Shut up. Please don't tell Kross. I had to work late at my other job."

"That depends. Are you going to finally let me tattoo you? You know I've been waiting to get my hands on you since you started," he says in his normal flirty demeanor. "I'm a great teacher too. I can show you more than how to empty the garbage or clean the bathrooms."

I've clicked with Wesson more than I have anyone else here so far. He's the most laid back one out of all the artists, though he's a little quiet in a group. He's become a friend, and one I'd hang out with after work for drinks, but that may change if he doesn't stop asking me out every time we're alone. He's cute enough, his brown hair longer and messy, stopping just over his ears, and I love that his body is almost covered in ink, but if something is supposed to happen it just does, and with him there is nothing there but platonic coworker love. No sparks. No sizzle. No burn. No electricity or humming in the air. Just lighthearted, easy conversation.

He takes a sip of his coffee. "I don't know. I'm too busy right now working two jobs. Maybe soon."

"You shouldn't be working two jobs, Delta. It's unhealthy."

"Well, bills have to get paid somehow. People do it all the time."

"If he's not paying you enough you should ask for a raise or quit. I see all of the shit he has you doing and it has nothing to do with learning to tattoo. Cassie doesn't even clean the studio. It's the responsibility of the artist to keep his own shit clean."

"Do you have a problem with the way I run my shop, Wesson?"

Tingles runs down my spine at the sound of that voice. I glance at the entry to the stairs, behind where Wesson is standing. There's a back stairway at the employee door that everyone uses to get to the studio, aside from whoever opens the front.

His eyes are already on me. He's standing on the second step, leaned forward with his hands on the frame above him, his tattoo-covered arm muscles more noticeable due to the slight flexing as he grips onto the wood. His black Hurley shirt is fitted, emphasizing the hard body I know resides underneath, and he's wearing a black cap. Everything on his body is black, aside from his faded jeans, including his earrings. I can smell his cologne from here.

I would so fuck his brains out.

I shake my head, trying to rid it of those completely inappropriate thoughts. He's my boss. It's unfortunate the one man that has me completely beside myself in years has to be the one I work for. That's my luck, though. "Good morning. Sleep well?"

Because you look like you slept well . . .

Fuck, shut up.

"Is that my coffee?" I guess he's going to completely disregard me like he usually does when I'm trying to be friendly in the morning. And here I thought I wasn't the morning person. He makes me look like a chirpy bird.

"Yes," I respond, handing him a cup as he steps down onto the main floor.

He grabs the cup out of my hand. "Since the two of you are having a meeting about my company why don't we finish it now that I'm here. What was it you were saying, Wesson?"

"Nothing, Kross. My intention wasn't to disrespect you. I just think she's ready to start learning more about being an actual artist and leave the maid shit for us all to split like we always have. It's been four months. If you aren't going to let her tattoo then why did you hire her?"

"And you think she's ready to permanently mark a client's body?"

"She can sit with me and watch. I'll talk her through it; with the client's consent of course."

He looks at me as Kross stares him down. *Shut up,* I mouth.

He briefly squints at me. "I'll save the hands-on practice for between clients. She can tattoo me."

Kross looks at me, anger showing on his face. "What do you think, Delta? Do you have complaints about your employment here, pay or otherwise?"

He's obviously heard way more of this conversation than I wish he had, and I didn't even start it. "No. Things are fine the way they are. I like my job."

Wesson narrows his eyes at me. I can see him from my peripheral vision, but my eyes remain on Kross. Call me a pussy for not taking a stand, but I will keep my job one way or another. He takes a sip of his coffee and walks toward me. "Wesson, go prep for your client," he commands.

Footsteps sound as Wesson runs up the stairs, leaving us alone. He hands me the coffee cup back. "Do I look like I want dessert with my coffee?"

I notice the label on the side of his cup. "Shit, that's mine. I'm sorry." I switch out the cups in his hand. "Yours is dark roast: black."

He steps closer, making me nervous. "I tried to call you last night to give you some practice. Where were you?"

"At work."

"At 3AM?"

"Yes."

"It went straight to voicemail. I've never had a problem getting ahold of you at the bar. Why was your phone off?"

Guilt consumes me as the events of last night and what I allowed Chuck to do to me on that desk resurface; though I don't know why. I feel like I cheated on my boyfriend and am lying after getting questioned, which is stupid. I'm not currently promised to anyone. Still, the truth remains that I shut my phone off after we had sex. I felt like trash. I've held out for two years just to give it away negligently. If my body were capable of producing tears I would have cried, but my heart hardened when I was just a kid, my tear ducts turning to stone. Crying never gets you anywhere. But last night I felt like a whore, lying there and spreading my legs to ensure an income, and because of it I let myself act like one for the rest of the night; dancing and stripping for money like I used to do. Only this time it didn't give me the rush like it did back then. Every hand that placed money in my underwear felt like coming in contact with disease. I'm not proud of myself right now, and that's a feeling I haven't had in a long time.

"My phone died," I lie. "I didn't have time to charge it between here and there."

He stares at me in a way he never has, as if he knows I'm lying. I'm not sure why I am, honestly. I don't want to give him any reason to think I don't deserve to be here. I'm just going through a hard time financially right now and I don't want any special treatment. I want to be treated like everyone else here.

He leans in. I'm fighting hard not to touch him. God, I want those full lips on me so bad. A man like him should not have lips that sexy. They're bite worthy. Four months around him is like enduring four months locked in a padded room with no food or water. I feel like I'm going insane and starving at the same time. "When Cassie gets here come upstairs." His hand grabs ahold of the front of my neck; firm but not tight enough to hurt me, his thumb resting on my jugular. I never look away. "No one," he barks, his cologne wafting into my nose, his eyes boring into mine. "Is going to train you or tattoo your body but me. If you think I'm joking test me. Deal with your boy toy. If I have to it'll be a lot less civil. Consider this the only warning."

I swallow. My skin is burning beneath his touch. "And if I want a tattoo?"

"Then you lay your ass in my chair and I'll give you one. The day you accepted this job you became my property." His eyes scan down my body in a way that scares me but spikes my adrenaline. My breathing becomes heavy, my muscles lithe. "My property is not for public use. From this point forward, another set of hands better not touch your body, much less anything else. I've dealt with men for less."

"What do you want from me?" My fucking mouth . . .

"When I'm ready for you to know, you will. Since the two of you took the liberty to discuss your employment, you're going to sit with me today." His thumb presses harder against my vein, my pulse pushing against the pressure he's exerting. "Oh, and don't lie to me again. Next time I can't get you I'm coming to find out why."

And then he turns and walks away, disappearing into the stairwell, and for the first time since he came down here I can breathe evenly and with ease. Slowly my bottom lowers to the seat of the chair, my eyes staring out the window at the parking lot.

My hand rubs where his just was. My skin is still hot. Something tells me there's more to him than meets the eye. He's dangerous, but in what ways I don't know. Still, as I sit here, I want his hands back on me . . . in any way I can have them.

Kross

I hate being lied to. There is nothing more disloyal than a liar. I am who I am on the principle of loyalty. It was all over her face. In her hesitation. She was with someone last night, but who I still have to find out, and I will, because now I'm fucking angry. Anger issues are something I've dealt with for years, and in its presence someone always ends up physically hurt. It's one thing that has earned me so much respect.

I look at the clock on the wall when Vinny walks through the door for his appointment. 9AM. Cassie should be here by now. It's been two hours since we opened. I stand and shake his hand as he makes his way to my chair. "You ready to do this?"

"You know it. Been ready since we did the outline a few months back."

Vinny is one of my regulars. He has been for about five years now, but he drives or flies to wherever I am when he wants ink. I've always been a mover. I don't stay in one place very long. Old habits die hard I guess. I open shop, grow my business, and then one artist that I trust ends up becoming my manager and I move to another location and start over.

My body may not be there but my fucking eyes are everywhere. I

LOVE *and* *War* VOLUME ONE

watch my books closely for every store, and it pays off. I also pop in randomly with no warning. Surprise is the best form of attack if you want to make sure everyone is doing what they're supposed to be.

I don't make friends with employees; even the ones that I seldom recruit for criminal activity, and for good reason. Money talks and that's what I use. No one screws me over. My form of punishment doesn't come with a happy ending. Maybe that's why Kaston has a little more of my trust than the average person. He understands jobs with special circumstances. Atlanta was my fifth shop to open and it won't be the last. When business here is strong and steady I'll move on. "How's Detroit?"

"Shit, Man. It was better when you were there. When you coming back?"

"Oh, you know me. When I'm not on anyone's radar."

He removes his shirt. "Yeah, and why I have to spend more money to track your ass down."

A dry laugh occurs. "I'll make it worth the travel. Always do. Let me see it."

He turns around, revealing the full back piece we started a few sessions back. A life size skull sits in the center, already shaded at the last multi-hour session. A cobra is wrapped around it, the tail stopping at his left hip and the head over his right shoulder, mouth wide with the fangs penetrating his neck. The skull I transferred from a sketch I did before his first session, but the snake I had to freehand because of the way it's wrapping multiple times around the skull and the natural curves of the human body.

Vinny's sessions always consist of hours in length and it takes multiple to complete a piece. He likes dark, detailed ink, and he spends the money to make sure it's the best. Today he's here for the coloring of the snake and this one will be finished. "It looks like it's healed nicely. You haven't lost any color."

He throws his leg over the slightly reclined chair and straddles it, sitting chest against the back, giving me access to the tattoo. "Always my plan, my man."

I take a paper towel and drench it with alcohol, rubbing it in broad strokes over the workspace of his back to sanitize it. "Did you still want me to sit?"

Her voice is low. Vinny and I look up at the same time. "That depends. Who are you, sexy?" Vinny's tone is curious, animalistic, his eyes staring at her mostly bare midsection that shows off her full side tattoo over her ribs. All she's wearing is a piece of purple fabric that looks like a band covering her tits and a pair of black short overalls in some material other than denim that stops just below her ass. I hate the way he's staring at her. Maybe I should set a dress code for her like my receptionists.

My eyes finally ascend from the chest level place they were, locking with hers. They are a deeper green than they were earlier. She sways to Vinny, holding out her hand. "I'm Delta. Trainee."

He pulls it to his lips, kissing the back of her hand. "Vinny, sweetness. Kross didn't tell me how juicy the peaches were in Georgia. He's been holding out on me. If you're going to be working here I may have to make a trip more often."

"She's taken, Vinny. Don't waste your time."

Her eyes return to mine, her cheeks reddening a little. "That's a damn shame. Lucky man."

"Pull up a seat," I say, before going back for my supplies, grabbing the black, latex gloves first. I pull them on. "You okay with her helping, Vinny?"

The sound of a stool being rolled over from the vacant station occurs. I grab a new needle, opening the package as she sits down beside me. "Yeah, Man. I'm good. I know you won't let me walk out of here fucked up."

He places his hands on his lap to relax his back, his forehead going to the chair back. "Is this where you want me?"

I load the needle in the gun and make sure everything is within reach to my right on the tray. "No, come here. Grab some gloves and put them on."

"Come where?"

I scoot to the very back of the large, round seat beneath me and nod her over with my head. She stands, still putting on the gloves, but doesn't move. I take a deep breath, getting impatient. Obviously, I'm going to have to physically plant her there. I grip her bare side and pull her toward me, instructing her to sit on the stool in front of me, my front at her back. She's tense. "Relax," I say just outside her ear, placing the gun in her right hand. "You can't tattoo if you're uncomfortable."

"You want me to tattoo him?"

"That's why you're here, isn't it?"

"Kross, that's a wicked and complicated piece. I'm okay with just watching. I don't want to mess it up."

I scoot the footswitch closer to her foot. "Make sure your foot is comfortable so that you have full control of speed."

Vinny glances over with a smirk on his face. "Damn, bro. You never specified."

I ignore his comment and turn my hat around to get the bill out of the way. My left hand settles on her inner thigh and I point as I instruct. "Everything you need is right here." My lips touch her ear to lower my voice. "Let the sound relax you. A little goes a long way. Do you remember me going over color blending and making you do it with the colored pencils?"

"Yes," she responds.

I guide her hand to the first tray of ink and load the gun, then position it in the center of his back so she can get the feel before making it to a more sensitive area like his neck. We're going to be here a while. Once she gets in some practice I'll take over and finish, but Vinny is the best client to let her practice with. He's easy going and trusts me as his artist after all these years. "The gun is your pencil. Use it accordingly. Look to your right."

She does, her cheek brushing against my lips. "See the photo of the cobra hanging from the tray?"

She nods. "This is where the artistry is necessary. Use it as a guide for pattern and color. After each section wipe the excess ink to keep your place. I've seen you look at a photo and redraw it. This is no different. And I've already done the outline. Think of it as really fun coloring. You'll get used to the vibration the longer you hold the gun."

"And you're going to be here in case I do something wrong?"

"Yes. I'm giving you your wings. Now fly."

"Okay," she says, her voice a little offset from the nerves.

Vinny turns back toward the chair back, waiting for the start. "Never thought I'd see the day," he mumbles.

My right hand drops to mirror my left on the inside of her thigh and I scoot against her to support her back. "Do you have your foot on the footswitch comfortably?"

"I think so."

"Position to draw. It's like learning to drive. Once you know the basics, the rest is practice."

She finally rests her forearms against his skin and the gun comes on— short bursts a few times as she gets used to the footswitch— the vibration sounding through the studio to match Wesson's. He glances up at her as he reloads ink, with a slight smirk, and goes back to the neck piece of the girl in his chair.

I watch her hand slowly color within the lines of the snake, doing just as I instructed. I run my company my own way. No one jumps to the top in a matter of days, weeks, or even months. To be humble at the top you have to start from the bottom. It's why I've never taught. It's a liability I don't want for myself, or my business. Tattooing takes time to learn, years to master, and steady growth along the way. It's just easier to bypass those steps and hire someone seasoned in the art, but there are times when you have to throw the rules out the fucking window and go with your gut. That's what she is. She walked in my shop four months ago with nothing on her mind but a single tattoo and the big mouth of a friend along for the ride. My instincts told me not to let her go yet, and here she is, still as passionate about it as she was when she walked in here.

I put her through hell to see if she could withstand the fire when she found out it's not like it appears on the tattoo reality television shows. Some days it's fun. Others every muscle in your body aches. On a rare occurrence when you've worked late back to back, or weekends, you wonder why the fuck you're even in this business. And then there are days when you get to witness the very emotion driven behind the tattoos you create, reminding you why it is you do this in the first place.

I squeeze her thigh, letting her know she's doing good so far. Within the hour every gun in this studio will be buzzing. This is the sound that I live for. It's what makes me happy. If happy is what I am. It calms my rage when nothing else does. Gives me a sense of belonging that was absent for so long. It's the only peace I've ever known, but it's also something I've always done alone.

I will admit . . . I could get used to this.

CHAPTER FOUR

Delta

I stare into the mirror at my station, taking a deep breath. It's only my second night and I'm already dreading walking out on that stage. This isn't my life anymore. I don't want to be here. I wish there were another way, but now more so than ever, I want to push through, because today was one of the best days I've ever experienced. Holding that tattoo gun made every hour of lost sleep worth it. The adrenaline rush was almost more than I could bear. I fucking loved it.

I can still feel him on me: his hands against my thighs, his front against my back, and his lips beside my ear talking me through every color choice, every blending technique, and how to properly work the gun. And fuck the smell. It won't go away. The chemical makeup of his cologne, his soap, and whatever else makes him fucking smell like him has seared to the insides of my nose, assaulting me with memories recently made.

I didn't want it to end. Today was an unforgettable twelve hours. I'm still stunned I was there for that length of time and didn't notice till it was time to go. For the first time it didn't even seem like work. It was fun. Walking into the studio I had no idea what kind of mood he was going to be in after what happened in the lobby. One thing I've learned about Kross in the last four months is that his mood edges on broody almost constantly. He's controlling, he's closed off, and he's a damn psycho when it comes to me and men, as of today, but dammit if he's not all I can think about.

I'm not sure what changed. That's the million-dollar question. Before this morning I can't remember a single time that he's laid a hand on me aside from giving me a piece of paper, touching my hand accidentally, or me bumping into him by mistake. We had that one hot moment where he said the weirdest shit in the sexiest way the day of the interview and then he went completely cold.

Now, suddenly, he's threatening me of being with other men and telling random clients that I'm taken, feeling me up as he teaches. I already miss it, but I have no idea if I should expect him to be distant again or play along with this little . . . whatever it is.

My fingers rub down my neck, remembering the way he gripped it this morning. *You're my property.* I want to be his property. I just want to be . . . his. The way he handled me so rough, not worried about what I was thinking or how I'd react, made me want to combust under his hold, and that's something I haven't experienced in a really long time, if ever.

The door opens. Chuck. He has a smile on his face, stalking across the room toward me. His palms press against my chest from behind, and then he tries to descend into my lingerie. I sit forward, not wanting his hands on me. Instead of taking the hint, he brushes my hair to one side and places his lips to my skin. I tense. "What's wrong?"

"Nothing. I'm just trying to prepare. Did you need something?"

He pulls the strap over my shoulder. "You know what I want."

Sadly, I do . . .

My bed dips and a sudden rush of air caresses my body, pulling me from my slumber. I blink into the dark, trying to focus on the mass of man in front of me. "What time is it?" I ask as he shucks his boxers and gets in my bed.

"Late," he whispers, pulling his body against mine, his erection pressing against my belly. I pull the cover back up to my neck to block the air in my cold room.

"I have school tomorrow. What do you want?" My voice is thick, in dire need of water. My eyes finally start to adjust from the intrusion into my perfectly good sleeping state. I was dreaming I was on a beach somewhere, and even though I hate the beach it was nice, because it was anywhere else but here.

"You know what I want, Delta." His hand softly lands on the curve of my ass, only covered by a thin sliver of cotton, before guiding his fingers to the waistband of my panties, pulling them down.

"Where's Mom?" I roll onto my back, knowing he's not going to let me go back to sleep until he gets what he wants. Since I gave him my virginity last month, he's made every effort to show up in the middle of the night if the chance presented itself. When he's not at his club . . . But he's always waiting when I get home from school. Always. At first the guilt was there, slowly trying to consume me because of the circumstance, but with every cut down, every neglectful act, and every absence when I know she's not at work, I let him have me again and again. With every slur and every slap,

I give him more. He's had me in every hole and in every square inch of this house. And with each time the guilt diminishes a little more. She's too self-absorbed to notice her boyfriend is fucking her daughter. The ironic part is that the more he looks and talks to me the clingier she gets with him. It's not because she has suspicions, she just doesn't want me to get any attention. She's jealous. She's scared I'll be prettier than her.

My mother is an attention whore. Sure, she's done fairly well for someone that's a single mother. If she actually classified herself as such. But she doesn't work for her family she works for herself. She provides the necessities for me and nothing more. I can't really complain. I don't do without the things some people don't have . . . like Lux.

I have food readily available. I have a house, a room, clothing, and a few nice things. I've experienced a little life at the hands of her boyfriends. But I go to school and come home otherwise. I'm a seventeen-year-old with no car because that would require her to actually spend a little bit of her precious time and money to take her only child to get a license, not to mention a car. She lives for the party, for the social life, and for the men. She lives like a woman afraid to lose her youth. She doesn't want to be a mother at all. I'm convinced if she didn't think my presence made her look better in front of men she'd rid of me all together.

He wants me.

He makes me feel needed.

He sticks up for me.

"She's in bed."

"What if she wakes up?"

"She won't. She's had a bottle of wine. You know she doesn't like to stay home."

"Why do you stay with her? She only wants you because you're younger than her and you feed into her warped view that you make her look more desirable. She's a cunt."

I push my panties off as they reach my ankles. He pushes my camisole up my body and wraps his lips around my nipple as he gets on top of me. "We all use someone, baby. She uses me for status. I use her for you. She came into my club looking for her prey, bragging about how great of a mother she was. All it took was one photo and I knew I wanted you. It's more than I can say about her."

And then I grab the back of his head and pull his lips to mine. It may be a low blow, but it's words I still need to hear, and if using my body satiates that need, then I'll use it. Some of it may even be my way of getting revenge on the woman that conceived me but never wanted me. She's tolerant, and I'm convinced that's worse. She may not have aborted me physically, but she did mentally, and I can't say the two are all that different.

So I guide his dick between my legs, and with one hard thrust from him inside of me, I make myself hate her a little more.

His hand cups my breast as I blink the memory away. Things I've had locked away are coming back as if the floodgates were opened with me coming back here. I pull his hand away and replace my strap in its expected position. "Not right now. Maybe after I'm done."

"We have plenty of time, and you've never denied me before."

My heart is starting to race. Panic is quickly setting in. I don't want to sleep with him again. The only way I was able to stomach it last night was imagining he was Kross. That's totally fucked up, I know, but it's true. I wanted it to be him so badly. And for a second I thought that I might actually orgasm, but as quick as I thought it was coming it vanished. Maybe because the images of Kross wouldn't stay but for a few seconds at a time, being replaced with the reality of Chuck—a face that I used to find so much comfort and even some level of happiness in, but he and I were doomed from the start. Our relationship was built on a false premise.

Maybe the images left me because Kross doesn't want me. It's a fantasy, and fantasy never lasts. Most days I feel like his experiment. But now, with everything that has happened today I'm confused. I feel like I've done something wrong—being with Chuck. No matter the circumstances for why we're together it always feels wrong. I need to figure out a way to get him out of here until I can work all this shit out in my head.

I stand and turn to face him, placing my palm on his chest. He grips my ass in his hands but I let it go to avoid questions. "Hey, I just want it to be special next time."

He leans his head into the crook of my neck. I turn my head, trying to keep the places Kross has touched untainted. I search far and low to find that innocence that lies somewhere deep, deep inside of me. Something that's been lost for a lifetime it feels like. My voice mimics a pitch that isn't me. "Remember how we used to? In a bed. No clothing between us. It was just the two of us and skin while you made love to me. Do you remember?"

His fingers dig into my skin as he grips me tighter. "How could I forget? I've missed it for close to a decade."

The conniving, vindictive whore I used to be resurfacing sickens me. "Tonight you can have it back. Let's go back to those times. Not here. I don't want to be your whore."

"You've never been my whore. I've loved you since the day I laid my eyes on you."

"Then show me."

He finally releases me. A sense of relief washes over me. I move just in time for his lips to press against the side of my mouth instead of my lips. "Okay. You're staying with me tonight."

He touches the ring through the center of my bottom lip. "I want you to go down on me like you used to; like I taught you. I want to feel this against my skin."

He taught you everything . . .

I pull my lip between my teeth, disregarding the nausea in my stomach. There is no way in fucking hell I am sucking his dick. He moves to the diamond stud in the lower corner. "I like how you've accentuated your lips. They always were one of your best features, second to those eyes. I used to love watching them roll back in your head when you felt me between your legs."

"That's because you paid attention to what I liked. It was your best feature."

"I'm glad you're back. I've missed you. Things will be different this time. There's no one in our way."

I'm really hoping that's not true . . .

"Let me get ready. We can pick this up later."

"Okay. I'll be out front watching if you need me. Trish is almost done. You're on in ten."

He walks out, finally leaving me to myself. I glance in the mirror, making sure my black, leather, thigh-high boots are in place, before taking off the satin slip I was wearing to cover up the leather bikini set underneath. I brush through my hair once more and paint my lips with maroon lipstick. I like the way it looks against my creamy skin tone.

I stare at the reflection of someone I don't want to be. No one ever did *bad* better than me. I perfected it in adolescence. It was a skill I used often too. I thought I was past those days. I really wanted to be out of this phase. This is what will pay my rent, though. Show them that bad looks good . . .

"When can you have it?"

The razorblade works at the line from both directions, ensuring it's fine enough. I bend forward, one nostril closed, and snort it from right to left until I can feel the fine powder at the back of my throat and all that remains is a residue on the glass. "How many you need?"

"Three dozen."

"Fully automatic?"

"Yes. How quick can you get them?"

"Two weeks."

"How sure are you?"

I glance at him to my side, staring into a pair of gold frame sunglasses, the lens light enough I can see his eyes. Gold jewelry accents his dark skin in multiple places, just as it always does. His hair remains tight to the scalp in braided rows. "As sure as I am that you didn't cut this shit for once."

He smirks. "Gotta take care of my dealer."

"I'll have it."

He slides an envelope down the length of the table. "Here's half. Other half will be ready at pickup."

"Of course. Be expecting my call. Transfer will be same place."

He sits back and drapes his arm over the back of the couch when the topless girl straddles his lap. We've been working together for about eight months now and still we don't know each other's names. That's the way I like to keep things and so does he. Meetings always occur in the same place: a private room in this strip club. In this business you learn where you can wheel and deal and where the traps are. The owner is a fucking sleezeball, but that's better for me. He has underage strippers and we both know it, so he keeps his eyes away and his lips closed.

I grab my beer and take a drink, staring out at the stage through the one-way window. It's empty. Stripper change. "Ride it, girl. You sure you don't want one, Man? I can put in a call."

I glance over at him, his hands on her ass and her hands on his head. She's lighter complected than he is, her hair long in tight curls. She's got a nice ass and rack, but I've learned very recently that I prefer a custom flavor I've yet to try. "Nah. I'm good."

"Whatever you say, Man. I'll just sit here and enjoy enough for both of us."

My eyes settle back on the stage. Leather and lace and long, black hair assault me. Lots of fucking black. The kind of darkness that I like. The kind that I thrive in. The kind I've never seen here before. My thoughts race. Too much like the kind that I've been fucking dreaming about for a while now, despite the effort to stop. My eyes linger on every line of ink visible to the naked eye.

The second I recognize the tattoos my jaw locks. I have one skill better than most: photographic memory. It's what sets me apart from the rest. I never fucking forget something once I see it, especially tattoos. And I have damn good vision, even at a distance. One thought registers: she lied to me again. I watch her dance at the end of the raised stage, and then her top comes off. She spins it around one finger before tossing it down on the stage, immediately going for the pole. She doesn't even look like a fucking amateur.

Before I can stop it my mind begins to fog and something that hasn't haunted me for a long time returns.

My eyes pop open. "Rachel," I say, looking around at the dimly lit room as I rub my eyes. She's gone. The table with the big lights all around the mirror is empty. The others are too. I'm alone. She was just there. Where is she?

The walls are shaking from the loud music again. I stand from the little cot in the corner and walk to the door. I stop in front of it, standing and staring. I'm not supposed to leave this room. Rachel said never leave. It's unsafe. I'm supposed to stay here. Why did she leave me? Did I forget to follow her? Maybe she tried to wake me up. I should go find her. I think. I'm not supposed to wander around.

I tug down on my cartoon shirt. My eyes go big. I cross my leg over the other and grab myself. "Don't go. Don't go." I wiggle, trying to hold it. I squeeze, trying to make it stay. My wee-wee hurts but I try to hold it anyway. Warm wetness runs down my leg. Oh no. I'm going to get in trouble. I need to find Rachel.

I push up with both hands in the air, standing on the tips of my toes to reach the doorknob. It opens and the music gets louder. I follow the bright pink tube that runs along the top of the walls, passing the closed doors. I'm not supposed to open doors without Rachel.

I walk out into a big room. Lots of pink tubes and some other colors glow, but mostly pink. They're bright and hanging on the walls. I can't read them. I don't know how. It's dark and I can't see good with the lights flashing. I've been here before. It looks different. I stay by the wall, trying not to look at the men I don't know.

I keep my head down as I walk past, toward the light, calling her name out, hoping she can hear me. I look up when I step on something by accident. My eyes get big. "Rachel."

She doesn't have her clothes on. She's dancing, but that's not the way she dances to 'The Wiggles' on TV with me. There are people here. Boys. Boys aren't supposed to see girls naked. Why are her clothes gone? Did they break? Did she have an accident like me? I look around. What's that metal thing? Is this where firemen live?

I shout this time, trying to make my voice loud. "Rachel, I had an accident."

She stops and looks at me, but then starts back dancing as she looks around. She doesn't look happy. When her head points to me, her eyes go big like when I'm in trouble. "Kross, go back to the room," she whispers.

"But, Rachel, I—"

"Run, Kross. Now. Run."

I turn around to do as she says and bump into someone. I look up. The first thing I see: a large cross, drawn on the side of his neck. He squats down. "What are you doing here, boy?"

"I'm looking for Rachel. I had an accident."

He looks up. His face looks mad. "You can't be in here. Come with me. I'll deal with Rachel later."

I look back at Rachel as she whispers my name. I've been bad. And now she's the one in trouble . . .

I snort another line, ridding my brain of the content with no context. It's like reading a damn chapter without the rest of the book. A movie ending missing the beginning. Memories with no belonging. I refocus to the girl on that stage. Black leather boots on heels. Lace thongs to match. Hair I want to pull hard. A neck I want to grip. And a beautiful body on view that belongs to no one but me. I bought it.

One emotion in my fucking high state takes precedent over the rest: rage. With cocaine that's never a good combination for me. She spins around the pole and my anger cannot stay in this one fucking spot any longer. "I take that back. I found one I want. We done here?"

"Yeah, Man. I'll be waiting to hear from you. Two weeks."

I salute him and walk out of the room. The one thing that has always crawled under my skin and desecrated me is a fucking whore or stripper. Don't ask me why. I do business here, but that's it. I look at them with anger in my veins, not pleasure. There is no way in hell she's going to be working here if she's working for me. I don't care what I have to do to enforce it. I always get what I want. Always.

Detta

I group my tits together and fold them in half. I'll count them later. Right now I just want to take these shoes off my feet. Dancing in stilettos sucks. They were not intended to be worn for extreme activities. Then again, maybe they were. I prefer chucks, high tops . . . Hell, anything flat. These are more Lux's style.

I'm sweating; burning up, even though I know Chuck keeps it cold in here. *Keeps the nipples out*, he said, and nipples make the customers happy. I roll my eyes at the memory of that conversation from my first night. I thought he was 'the shit' back then. My way out of a shitty, unwanted existence. A way to live on my own. And it was . . . Until I wanted better for myself.

My thighs and calves are burning. I'm ready to go home and shower, to crawl into bed with a movie in the background as I fall asleep, but unfortunately that won't happen anytime soon for me. I still have another set later.

I walk into my dressing room and shut the door. "Lock it."

I nearly jump out of my skin at the sound of his voice, my hand immediately snaking over my breasts to cover them. Reflexively I lock it without questioning him. His tone is a little . . . harsher than usual, and his irritation is nothing new to those that work for him.

I look at him sitting in my chair, hunched over, legs spread wide with his elbows to his thighs, holding a lighter between them—my lighter, in fact. In a hypnotic rhythm he strikes it, causing the flame to emerge before letting it go. He's looking at it and not at me, as if he's trying to cool some sort of fury inside of him. My heart begins to race. I can feel my pulse beating along every passage in my body. My nerves spark like two wires being touched together with opposite charges. My oxygen tries to recede back into my lungs. I force the words out. "Kross . . . What are you doing here?"

He looks up at me, a cold, stone-like demeanor present, emotion absent. The words come out as controlled as he is. "Come here."

His eyes look different—determined, angry maybe. My feet automatically move toward him. I should stay where I am, but instead, I quickly tread across the floor to where he sits. The second I get to him he stands and grabs my neck so fast I can barely blink between movements. He forces me to sit on top of my vanity, head against the mirror as he comes between my legs. "What the fuck are you doing here?"

I grab his wrist as a reflex. "Kross, I'm working."

He looks down my almost-naked body, his judgment cutting into me like a serrated edged knife. If I didn't already feel like trash I would with just that look. "I can see that. What happened to the damn bar, Delta?"

He's seething. Fear sets in. Little to nothing scares me. I've worked for him for a while now. I've seen him on a daily basis and in many different moods. I've never heard this tone before. It's bordering on psychotic. And his eyes. What's wrong with his eyes? His grip tightens, but still not enough to hurt me in ways I can't take or cut off my air. Because even though he's holding me in a way that most would deem abusive, no bone in my body feels like he would physically hurt me. The only thing my mind can process is the fact that he's close, and that he's touching me in a way I've wanted him to since I laid eyes on him. He's looking at me like I'm his, like he's angry with me. I stare into his eyes, unable to look away even though I can't read them. "Answer me."

The words tumble out with no remorse. "He cut me for always being late. Demoted me to a fill-in as a form of punishment. I'm not working as many hours. I'm behind on rent. If I don't come up with the money I'll get kicked out of my apartment. This was an easy rehire, so I had no choice."

"Rehire? Fuck, Delta. I pay you," he grits.

I fight to speak against the constriction of my throat. "Minimum wage. I'm not a college kid chasing a social tag. It's not enough to cover bills." I cringe inside, not wanting him to know the shit I'm dealing with. It's personal. It's fucking embarrassing. I try to sit up, but he pushes me back against the mirror. "Look. I'm making it work. What the hell does it matter? It's not interfering with my schedule at the shop."

"Why didn't you come to me? I specifically asked you this morning if you had any problems with your pay." He's staring at me, eyes deadpanned, not even blinking.

My anger is spilling out in waves. "Because I want to earn my spot just like everyone else. I'm going to show you one way or another that I fucking deserve to be tattooing beside you, and I'll do whatever it takes to do so."

His lips crash against mine, hard, roaring sounds ripping from his throat as his hands grip behind my knees and pull me to the edge of the table. His fists close around the waistband of my black thongs so hard I'm probably going to have bruises on my hips from his knuckles. He removes them. I grip onto the table's edges, holding myself steady, and internally chanting for him to continue.

Damn he can kiss. It's rough, hard in nature just like him, but then his lips are so soft, cushioning mine for every strike. His tongue enters at the right moment, leaving long enough for you to want it back. I can hear his belt buckle—the jingling sound before his zipper follows—my insides rejoicing in anticipation. He angles my bottom and then I feel it. He enters me. With one clench my body molds around him, an auto response to something I've been dreaming about. I moan into his mouth, not expecting his size. Truthfully I expected him to be smaller because of his large build. Judging on past experience. It's a hard habit to kill. But I guess it's true . . . What they say about those who assume. It makes an ass out of you and me. This time, me. All he's done is shove his cock inside of me and already he's satiating a need I've had for so long—the very act that drove me to this neediness to begin with. I need this. I want this. Already my pussy is panting. And it's only just begun.

He pulls my foot up onto the table and pounds into me. His lips trail down until his teeth sink into my neck, and then he crosses my leg over, roughly turning me around without pulling out. "Fuck!"

He pulls my hair as he drives inside of me over and over again, deeper this way. He grinds against my backside, his thrusts slowing, until he's completely still. He jerks me up, grabbing my breast in his tattooed hand, his teeth skimming my neck once again, until his mouth is outside of my ear. "You want to live like a whore you get treated like one. Respect is earned, and not just in my shop."

He pulls out and immediately I hear his pants being pulled back up, leaving his seed smeared between my thighs. I turn around, our eyes locking. Anger is rolling off of him in waves. That much is clear. And even though I didn't orgasm like I had hoped, my pussy is throbbing, the hungry bitch wanting more. "I guess I'll see you in the morning then?"

"No. Put on clothes and get your shit. You're coming with me."

"I can't leave yet. Did you not hear anything I said? I thought that was you understanding."

He closes in on me, his jaw ticking. "Did you not hear anything I said this morning? I don't share my fucking property. As long as I write your checks and you call my shop home, you're mine. Rightfully owned. That was me dotting the i's and crossing the fucking t's. To make myself clear, you won't need your apartment, because obviously I have to babysit my employees."

"Don't be a dick. Last time I checked I'm an adult. I don't need supervision."

"This is the way it's going to go. And if you don't like it you're free to walk out the door you walked into that night. The one that has my name on it. Which option you choose doesn't matter to me. Should you choose to stay, you're going to live with me for now. Pay is earned just like my respect. I didn't get where I am by being a pushover. You're still an apprentice. Just because you're a hot piece of ass in the shop all day doesn't mean you get special treatment. All of us have put our time in somewhere. But right now you work for me. When I say be there, you ask what time. When I say stay don't question how long. If I tell you to jump you ask how high. That's the way this works. I keep business and play as separate as

CHARISSE SPIERS

church and state. I'm not going to show you favoritism just because I'm fucking you before bedtime, so instead, I'm eliminating your biggest bills."

"No. I can't do that. I've never—"

"It's not optional. Do you want this job or not? No employee or girl of mine is going to be showing ninety percent of her body to other men. What part of my property isn't for public use did you not understand? Until you walk away, you are mine."

My mouth isn't going to win me any tokens here. But it just won't stay shut. "Well, maybe I was a little confused at what specifically you meant by me being your property," I bite back, tired of his angry tone. "Boss and bed mate are two totally different things."

"All that apply. Are you still confused or was my dick enough of an explanation?"

I cross my arms over my chest; my leg cocks out to prove my mouth isn't going to shut anytime soon. It used to piss my mother off I'm sure it's not going to stop for him. "That depends. Is this mutually owned exclusive property?"

"One is more than enough for me."

His response catches me off guard. I'm sure my face shows it. I'm trying really hard not to smile. When a knock sounds at the door it becomes easier not to. "Delta, baby, let me in."

"Shit."

Every inch of his body becomes rigid. "Let me guess. The reason for your phone being off lately?"

"It's a long story that I can't explain right now."

"You fuck him?"

"That's completely irrelevant. I needed my job back and I've known him for a long time. This shit right here happened today. You cannot ask me questions regarding things prior to you telling me you wanted something between us."

The doorknob wiggles. "Delta, unlock the door."

"Put your goddamn clothes on. We're leaving."

I quickly unzip the thigh-high leather boots, tossing them on the floor. He stalks to the door and I grab a pair of denims and a tee shirt, pulling them on. Then I step into my high top sneakers, quickly working the backs over my heels. Kross disappears out the door and then I hear something fall into the wall. I grab my stuff in a hurry and take off running. "That was her resignation. Try to contact my girl and I'll rip you apart motherfucker. You know I'm good for it."

He looks at me, anger blazing in his eyes. "Let's go."

I follow behind him, passing by Chuck sitting on the floor against the wall, holding his eye with blood trickling down his cheek. I'm not even sure that this is realistically happening right now. I could be dreaming for all I know, but what I'm sure of is that if it's a dream I don't want to wake up, because even without orgasm that was quite possibly the best fucking I've ever gotten.

Living in a house . . . with Kross. Holy shit.

CHAPTER FIVE

Delta

He pulls up at a rather large house a good stretch outside of town. It's secluded. It's private. I'm not even sure why that surprises me. I guess I just imagined him being an urban living kind of guy. You know, the middle of the city, walking distance to all the hot spots. Maybe I should just stop stereotyping him completely, because he keeps proving he doesn't fit in any of them.

His truck smells good, like his cologne mixed with something clean. It smells like him. That smell will cling to my nose forever. I glance over at him. I've tried to keep quiet by looking out my window the entire time. He doesn't seem like much of a talker. "What's on your mind?"

He hasn't looked at me this entire time, and he still isn't. He just presses the button to raise the garage door and pulls in. "Are you sure about this? If the dancing—"

"Fucking stripping. Don't try to give it class it doesn't deserve."

I roll my eyes, and then recite the speech I've heard a thousand times by the girls at the club. "That's not the accepted term for those that choose it as a form of living, but I'll humor you. If the 'stripping' is really going to bother you I can just try and get my job back at the bar and we can work out a schedule. I don't have to move in with you."

He kills the engine, still staring straight ahead. "Once I make a decision I don't go back on it. Seeing you up there was a kick to the balls. I've had time to cool down, but other men looking at you that way makes me angry, and a bar isn't that much better. I'm not sure why it does, but I don't do well with anger. Someone recently reminded me that I couldn't control what you do if I don't make you mine, so here we are. I've ignored you for four months because I'm your boss. I'm over it. I'm going to say this and then I doubt I'll talk about it again, so listen closely. I'm not an easy guy to live with. I'm an asshole really, and I'm set in my ways. You won't change me. There's no point in trying. I have no emotional capabilities. Don't do that shit most girls do. Leave your heart out of this relationship or you'll end up resenting me. I likely won't talk about my childhood and I expect everything you see or hear to never leave your mind in any way."

"My heart was never part of the equation. I lost it a long time ago," I say without thought before doing so.

"Good. I guess that settles it then. Let's go and I'll show you where you'll be sleeping. We'll get your shit later."

I follow him out of the truck to the door. I walk inside, purse in hand. Everything is dark. He turns on the light and I realize we're in the living room. I'm in grunge heaven. Blackout curtains cover the windows and the couch is black leather against a dark gray wall. The throw pillows are all dark in theme with the decorative fronts: some words, some skulls or a monster of some form, and some directly related to rock, but all implying a dark undertone. A big screen television is mounted to the wall over the mantle of the fireplace, an electric guitar hanging to each side, though each different in looks. He has two recliners in front of the wall directly across from the television that match the couch, with a gun cabinet sitting between them, a lock hanging on the outside.

"Sweet crib."

"What were you expecting?" I jump at his voice just outside of my ear. Fuck, how does he do that? "Floral and subtle colors?"

A dry laugh escapes. "Maybe no decor at all. Definitely messy and bland."

"I'm pretty specific in my likes."

"I guess that makes two of us."

He grabs my arm and tows me toward the staircase. "Everything is pretty easy to find down here. You can wander anywhere except my bedroom and the basement without me here."

One by one we climb the stairs until we reach the top floor. He opens the first door on the right. It's a bedroom the same dark gray as the living room; only white, fluffy bedding is on the large dark-stained poster bed. It's fully furnished, but otherwise plain. "This is your room. Do with it what you want."

"Okay."

He tugs me into the door across the hall. It's a large bathroom with a freestanding soaker tub, the focal point for the whole room. The shower is separate. Aside from the black towels and the dark tile, it too is plain. "You can put your shit wherever you want. Everything you need for a shower in the meantime is in the linen closet. My bathroom is downstairs attached to my bedroom, so this is yours."

"Thanks." I start to back out of the bathroom and he grabs my shirt, pulling me back in, before shutting the door. He reaches for the bottom of my shirt and pulls it over my head. "What are you doing?"

"You're going to shower the filth off of your body."

He backs me against the door. His eyes fall to my chest, before returning to mine. He jerks at my shorts with one hand, pulling the button through the slit, and then he pushes them to the floor, leaving me naked for the second time tonight. I have no idea why he's undressing me. "Are you showering too?"

"Not up here."

"Then why are you removing my clothes? I'm a big girl."

"Because I'd rather be the one to finish you off than to think you're up here masturbating."

He never leans in like he's going to kiss me. His hand cups between my legs and two fingers enter me. I stare at him, my breathing starting to heighten. My legs part a little, giving him more room. He fingers me, but only for a few seconds before his fingers travel between my lips to my clit. Him staring into my eyes as he does it is more nerve-racking than anything I've ever experienced. I want to look away, but then I don't.

He rubs me in a quick motion and pressed firmly to my clit, adding a pressure I like. "Shit."

He grips my thigh and pulls my leg up to his waist. I can feel it better. The back of my head slams against the door. "H-o-l-y fuuuuck."

His lips slam against mine in the middle of my orgasm, hard and rough. My hands go for the back of his hair, gripping fistfuls as we kiss. He bites around my lip ring, turning me on more.

The feelings consuming my body fade almost as quickly as they started, leaving me in a blissful state, my eyes heavy. His lips slow when his hand stops, but he doesn't immediately leave. He breathes heavily against my mouth, until finally, he pulls away. "Get some sleep and meet me in the kitchen at 7AM. We're taking the day off to get your shit in order."

I move out of his way when he reaches for the doorknob. Just as cold as he was at the beginning, he leaves, shutting the door behind him. My back falls against the door and I slide down, until I'm squatting just above the floor. My hands go for my face, trying to process what all has happened tonight. "Fuck," I whisper, remembering the unprotected sex from earlier.

I drag my purse over from the spot I dropped it as he took my shirt off, digging through it until I find the Plan B emergency contraceptive I keep with me in case something happens. I used to be on birth control, but I only remembered to take it when I was sexually active, which basically means it's not working, and dealt with the uncomfortable symptoms I had from it unlike most people. When I stopped having sex there was really no point anymore. I always just kept this as a backup and I've never let someone inside me without a condom. That was really stupid.

I place the pill on my tongue and stand, turning on the water. There is already a stack of small paper cups beside the sink. I grab one and fill it with water, making it easier to swallow the pill. If this is going to happen more often I should probably consider getting back on a regular birth control in some form.

I turn and prop against the counter, looking around the room. The tub looks the most appealing of anything. I think I may. I haven't soaked in a hot bath in a while, and after today . . . I think I need it.

CHAPTER SIX

Kross

I stand at the kitchen counter, glancing at the clock: 6:58. I can hear footsteps tromping down the staircase like a damn Cyclops. If she's going to go anywhere with me we're going to have to work on some things, because that shit is not going to cut it. That kind of noise will give away a person in the matter of seconds; precisely the amount of time it can take to get your ass killed or caught. I pull two mugs down from the cabinet and fill them both with coffee from the pot.

She walks around the corner, hair on top of her head and dressed in a tiny pair of pink, spandex shorts with a black and gray band tee shirt to accompany a pair of sneakers. Her eyes are heavily lined in black and her lashes look like spider legs they're so caked on with mascara. I still don't get women and makeup, no matter how much I age. They will never understand the term 'less is more' or the fact that all that shit painted on their face is the same as false advertisement for many.

She glances up at me as I slide one cup across the bar, her face in a pout. "Are you fucking serious?"

"Cursing like a sailor so early? Must be a good day."

"Do you just wake up looking this hot? It's a little insulting to those of us that look like crypt-keepers if we're woken before like ten."

I look down at myself and take a sip of coffee. "Looks like clothes to me. I'm not sure I see the specialty. By the way, they are made to cover. If you bend over your ass will fall out of those shorts. And it looks like a second skin."

"What's the point in having ink if you're not going to show it off? I like my thigh tattoo. I saved for a long damn time for it. It's getting seen."

"Do you know how many guys will actually be looking at your tattoo? I'm going to say about five percent and that's probably because they're not into females."

She rolls her eyes and picks up the mug, her eyes going for the coffee pot. "Have you never heard of a Keurig? That thing is old school."

I glance at it, half full of coffee. "Who said old school was a bad thing? I'm a simple guy. It works just fine without me spending unnecessary money for a fad."

"You would say that. It's less wasteful, not a fad." She takes a sip from her cup and immediately starts coughing behind the swallowing sound. "Poison. It's fucking poison. What the hell is that? I don't want hair on my chest."

I'm already half a cup down, but as I take another sip I grab the bag of grounds and set it before her. "Coffee. That shit you pay a ridiculous amount of money for is not coffee."

"At least it tastes good." She picks it up and reads the writing on the black bag. "Well you can't accuse them of false advertising. Why would anyone buy coffee from *Death Wish Coffee Company?* Are you trying to find your way out peacefully or something? Although I must say, I like the skull logo on the packaging and black is my favorite color. Where did you find this?"

"Online. I'm up a lot."

"You don't say. I was starting to think you were secretly a vampire."

"I can sleep when I'm dead."

"Which could be soon if you don't sleep enough. It's fact that our bodies need six to eight hours of sleep to properly function. But I'm more of a ten to twelve hour kind of girl. Why are we up so early if we're taking the day off?"

"Because we're taking one day off. Not multiple. And we have shit to do."

"I really don't have that much stuff, and we have all day and night since you never seem to need sleep."

"I work at night."

"I thought we were *taking the day off?*"

"You talk a lot to not be a morning person."

"You don't talk enough to be a person."

"I only say what I need to."

She walks around the bar toward me, eliminating the great big counter between us. I watch her as she does. She glares at me, and then she grabs the bottom of my shirt and rubs her hand up the left side of my front, stopping over my heart. I flinch at her touch. "I'm still not convinced you're human."

Being touched leaves me in a state that I don't like. I grab her wrist and remove it. "I never said I was. Are you going to drink that or let it go to waste?"

She steps closer, staring at me still. "So you can touch me whenever you want but I can't touch you? Is that how this is?"

"It's nothing personal. I just don't like it."

"What if I said that's not going to work for me?"

"I don't know what to tell you other than to deal with it."

She grabs my belt in her fist and pulls me toward her, forcing my cup back on the countertop. "I think you've underestimated me a little. I don't back down that easily, Kross." Her hands dip under my shirt again and slide slowly up the front. I swallow, trying to breathe through the fucking anxiety building with each inch she climbs.

A flash occurs, drowning out the present more quickly than I can blink it away.

"I thought I told you not to come out of your room without permission."

"But I had to use the bathroom."

She stalks toward me with the cigarette hanging out of her mouth; the belt ends in her hand. "You don't get it, do you? No one wants you. Your parents didn't want you and no one else wants to adopt you. You're only here to make me money. This is my house. You abide by my rules."

The leather swings forward and licks the center of my chest, stinging. I back up, but she follows me, the ashes from her cigarette falling on the floor. She swings again, harder this time. The belt hurts, but not as much as her words. She uses them often and most of the time laughs right after.

I continue to my door. When I turn the belt licks across my back, knocking me forward with the arch of my spine. The door slams and I can hear the keys jingling as she locks the door from the outside. I turn over, my hand rubbing along the red stripes now on my skin.

Tears fall down my eleven-year-old cheeks, trying to remember my parents. I've tried over and over again, but nothing ever comes. And the result is always the same. I bang the inside of my fist against my forehead repeatedly, angry that I can't remember. Maybe it's best that I can't, because they left me here . . . in Hell with the devil's wife.

"Stop!"

Her hands drop with the thunder of my voice, her eyes wide. She backs away from me. Fuck. I'm not used to this. I place my fists on the bar, my eyes downcast on the quartz, breathing heavily. "Come here."

"No. That's okay. Sorry I pushed."

"Come the fuck here."

"Kross, it's fine."

"Don't make me repeat myself again."

I can see her feet as she approaches. I grab her shirt and pull her in front of me, her back against the counter. She props her elbows on the bar, arching away from me. "I have issues," I say.

"I understand. We all have demons."

"I've never done this," I continue.

"I won't hold it against you."

"I'll try to be less of an asshole."

"I'll still be here even when you can't," she says, staring into my eyes.

That statement grips me in a way I don't understand. "Touch me."

"I don't have to. It's okay."

I remove my shirt and lay it on the counter. She glances at my chest. "Your body is beautiful."

"Touch me. Slowly."

Her hand comes toward me, hovering about an inch over my skin. My breathing spikes again, but my eyes remain locked with hers. It finally becomes flush with my chest. My heart is racing.

"They can't hurt you. Whoever did this to you." Her fingers find my scar, covered in ink, and then it starts.

"You stole from me."

"I didn't take anything. I've been in here."

"Don't lie to me, you little bastard. Where are they?" She's *yelling in the doorway of my small cluttered room.*

"Where is what?"

She walks toward me. The smell of cigarettes filter through my nose. *"You took them. Where are they?"*

"I haven't taken anything."

"Maybe I just need to remind you what happens when you lie." *The cap opens on the lighter and the flame stands tall at the turn of the metal. She continues moving toward me.*

"I'm not lying."

"Is that why your parents didn't want you? You were a little shit-stirring liar, weren't you?"

I watch the orange and yellow waving back and forth with the air in the room. When she reaches me, she squats to my level. *"I don't have parents."*

She laughs. *"Everyone has parents. Yours just didn't want you. You were a bad seed from the start. They saw it and ran. Now I'm stuck with you."* *An ugly smile spreads on her face, showing her off-white, slightly crooked teeth. Her blonde hair has taken on a yellowish color from the smoking. She's middle-aged, but looks older than her physical age by the tough texture of her skin. She's skinny because her cigarettes are more important than food. "You like fire? Do you want to hurt me with it? I bet you want to watch me burn, don't you?"*

I remain still, ignoring her. The flame goes out and then the hot metal presses against my chest, adhering to my skin. It hurts. It smells bad. I want to scream, but I don't. "He doesn't even cry. I knew you were a little freak. I will find them. If my cigarettes come up missing again it'll be worse next time."

She rips it away, as if she ripped the skin with it and then leaves, locking the door once more. My hand touches the place that hurts and my other one goes for my mouth. I bite down hard as I scream, trying to smother it.

My shoulders tense and bow as the anger moves through my body, looking for an outlet. She jumps on my front and her lips collide with mine. I can feel the metal from hers skimming my skin. Sounds of her frantic breaths come in steady waves. "Open your eyes. Look at me. I need you to see me."

My hands grip onto the back of her thighs to keep my balance. I blink; unaware they were even closed. "I'm fucked up. I'm a monster in disguise. You should run while you can."

"I think I want to stay."

"You're going to regret it. I can't be the type of man a woman wants. I'll never want the same things. I'll use you. I'm a bad person."

"Says the person that cares whether or not I'm homeless?"

"No one should be on the street. And no woman should be selling her body to stay off of it."

"So you would just let anyone move in with you?"

"No. You work for me. It's different."

"Any woman could work for you."

I shake my head. "I don't hire women in the studio. Conflict of interest."

She starts to smirk, but then it falls back into place as if it was in error. "Well, I can't be the type of woman a man wants, so I guess we're on the same page. My heart was burned in adolescence, and all that remains is a black organ with barely a beat, so you don't have to worry about me falling in love with you. We can just be two fucked up functioning addicts together."

"Okay."

"Lux had terrors. I'm not new to this. Tell me what makes it better when they bother you," she whispers. My fingers slip beneath her stretchy shorts.

"Tattooing."

"Let's go get my stuff, and then you can work on my sleeve. I'll even let you choose what to add."

"But first, do that again."

"Do what again?"

"Chase them away."

Her eyes fall to my lips as she leans in, and then she kisses me, her lips soft against mine; something I've never experienced before, and something I never thought I would like . . . until now.

CHAPTER SEVEN

Detta

I accidentally roll onto my newly tattooed arm, the sting waking me up. To relieve it I turn on my side, allowing it to drape over my body, before searching for the old, ratty, one-eyed stuffed puppy I never sleep without. When my hand finds it not far away from me I snuggle it against my body. At least he keeps it cold in his house—the only way to sleep.

"Aren't you a little old for stuffed animals?"

I jump at the sound of his voice, my eyes popping open. "Fuck, Kross. That's creepy as hell," I say, groggy, trying to focus on the dark figure standing against the doorframe. I really should buy a gun, a knife, something to protect myself. I've never been a fan of weapons—didn't think I'd ever be in a place in my life that I'd need one—but maybe Lux was right. You never know what kind of

This one I may want stalking me, though. Just a thought.

He walks inside, not stopping until he's sitting on the edge of the bed beside me. I scoot back a little to give him room. "What time is it?"

"2AM."

Things finally start to register in my half-sedated mind. "Why the fuck are you awake?" I tug on his thin, black, long sleeve shirt at his back. "And dressed? Long sleeve at that . . . It's October and we live in the south."

"I told you I work at night."

"The last appointment at the shop was 8 o'clock. In case you forgot you were shading in the rose on my arm when they left."

"How serious were you this morning about wanting to stay?"

Let's not tackle B. No, Kross Brannon jumps from A to C.

"Serious enough to fucking live with you. I'm a loner. I don't 'live' with people. Not even Lux. And sacrifice my much-wanted sleep, apparently. Why? This is not important conversation at 2AM. Are you going to make me regret this? I haven't attempted to live with someone since Lux and I first moved here. I like my own space. That didn't work out too well. We're totally different in that sense."

"Stop talking. Get up and get dressed."

"Damn. You're a pessimistic asshole. For what?"

"There's somewhere I have to be."

"I'm not stopping you. Just pretend I'm not here between the hours of midnight and 6AM since you eliminated the only reason I had to be awake at those times before and expect me to wake up at the butt crack of dawn. I thought one of the perks of having a cool-ass job was to have less structured hours."

He stands to leave and I pull the comforter up to my neck, my eyes already closing. The second they start rolling back in my head he jerks the covers off the bed completely, the air kissing my skin and leaving chill bumps. "Fuck! What?"

"I tried to play nice."

"If you wake me up expect the bitch to come out and play. She's not pretty either."

He straddles me and turns his hat around. "It wouldn't be the first time I've dealt with a bitch. This one I know how to make disappear."

He rips my panties at the thin string on my hip and peels the front down, not worrying with the other side. Before I can fully wake up my thighs are on my stomach, my knees at my breasts, and his lips touch down on my . . . "Shit."

His warm tongue slides between my lips, stopping on my clit. He alters flicking and sucking, both quick changes, and staying at the exact spot I need without moving. My hand goes for his head, recoiling when it grips around his hat instead of hair, going for my own breasts as the loud moans exit my mouth. "You're really good at . . . that. Fuck."

He bites me and I'm fucking done. The second his tongue rubs over it in short quick strokes the orgasm comes, fast and hard. As I start to come down he shoves his tongue inside of me, making it last a little longer, and then rolls it so I can feel it, before slowly pulling out. "God bless America."

"Leave our country out of this. Get up and get dressed."

He gets off the bed; every damn fine inch of him. I groan when he starts to walk away. "I hate you."

"Good. Meet me downstairs in five minutes. Wear black and quiet shoes. Your coffee will be waiting."

He starts to open the door. "I'm only going because of your

choice of wake up call."

He shuts the door without acknowledging me. "Add milk to my death coffee!"

"Five minutes," he yells back.

I shamefully drag my post orgasmic body out of the bed and walk to my dresser that was just filled at lunch with all of my fold-up clothes. The panties fell to the floor as I stood. I failed miserably, disappointing independent women everywhere. We are supposed to have all the control over sex. That's the way nature intended.

He didn't even act like he wanted sex. He just waltzed in here, ate my pussy like a fucking champion, and then walked out without me even knowing whether he had a hard-on as a result. Furthermore, he hasn't initiated sex again since the club when he just fucking took it without asking. I'm not complaining. I want it again. I'm pathetic. I've gone two years without sex just fine and suddenly he gives me a damn quickie and I'm like an addict. Makes no damn sense.

My head falls back as I remove a pair of black yoga pants from the drawer, slowly pulling them on without bothering with panties. Work tomorrow is going to suck. Why the hell did I agree to this? Oh, because the damn sexy tattoo God gave me a little attention and now I'm like a puppy waiting for table scraps. Doomed. I'm fucking doomed.

Kross

I look back through my side mirror as the black suburban pulls in behind me. I glance over at the passenger seat, the taste of her still lingering on my tongue. Her smell clings to my scent palate in a way nothing ever has. Her head is leaning against the window and her feet are folded in the seat.

Don't ask me why I fucking brought her. I don't just bring people into my business. The more people that know increases my chances of getting caught. I don't get caught. Ever. Too much is at stake if I do. I'll kill before I will. Done it before. The only way to keep respect is to have people fear you. To instill fear in someone is to fear nothing and prove you aren't a pushover. Sometimes you have to make an example out of someone to do so. And I haven't feared anything in a long time. I just hope she can keep her mouth shut. It'd be unfortunate to execute someone with such God-given talent. Someone that makes my mouth water simply by existing. The only way to truly know is to test her.

She looks at me when I kill the truck. I grip the back of her neck, having told her basically nothing this entire drive. To ensure she pays attention, I force her head to look up at me. "Don't say a fucking word; don't stare at them, stay by me, and the second this is done never speak of it again, not even to Lux. Do I make myself clear?"

"Okay."

"Let's go."

I open my door and get out, waiting for her to round the front. They stay in the suburban, watching me, as I walk toward the storage unit they pulled next to. I glance around before stopping at the appropriate one. After this deal I'll cancel this unit and move on to another. I never keep anything long-term. Habitual behavior is what gets people locked up. I don't do well in a cage. The demons then come out to play.

They open the doors to the SUV when I shove the key in the lock, pulling it off and lifting the door. "Get inside." She does as I say and I wait for the two men to enter before me, and then I file in behind them, shutting the door and turning on the overhead light.

"They all here?" the one running this operation asks.

"Yes. I got the full order."

"Who's this?" He nods at Delta in the back corner, his hand on his piece under his shirt that's strapped to his waist. "You didn't mention someone else."

"She's with me. You don't have to worry about her."

"I don't like surprises."

"If she runs her mouth I'll kill her myself."

"Let me see her dirty."

I stare at him, his hand still on his gun. He doesn't scare me, but if he gets pissed off she'll be the one he aims for. He knows he can't take me down. "Delta, come here."

She walks toward me and I hold out my hand. The one staying quiet places a small, clear bag in it. "It's already ready to go."

She's looking at me, questioning me without even opening her mouth. I reach into my pocket, pulling out the cheap BIC pen and then disassemble it, keeping only the hollow cylinder. She takes it as soon as I hand it to her, waiting for instruction. I pour two lines, snorting the first one, because there is no way they are leaving without the full bag being gone and I'm not letting her do that much blow. They are the runners for one of my biggest buyers. You don't move that much inventory without being serious about using it if necessary to cover your ass.

I wipe the residue off my nose and pull her to the box in front of me. "Snort it."

I can feel her shaking as she looks at it, but without hesitating she places one side of the narrow pen casing to the end of the line, the other at her nostril, and does it, inhaling it all and leaving nothing behind. Her hand immediately starts wiping at her nose and she keeps sniffing. "You ready to do this?"

"Let me see her chest, bruh. I don't play."

He's pissing me off. I turn us, keeping her back at my front, before gripping the bottom hem of her shirt and lifting it to her neck to show him she's not wearing a wire, then slowly turn her for him to see the back. "Now quit harassing my girl and let's do this before I cancel the order. I'm sure he's made you well aware not to fuck with me. No one else can fill that kind of quota on short notice. I'll tell Hector myself his two goons couldn't do the job and he can come see me if he has a problem with it. Do you want the shipment or not?"

He walks forward, the gold cap on his tooth showing through the smirk he has on his face. He's looking at her in a way that makes me want to rip every tooth from his head one at a time. He grabs her chin in his hand. She tries to turn away, but he's gripping her too tight. His tongue runs along his teeth as he looks at her. I swear to God if he touches her with it I'll cut it off. "We good, Man. Just gotta protect boss-man. You sure do know how to pick 'em. I bet this one is fun to look at while she rides."

My eyes close, my jaw working overtime, the cocaine filtering through every vessel. I open them, ready to shred something from the anger quickly building. "You have about a second to remove your fucking hand from her or I will kill you with the very gun strapped to your body. If you think I'm incapable keep up your shit. I've been doing this a hell of a lot longer than you have."

He drops it. "Open the boxes and we'll pay and be on our way."

I open the one in front of us and grab the 9mm sitting on top, tossing it to him. He inspects it and places it back in, waiting on me to open all of them so he can see inside. After the final one he grabs the small duffel from his partner and tosses it to me. "It's all there."

"I'll check."

He sucks his gold tooth. "Load them, Dwayne."

His partner lifts the unit door and walks toward the truck, taking one box with him. "Delta, get in the truck."

She doesn't even let the last word exit my mouth before taking off in a sprint toward it. Before he can wrap his eighth grade educated mind around what I'm about to do, I close the door and move behind him, grabbing his black hair in my fist, the point of my knife already pressed into the rosary beads between the praying hands over his jugular. His hand goes to his gun. "Try it, motherfucker. I'm much faster than you."

I smell along his neck—fear—watching the blue line become more visible as the blood pumps harder and faster through his vein. I press the tip into the skin, along the edge of his vein and pull downward, purposefully missing it, but hard enough to watch the blood seep through as his skin parts from the cut. "I may be his dealer but I don't work for anyone, especially not someone like you that's easily disposable. Who do you think Hector will get rid of if you fuck up his vendors, huh? Me or you?" He grits his teeth, bucking against me, earning him another slice. "If you ever fuck with something that belongs to me again, specifically that someone, you won't walk away alive. One centimeter over and I can watch the blood drain from your body one beat at a time. I'm not a man of second chances. Next time I'll bury you where no one will find you. Get your shit and lock up. I'll be watching."

I release him and disarm him as I shove him forward, before walking to the door, lifting it once again. Delta has her fingertips in her mouth, staring out the truck window at me when my eyes land on her. "Tell your boss to expect my call."

And I will, because if he sends that stupid-ass motherfucker back his head will return in a box just like the inventory he was sent after.

Della

I jump out of the truck y he pulls into the garage, my heart pounding in my chest, still scared shitless. I can feel him at my heels all the way to the door. He unlocks it and I walk inside, angry. I haven't said a word the entire ride back to his house. It takes a lot to scare me, but I was fucking terrified back there and I had no prior warning of what I was walking into.

I stared at that roll-up door with the truck locked, hand on the button waiting for him, wondering if he was dying, if they were going to come after me, what they would do to me if they did. Between this fucking high I've never experienced and the fear of what could have happened, I'm wound up. "You ready to run yet?" his voice booms from behind me. "Not the good little tattoo artist you thought I was, am I?"

I stop in my effort to go to my room, my breathing heavy and my emotions running wild. I turn around, wanting answers. "You're a fucking arms dealer? A gunslinger like the shit we see on T.V.?"

"Yes."

"What's the point in your tattoo shops then?"

"Part cover-up, the other part legit. Tattooing is real for me. I just use it to my advantage. That's all you need to know."

"Here I was thinking you're this special brand of man, gifted by the tattoo gods and the entire time you're just a criminal in disguise?"

"That's your problem, not mine. Don't remember telling you I was clean. I didn't seek you out. You came to me. You walked into my world, baby."

I'll admit that stings a little. But it's true. Now here we are and I feel like I'm drowning at the thought of walking away. I need to know what I'm dealing with if I stay. I've never been in trouble with the law.

"What else do you deal? Drugs? Women? Please say no."

"No. Not anymore. Drugs got boring. And do I look like I get off at the idea of selling pussy to the highest bidder? Human trafficking isn't interesting to me at all."

My hands go to my face. I feel like I can't breathe. My chest hurts. Is this what a panic attack feels like? "Fuck. Not anymore? How often do you *use* drugs, Kross? Because you didn't look like an amateur back there."

"Just like you didn't look like an amateur on that pole."

I feel like I was just kicked in the stomach, but I fight to ignore it. "How often?"

"When I need to. I have an image to keep. It's no different than undercover cops in the middle of drug rings. They do it all the time to slip in unnoticed. That's why they wanted to make sure you weren't wearing a wire. There is no such thing as a clean dealer. It's part of the life. You can't have one without the other."

I laugh, my body heating. "You're comparing yourself to a cop? Someone trying to get crime off the streets?"

"I told you I was a bad guy. You won't change me. There is no way out for me. I'm in too deep and I like what I do. From the first day you walked into my shop I've been the same. I never pretended to be the fucking guy a girl falls in love with or rides into the sunset with like the lame ass movies. I'm the kind of guy that leads you to an ending like Bonnie and Clyde."

Thoughts race to find their place. "At the club were you . . . when we . . ."

"Was I high when I fucked you? Yes. Doesn't mean I don't remember it."

My heart sinks a little. I've always been told you do things you wouldn't normally do when high. God knows I have drunk too many times to count. Drugs are a foreign place for me. Would he have still fucked me had he been sober? Would it have been different if he had? I think a part of me would die a little if the answer to question one were no.

His massive body takes up so much space. Every muscle has volume under his skin. I stare into his brown eyes, the fear-driven adrenaline pumping through my body. Feelings I don't understand are going on inside of me, creating a whirlwind effect. Even high out of my mind he's still the sexiest man I've ever seen. The risk of becoming an accessory to God only knows what kind of charges doesn't even make me want to end this. I think it's going to take a lot more than drugs to change the way I see him. And I don't know why. I've always played it safe where Lux liked risk and adventure. Regardless of how much I want him physically, I've got to be crazy to stand here and listen to this or to continue any sort of involvement with him knowing everything I do now. The words fly out of my mouth before I can think of them. "Why did you take me there? Was this a test? To see if you can trust me?"

"Yes. You said you wanted to stay. This is what it requires if you do. You need to know what you're walking into, but even if you leave, I meant what I said back there. If you open your mouth it'll be the last time. I don't trust people. I'm giving you one chance.

There are some things I can't let go in the position I'm in."

My hands go to my hair and my eyes close, my fingers nervously twisting the black locks. These are the women that end up on Unsolved Mysteries or the news, or worse, missing without anyone noticing. God knows my mother wouldn't. When my eyes open he's standing right in front of me. "Does Kaston and Lux know?"

"Kaston, yes. Lux, likely. If I know Kaston she's already been threatened. Those that live lawless have certain rules to stay that way."

"Is Kaston?"

"A client."

"What kind of client?"

"That's not my business to tell."

"She's been keeping secrets from me?"

"Just as you would be . . . You're either by my side or not in this at all. The choice is yours, but you can't be on the fence. She made hers months ago."

My lungs are closing off. I feel so betrayed. I've never kept anything important from Lux. I'm a little insulted she wouldn't confide in me. We've always told each other everything, bad and good. I'm hurt that they've all had secrets I was left out of. "Have you ever killed someone?"

"Yes."

That is a terrifying revelation. I think somewhere I was hoping he'd say no. "That guy back there?"

"No, but I wanted to. He touched you."

My lips tremble. "Would you ever hurt me?"

"Only if you betray me. But you always have a choice."

Through each question his eyes remain locked with mine, never swaying, never hesitating, proving they're truthful answers whether

I like them or not. "Would you ever let someone else hurt me?"

"Never."

My heart rate increases again, my body humming in awareness that he's near. The questions continue to come, even though I should just shut up. "How many girls have you done this with? And what did you do to them when it was over?"

"None."

My shoulders fall. I'm becoming more defeated with every answer. "And how long have you been a criminal?"

"I started at fifteen. But before I was into other stuff."

"Then why now? Why take me?" It comes out in a whisper; not at all how I thought.

"You appeal to me. I want you. Even when I told myself no."

"How long have you wanted me?"

"Since the night you walked into my shop."

My jaw locks, trying to understand him, and unable to stop while he's actually giving me answers. "So the hot and cold?"

"How I deal with things."

"And if I stay above all else?"

"I don't know. Best case scenario I'll never let you go."

"Love?"

"War."

"Meaning?"

"Neither have predictable outcomes. That's not a question I can answer. I can't promise feelings I don't understand."

"If I show you?"

"I guess you'll see. But I wouldn't get your hopes up."

"Okay."

"You should get some sleep."

"No."

"It's late."

"You proved you didn't care about that when you woke me up. Show me you want me. I want to know I turn you on too."

"I thought that was obvious last night."

"You were high."

"I still got up."

This is not going the way I wanted it to. I hate the way this feels. It's one reason I gave up sex. I hated trying. There are so many things I'm sure of myself in, but this—initiating things with a man I want—I'm insecure. The guys that wanted me bored me, and the ones I wanted were the ones that never gave me a second glance. I've had attention-seeking issues my entire life. I craved male attention. I have no father and a mother that doesn't care. It's how Chuck and I started. He gave me attention when I needed it the most. Maybe it was wrong, but then again, maybe there's something wrong with me. Either way, I was left alone a lot. My mom wasn't as bad as Lux's mom, but she wasn't in the runoff for the mom-of-the-year award either.

I'm just the result of a bad decision she made in life, and she didn't mind telling me on a regular basis after consuming several glasses of wine when she had no plans. I never knew my dad. A drunken weekend in a military town full of training soldiers and nine months later I was born. She didn't even know his name, if he was married, or if he had other kids. By the time she found out she was pregnant he was long gone to wherever he came from. Between working and her social life there was little time for me, so every person that threw me a bone I clung to. It's the part of me that I hate. Lux was always so sure of herself and what she wanted, despite every shitty thing that happened to her. Once we left home she blossomed, became assertive; the bitch on heels that took life by the balls, regardless of what it made her look like. She is a female alpha extreme. Used her body as bait. I envied that in her. Me, I'll always be a beta, second best, regardless of what I wish I could be. My insecurities will come out no matter how hard I push them away.

"If you don't want to just say it so I'm not wasting our time and I'll go to my room."

He's just standing there, staring at me, making me feel fucking stupid. Rejection is what feels the worst being a girl. Wanting someone and them seeming completely unaffected is an ego-kill. I roll my eyes and turn for the stairs. He grabs my arm, almost pulling me down as he jerks me backward. "You need sex to know I want you?"

His question is not making matters better in the insecurity department. But the curiosity in his tone and the heaviness of his eyes make me feel even worse. Maybe we both really do have issues. I just don't know what his are yet. As bad as I don't want to admit it . . . "Yes."

He walks me backward until I'm pushed down on the dining room table, taking off my shirt as he goes. I never put on a bra earlier and my pants take no effort for him to remove. I prop up on my elbows, watching him as he removes his shirt. My eyes always get lost in his ink, trying to study what they mean or how they came to be.

He unbuckles his belt and drops his jeans quickly, stepping out of them. His hand goes for his dick, covering it—at least trying to. I don't know why a man with a dick that felt like his did would be trying to cover it, as if he's modest of his size. His hat gets tossed on the floor with his pants. It's the first time I've seen him naked. I sit up, mesmerized, my eyes slowly memorizing his body and fixated on every dip and bulge of his muscles. He grabs my hand and wraps it around his erection as he steps between my legs. "Is this proof enough?" he bites out, his voice deep and rich.

I stare at it in my hand, as if it's not real and this is all a dream. "Were you hard when you went down on me?"

"Yes." My eyes never falter; my hand slowly becomes acquainted with it. "What are you staring at?"

"You're big."

"And this is surprising why? A lot of guys are."

"You're buff."

"What does that have to do with anything?"

"Well, it's just that in my personal experience the guys with the biggest muscles are packing the smallest punch down there."

He grips my legs and pulls me to the edge of the table, leaning over me until my back is flat against the wood. He pushes inside me much slower than he did last night. "I will never be like any of your experiences."

My hands rub along the tattoos on the side of his neck until they lace together at the back. I pull him toward me, but before our lips meet, I return: "I'm kind of hoping for that."

He doesn't go slow, but he goes slower than he did last night. I wrap my legs around him; my feet settling on his ass, and with each thrust my black nails scratch against his skin, the moans smothered between our lips. His hands dig into my ass and he lifts my bottom off the table, driving inside of me at an angle.

My toes curl. My breathing is out of control, forcing our lips apart. "Fuck. Right there."

His lips close around my nipple and he sucks. "Holy shit. Please don't stop." The bliss I haven't felt in so long overtakes my body. He hits against it again. "Fuuuuck-ing finally." The words turn into loud moans and my breathing stops. I'm sweating, my eyes rolling back in my head. He bites into my nipple before my orgasm ends completely, his movement ceasing, and as it does his fingers relax from the pain they are causing clenched into my skin. He kisses me first this time and slowly pulls out. Before he stands and helps me off the table I notice his erratic heartbeat, saying what his mouth can't and putting my mind at ease over his anti-theatrical come moment. "Meet me in the kitchen at 9AM."

And then, just like that, the coldness is back. He walks away, disappearing down the hall until he walks into a room and slams his door. One step forward two steps back, because every part of me wanted him to invite me into his bed, but instead, I end up climbing the stairs until all I can do is pick my comforter up off the floor and bury myself under it, because I know for sure that for me, this is going to end beautifully or like the remnants of war with no survivors.

CHAPTER EIGHT

Delia

I sit in the vacant chair with the tip of a pencil in my mouth as I get in a comfortable position, pulling my legs up so that I can rest the sketchpad against my thighs. I look down at the drawing I started working on this week, deciding what I want to add. Trash has all been emptied, sharps containers aren't yet full, every station is fully stocked and everything is orderly within the studio. It's peaceful; tattoo guns buzzing all over the room.

It's been two weeks since the night at the warehouse and the amazing table sex that followed. From that point forward things have basically gone back to the way it was before I moved in, with the exception of us sharing a house. Most mornings I slip out of the house before his scheduled *meeting time*. He always has something to say about it when he walks into the shop, but it's hard to ride with him to work when I want him constantly, and the way I see it since he doesn't want to act like we're a couple then no one should think we are either. This is me backing off.

Some days, when I stay busy, it makes it easier. He's let me do several transfers to the point that I've almost perfected it, I practice tracing on the light table daily, and occasionally he lets me help tattoo on customers he knows to get the feel for the gun. Sanitize and moisturize have become part of my job skills. I haven't figured out if he doesn't like to do it or if he's just finding some way to include me. Even when he does, you would never think we've slept together. He treats me just like he treats everyone else, and that both makes me happy and disappoints me at the same time.

I drag my pencil across the paper, outlining the add-on. Yesterday I shaded the skull, leaving it in gray scale I love so much. It's my personal preference on ink. I like color in moderation, but to me, too much looks cheesy and low quality on the body with the end result. I'm not fond of blues either, because it reminds me of a really faded tattoo after years and years of wear. Both are definitely personal preferences, because people walk in here all the time with nothing but color from neck to legs.

My hand moves in swift strokes back and forth as I finish the electric guitar he's holding in his boney hands, giving it sick details like the fire coming from his fingertips as he plays. I've found that I love drawing when everyone's stations are full, because it's easy to get lost in the buzzing sound and light conversation around the room. Once I'm finished with the guitar I'll move on to the wings of the raven I want spread behind him. The feather details will probably take me a while.

My hand stops when I feel hands touch my chair, a body over me. I glance up at Remington hovering over me, his Mohawk more noticeable with the way he's leaning and looking down. "Nice.

That'd make a fucking awesome back piece."

Remington is a little more on the reserved side. He stays pretty booked up, but he talks from time to time when you least expect him to. Usually when he does it's about tattoos, music, or something going on in the city involving one of the two topics. Honestly, between him and Wesson he's the hotter one. The steady lineup of girls trickling in after some concert or something he's attended tells me he probably stays just as busy touching bodies in his spare time as he does with a needle in hand. And from what I can tell, his type leans more toward Cassie: not punk or dark in the least. He's probably tattooed more flowers and butterflies than anything else.

I look back at the drawing. "Maybe. I haven't decided on my thoughts yet."

He grabs the pad from my lap and stands upright, holding it in front of him. My head rolls backward after glancing at his empty station. "You got rid of the giggly one so soon?"

He smirks at me. "It doesn't take long to do music notes on watercolor."

"I've never known someone to find getting a tattoo ticklish. I think she just wanted in your pants."

"Probably so," he says dramatically, still looking at the drawing. "They usually do want seconds." I bite back a laugh and roll my eyes. Guys are clueless, but then again, I usually get along with them better than girls. Females are a species I usually don't understand and I am one. Too catty and drama-driven for me. Lux and I are just different than the rest; always have been. I'm not sure why he's so intrigued. It's not done. "But at least she's not a screamer. Giggling is so much more pleasant to endure."

"You're a pig," I laugh. "Are you going to give that back?"

"I'm deciding."

"On?"

"Whether I want it permanently or not."

"You'd get my drawing tattooed on your body?"

"It's pretty sick. I like your style, which brings me to my next question. What are you doing tonight?"

"Nothing. Why?"

"You're not going to do nothing. It's Halloween."

"What should I be doing then?"

"Going to a haunted house with me."

"Do I seem like a person into scary things?"

He turns the drawing around. "You draw this shit. You should be."

"She has plans, Remington."

I turn around at the sound of Kross' voice. He's still tattooing a small Buddha sitting among Lotus flowers on the lower back of the girl in his chair, never looking up. "I'm pretty sure she just said nothing," Remington returns, unfazed at the tone of his voice. I know it. It's a warning.

"She's working."

"It's fucking Halloween. People like us don't work on Halloween. It's like our special holiday that only comes around once a year. It would be a sin to miss it. Let her off early. I'm sure Cassie would be willing to stay for any late appointments. She hates scary shit. I already tried."

"This is my last appointment," Wesson says, rubbing the jelly on the top of the foot he's been putting script on. When did this turn into a community shop discussion? I never said I wanted to go, even though this is my favorite time of year. I love the sculpted pumpkins and spider webs, the ghosts and goblins hanging in yards, and dressing up is the most fun of all. In the past, I've always been at the bar and it's a big deal. If I was off it was always popcorn and beer while I indulged in a marathon of all the scary classics like *Halloween.*

Joey walks out of the piercing room and sits on Remington's stool as the girl in front of him starts walking down the stairs. "I heard haunted house. We could close down and all go. I looked at the schedule earlier. Kross' is last to go. It could be fun. I bet we could even get Cassie to tag along if we're all going and get drinks before."

Kross finally looks up to load his gun as he wipes the last place he added color. I display a teeth clenched grin, hoping he's not angry. I did not start this discussion. I was minding my own business, but they're also talking about it in front of a customer and I know that's something he hates. "You want to go?" he asks, surprising me.

"I think it'd be fun for us all to go out together, regardless of what activity it is."

His eyes never leave mine. "If Remington can get Cassie to participate I'll close; otherwise every fucking one of you can stay for walk-ins until midnight."

And like a heard of zebras scattering at the sight of a lion they're gone, all three of them running down the stairs. I just shake my head, because all three of them are grown-ass men acting like teenage boys. Being with Kross on Halloween . . . Shit, I'm excited.

Kross

I turn the television off and stand: aggravated it's taking her so long. I walk to the bottom of the stairs. I don't like being forced into a decision, and that's what this feels like, because I sure as hell wasn't letting her go with Remington alone. He's a whore. He's also open about it. He uses his skill in ink and his tattoos as an attractant, not a part of him. He's just toned his stories down since Delta was hired, bringing a girl into the studio. And I felt a little more like an asshole saying no than I normally would, because that's what I've been for the past two weeks. She knows it and I know it. When shit gets too weird for me I don't deal with it. I don't know how, so I just keep my distance until it deals with itself instead. That conversation freaked me the fuck out. Since her I've had to talk more than what I'm comfortable with. The sex that followed just added fuel to the fire. Her pussy feels too good to be normal. The sounds coming from her mouth as her nails dug into my skin had me hanging completely on the fucking edge.

Sex has never been that big of a deal for me. I wasn't seasoned in it like most guys are. I have my reasons for steering clear of it. From the time I was a teenager there were far more important things to deal with than to find some random-ass girl and have to work at getting in her pants for five minutes of fun. I don't lie or play games to get it. I don't have time for all that shit. The times I got laid it was readily available and offered on a fucking silver platter, so I took like any guy would, and most of the time it was months between occurrences as well as quick and effortless on my part. It barely even fazes me until it's at least been a month; yet still, even though I'm generally an asshole by association, it surprised me she had to question that she had that effect on me. I've gotten hard over less. Just like every other man with a dick, I too get turned on, and have on several occasions since I met her.

I bang on the wall. "Delta! Are you ready? I have shit to do later," I shout up the stairs. All I can hear is heavy metal blaring, easily recognizable as Five Finger Death Punch: *This is my war.*

My feet start to move, one by one climbing the stairs. Her door is shut, but as I grip the knob I realize that it's not locked. I push it open, looking in the wrong starting direction. When my eyes scan the room they stop at her bed. Her foot falls from the propped position on the mattress and she turns to face me. "I'm assuming you're ready?"

I swallow, my mouth a little dry. "It's more than I can say about you. What the hell is taking so long?"

"Oh, I'm ready," she says. "I just need to get my whip."

I look at her, all of her. "What? Fuck no."

Her eyes fall to my crotch, and then a smirk appears on her face. "Is there a problem?"

"You're missing your clothes."

She glances down at herself. "I'm pretty sure I have everything."

She walks toward me, but before she can pass I block the frame with my arms. "Move out of my way, Kross."

"I will when you put some clothes on."

"I'm wearing them."

"You aren't leaving this house in that."

"Awe, that's cute. Did you forget I'm a grown-ass woman? I'll wear what I want. You may be my boss at the shop, but off the clock I'm a free agent."

I walk forward and push her further into the room, slamming the damn door. "Unless you want to add accomplice to murder to your rap sheet I suggest you change."

She stares into my eyes, not backing down. "I'll take my chances."

I grab her neck, turning her eyes upward. "Don't. Test. Me."

Her hand grabs at my dick over my jeans, matching my grip on her neck, the pain only making it swell more. "You haven't fucking touched me in two weeks. Don't you dare come at me like my boyfriend."

My chest feels heavy, the anger filling it. Like I'm possessed I grab her ass and lift her, walking toward the bed and tumbling down on it, my lips taking hers. She looks up at me when I stand on my knees, ripping the top open as I do, the hooks sounding as they tear through the loops. She's not wearing a bra because the corset top was so hard and tight against her body. "You want a boyfriend?"

My tone is reflecting every ounce of the anger coursing through my bloodstream. "Only one that's going to man up and act like a fucking boyfriend. If he's only going to be one occasionally behind closed doors then I'll pass," she seethes, getting angrier as we continue.

I remove my knife clipped on my pocket and slide it from the inside, flipping it open with one motion. The tip grazes along the black thigh-high pantyhose of her inner thigh, starting above her boots; slowly snagging the fabric until they aren't wearable, continuing to where I want it. She inhales deeply when the blade skims her lips, and in one swift jerk slices through her bottoms between her legs, baring her pussy for me. "I hope you know what you're asking for," I bite out, my eyes locked with hers as I throw the knife at the wall.

She turns her head when the blade drives through the sheetrock across the room. When she returns, her hands go for my belt, quickly working my jeans down my legs. "I want you to fuck me so bad."

I thrust inside her, hard, grinding my hips against her. "This how you want it?"

Her back arches. "Hell yes. Hurt me."

I still. "No."

She locks her legs around my waist. "Don't stop. Please."

My arm locks at the middle of her back and I flip us over, pulling her onto my lap, and then I push my jeans further down my legs. I sit up and remove my shirt, tossing it aside. "You want it more than I'm giving, then show me what I'm missing. It's your turn to fuck me."

Detta

His hands settle on my thighs, waiting for me to ride. I unhook the straps at the top of my stockings and pull what's left of the mutilated bottoms to my dominatrix costume up my body, removing it over my head. He grabs the base of his dick and holds it in position, allowing me to sit down on him. Both of his hands grip in my long, black hair. I pump up and down slowly a few times, and then push at his chest until he lies back.

I begin, using the heavy music playlist shuffling as a pacer. With each scream of lyrics I grind harder, rougher, rocking against his solid core. My body automatically leans forward until my hands meet the sheets when I find my G-spot, focusing on it to hit it just right. His dick becomes my tool. I want this. It's been so long since I've given myself a deep orgasm with a man's body. I can already feel it building. "Right . . . there."

My eyes open as it starts, slowing my hips already so I can savor it. He's watching me, my face slowly contorting with each feeling racking my body. His hands return to my hair, tangling within it, just before he pulls me closer. "I don't think I've ever told you that you're beautiful . . . but you are."

Then he pulls my lips to his and he kisses me in a way that shatters my soul. At the moment there is nothing left inside of me that's whole. Everything remains in pieces, because I've never actually believed someone when they called me beautiful before, but that, in its reverent form, has the power to bring back the dead.

And just as it becomes too much to bear, I sit up, and fuck him with everything that's left, because I don't want him to stray. There is something wickedly beautiful about him—the bad and the broken.

Kray

I park the truck, waiting on the others to show up. "I like that outfit much better."

She's smiling at me when I look at her. "The only costume I had was ruined. Ripped up jeans and a tee shirt with fake blood was all I could come up with. Besides, I don't know what the big deal is. I've worn that costume before —why I had it on hand."

"What you wore, who you did, or where you went before your cunt was hungry for my cock I have no control over. Now I do. It ended up exactly where it belongs. The trash."

"Funny. I was under the impression guys thought that kind of thing was sexy. I guess I was wrong . . ."

"Secrets are to be kept, not shared. I don't want other guys looking at your body like that. I kept my mouth shut over the pink underwear you called shorts."

"Because you can avoid it with more clothing? And you did not keep your mouth shut; you just let it go. People are going to look if they want to. You don't show much of anything and I see the way girls drool over you while you tattoo them."

"I wouldn't know anything about that. When I tattoo I'm inside my head not staring at the tits and ass of who's in my chair."

She rolls her eyes. "You're the only guy I would actually believe that coming from. Getting your attention is hard as fuck. But you're missing my point. If someone wants to think of me that way there is nothing you nor I can do about it."

"I can lower the ratio this way."

"Because you're crazy like that."

"Call it what you want."

"I don't know why it bothers you. My body isn't that great anyway. I just don't give a shit whether other people think so or not."

"Delta, have you lost your damn mind?"

"It's still there as far as I know."

"Your body is fine."

"That's what I'm saying. It's average."

She digs through her purse and pulls out a cigarette and lighter, placing the filter between her lips. I grab it before she gets the flame to the paper. "Your body is fucking perfect. If it wasn't I wouldn't want to keep it for myself, so stop trying to destroy it."

I snap it in two and put it in the trash bag. She dramatically tosses the lighter back in her purse. "Are you kidding? That was a perfectly good cigarette you just broke. You're going to force me to snort cocaine but you're not going to let me smoke? That is hardly sensible."

"That will not become a habit. Drugs are part of the job not a pastime. Recreational use will never happen as long as you're with me. I don't tolerate addicts. These are permanently bad for you. Just research the ingredients. You may need your body for something one day aside from looks."

Her head falls back against the seat. "God, you're nuts. Why do you have to be so damn hot . . ." She turns toward me. "I haven't had one in hours. You can't expect me to just quit cold turkey. I've been smoking since I was sixteen. I promise I'll try."

I open my console and hand her the pack of gum sitting inside. "It's just an oral fixation. It'll only control you if you let it."

She snaps her fingers, getting angry. Too bad anger is something I handle very well. "Oral fixation my ass. I need it. My nerves need it, especially to deal with your secretive lifestyle. Unless you want me to resort to sucking your dick every time I get a craving then leave the smoking thing alone. Gum doesn't do shit."

I stare at her, my hand pressing down on my inner thigh. "You can't just say that kind of shit to a guy."

"Kross, I accepted your bad habits. It's kind of hypocritical to not accept mine."

"You're not going to keep putting that shit in your lungs. If you want to kill yourself with someone else then fine."

She glares at me. "It's really unfortunate you have such an amazing dick that you know how to use so well."

"If I have to fill one hole to keep that out of the other that's fine. Stop being dramatic."

"Speaking of, what are you going to tell them when they get here and ask why we're together? I could have driven myself."

"The truth if anything. No reason to lie."

Remington's truck pulls up next to mine, Wesson sitting in the passenger seat. "Which is?"

"You're with me. Let's go."

"Like my boyfriend?"

"That's what was discussed, wasn't it?"

"I hardly thought you'd take that seriously."

"You thought wrong."

Detta

I scream when a hand reaches out and touches me as we walk through the dark house, running into Kross' back, my heart pounding. "Shit."

I've been holding the back of his shirt in my fist just like everyone else in this single file line the entire time. He's in the front and hasn't even flinched. I think I underestimated this a little. It's much worse when they're popping out of corners and touching you instead of being trapped behind the television screen. The creepy haunting music is blaring. I watch scary movies on mute just to avoid this. It's always less scary without it. Even the house looks fucking abandoned. It reminds me of the Blair Witch Project. I was not the same for a really long time after watching that twisted, fucked up shit. Creepy wooded areas at dark are nowhere on my radar.

A flashlight beam blinds me. I turn my head, realizing a fucking clown with sharp, pointy teeth, blood running down the corners, is holding it, waving a bloody knife at me. "Fuck you!" I scream, taking off in the opposite direction, lost in a maze of darkness and lights and sounds, completely leaving the line behind against the instructions at the beginning of the tour.

A hand grabs my arm in a dark spot, causing me to kick, jerk, scream, and hit as I'm pulled through a door, my eyes clenched shut. I can't breathe, my chest feeling like it's caving in. The adrenaline pumping through my body is making my head hurt. His body wraps around me, holding me to his front, and then he starts laughing. A real laugh; something I've never heard out of him. It's a beautiful sound.

Laughter.

I wasn't sure a trait of something so light and happy existed in such a man as him. In all of his coldness and arrogance I never thought I would experience it. Dry laughs don't count. It's as if a small window has opened in a room of darkness with a beam of light shining through and he's letting me see the tiniest bit of what lies within him. It may not be sunshine, but moonlight is good enough. And in consequence, I melt into his hold in a way I've never done with a man, and I soak it all in.

Safe.

I feel safe. My arms wrap around him and I finally open my eyes. We're outside. The chaos has ended and what remains is nothing but peace. He feels stronger this way. I stand completely still, feeling and listening, all of the fear disappearing. His laugh runs dry, but the slight smirk sets in place. "I thought you were supposed to be a badass."

"Shut up. I never want to discuss this ever again. I don't do fucking clowns. Everything else I can deal with."

"What? Why? They hardly belong in a world of horror. They're completely harmless and more of a happy kid-friendly circus thing than anything else."

"You have your opinions and I have mine. They're scary. They live under beds and probably in closets, waiting to show you that they're anything but 'kid-friendly'. Haven't you seen Stephen King's, *It?* And before you ask, no I didn't watch the remake." I pause, realizing he's not tense in the least. "Does anything scare you?"

He actually pulls me tighter, surprising me, the smell of his cologne attacking every feminine molecule in my body, making me crave more. I never want this to end. "The scariest things are disguised as normal people, Delta. That stuff in there is a walk in the park compared to what I'm scared of."

And this is the moment that I realize his demons are so much more real than I originally thought . . .

CHAPTER NINE
Kross

I pull the utility truck to the gate, waiting for them to open it. I look at her, biting her nails as she stares out the windshield. "You good? You can't act all nervous and shit."

"Is this one going to be like the last one? Is he going to want to see my body and all? That made me feel dirtier than stripping ever did."

"No. He's a smaller dealer. He deals with me face-to-face himself instead of sending hyped up little boys with guns that think they're fucking untouchable. Besides, I dealt with that little punk. This one's already seen your body. He's the reason I was at the strip club to begin with."

"You won't leave me, right?"

I grip her chin and force her to look at me. "I will never leave you with someone else. I'll take a bullet before I do."

"I don't like that alternative."

"Just the way this world works. Can't take the good without knowing about the bad."

She breathes out. "Okay. Can we do something fun after this? I'm still freaked out about the clown ordeal. It's a full moon, and now this, all on Halloween. If I see a black cat or hear something howling I'm going to flip my shit. I just need something happy before I go to sleep."

"Are you scared?"

"A little. I don't want to get in trouble. I've never been involved in something like this. I was bad in other ways. And I tend to have nightmares when I'm freaked out."

"Okay. We'll figure something out."

The phone rings on my console. I pick it up at the same time the gate starts to open automatically. "Drive around back and pull inside. The door will be open," he says, disconnecting the call.

Just as he instructed, I navigate down the drive toward the oversized shop he has on the back of the property, pulling in the open bay. The metal door lowers when I kill the truck, closing us in. "What now?"

"He's waiting. Get out."

We both file out of the truck together, meeting him at the front. I extend my fist; meeting his as he finally cracks the mask he's wearing. "What's up, Man?"

"Same as usual. Tracking down your shit."

"It's always well appreciated," he says, before dropping his hand and glancing at Delta. She's standing with her arms awkwardly crossed at her chest. I shake my head. For someone well on her way to being covered in ink and fine as fuck she looks like a scared mouse shaking in a corner. Again, we have to work on some things.

"Ah, now I know why you didn't want my chocolate. You were busy dipping your hand in the honey jar."

"If I didn't someone else was going to," I respond honestly.

He migrates toward her, pulling her into a side hug. "Baby, do you know what you're getting yourself into with this one? He's up to no good. It's only a matter of time until he screws something up, and when he does you just bring your pretty little ass over here and I'll fix it. You know what they say: once you go black you never go back."

She starts laughing, instantly relaxing. "I'll keep that in mind."

He looks back at me, his arm still wrapped around her. My smirk slides into place. "Don't put that shit in her head. I don't need her thinking about your dick. She disappears I'm coming after you first."

"You just better be on your best behavior, my friend."

"Always am."

"You heard that. He gives you any trouble you let me know. I'll put a boot in his ass."

Our eyes lock, her bottom lip sliding between her teeth. I've never been into mouth jewelry before, but I think she's pulled me to the other side, because I wonder how that lip ring would feel rubbing up and down on the underside of my cock. I clear my throat. "So you ready to do this?

"As soon as you try this new blend with me. I need your input."

He walks off, expecting us to follow, so I place my hand on Delta's shoulder when I step up beside her and guide her along behind him, walking toward the door at the back. I'll be honest. I'm a little ready to go home, and that's not usually the case, because solitude is enough to drive the strongest person mad when memories resurface at those times the most. The more she's around the less of a Jekyll and Hyde effect I have to deal with, and I kind of like it.

Delta

I really liked him. He's funny. My head rolls toward him as he pulls into the driveway and mashes the button on the remote attached to his visor to open the garage. It's late. We had to take the box truck back to the shop and switch it out for his truck. Everything is peaceful and slow, my brain lazily thinking. "I was expecting militia style guards and heavily armored premises after what we went through last time."

He pulls in and parks. "You watch too many movies. Crime isn't always theatrical. The obvious always get caught; unlike in films where everyone is guns blazing and owning the fucking streets. That's fake. The likelihood of you personally meeting those types of men is slim to none. They don't like unexpected company, trust no one, and rarely show their face. They have families just like normal people. They're more like ghosts. When I have those meetings it's very intricate and well planned out."

The closing of the garage door doesn't even faze me. I stay put in this comfy seat, kind of sleepy. "So Ludacris' twin back there . . . What's his story? I'm cool with hanging out with him."

He looks at me like I'm crazy. "We don't 'hang out' with clients. That's bad for business. You always keep your enemies closest. That's all that is."

"Didn't seem like an enemy to me." I shrug my shoulders. "And I'm supposed to just know this stuff? In case you forgot I'm the new girl."

My eyes burn into his, dazed at their depth and darkness. I wonder how he'd act if I just straddled him and took what I want. "Wouldn't matter if he had a story. May not have one. He's a smaller inventory dealer of a little bit of everything. Keeps him off the radar of the DEA but still pulls in a hefty profit. Not every criminal is bad, Delta. We just choose to be outlaws and do bad things."

"I really like you sometimes."

"You're high."

"I meant it. I'm totally fine. This is different than the Cocaine. I just kind of feel mildly drunk and hungry. I'm in no hurry to move. I kind of like it. I am completely living the Bob Marley life right now. It's great."

"That's *kind of* weed for you. You need to go to bed."

"You're an ass."

He smirks at me. "You really like me sometimes but I'm also an ass?"

I smile. "Yeah . . . It's a vicious cycle."

"Do you need help getting up the stairs?"

I sit up when he kills the engine and opens the door, getting a little bit of perkiness back. "Hell no. You said we could do something fun."

"You need some sleep."

"It's a holiday. I'll sleep later."

"Technically it's not. Halloween is over."

"Not until I close my eyes it's not. Don't be a pussy."

"A pussy huh? Fine. Let's go."

I follow him inside. He doesn't stop until we reach the living room, grabbing the remote by his recliner and turning on the television. "Strip."

I would have never taken marijuana for a hallucinogen. "I'm

sorry. What?"

"You better be naked when I get back." He walks down the hallway, entering the first door; not his bedroom. Considering he's never been this open and wanting to hang out, the clothes are coming off. My shirt almost rips from grabbing the torn segments of fabric as I remove it. I push my jeans down my legs and step out, standing in my bra and underwear. If he wants these off he'll have to remove them himself.

He walks out with a guitar strapped over his bare front and another in his hand, wearing nothing but boxer briefs—black, Diesel brand at that. Designer underwear is a massive turn-on for me. If a man cares enough to shop for underwear you know he takes care of his shit. Boxer briefs are by far my favorite. They are tight and sexy, unlike boxers, without looking like panties, because to me those nut-huggers are an instant drying agent. Dear lord help my soul. "No fucking way."

"Ever played?"

"Hell yeah. I'm crushing on you really hard right now."

He hands me the spare, my favorite smirk set in place. "Do you have a thing for guitar players?"

"No, I have a thing for rock." I'm cheesing really damn hard right now.

"I noticed today. That's why I thought of it."

"But I would have never taken you for a gamer."

He walks toward the built-in cabinets, opening it to a shelf full of cases. "Assume always starts with an ass."

When he finds the one he's looking for he puts it into the game system and backs toward me. I pull the strap over my head and settle the guitar at my front, getting a feel for it. "Speaking of asses; yours is kind of hot. You have a lot more back there than I thought."

"Checking out my ass, Rohr?" I love when his voice is deep, lathered up with alpha-male, testosterone-backed goodness.

"Yes. Yes I am," I state shamelessly. "It's damn fine. I can appreciate a good-looking backside when I see one."

"As much as I like knowing my ass is appreciated, get your head in the game. I'm the Guitar Hero king. You will never beat me."

"You sound a little sure of yourself, Kross."

"I just know the truth."

"So why did you want me naked?"

"I just wanted to look at your body, tattoos and all. Ready?"

If that doesn't make a girl feel sexy I don't know what does . . .

"Care to place a bet, *Brannon?*"

"Hit me with it. It'll be an easy win for me."

"If I win, you have to sleep with me and cuddle, but if you win . . . you can tattoo your name on my body."

"I'm not a cuddling kind of guy."

"That's what makes it a bet. It's not supposed to be something you like if you lose. I don't really want a man's name tattooed on me to wear forever, but I'll take it like a champ if you win. Besides, I thought it was an easy win for you. Getting scared you might get beat by a girl, *baby?*"

He closes in on me, guitar to guitar, his lips almost touching mine. "Better get a spot ready."

"This could go either way. Let's rock and roll."

Our smiles spread at the same time and we take our stance facing the big screen television. The game introduction starts. My hands are ready, one on the neck and the other on the base front, fingers positioned on the buttons. The first song comes on: Avenged Sevenfold — *Bat Country,* a personal favorite band for me. I haven't played this game in a while, but I've always been good at hand/eye coordination.

The notes start scrolling up the screen, instructing what color button to press. I'm a little rusty, but immediately fall back in when I miss one. I can see him getting into it out of the corner of my eye. It's a little distracting because it's really fucking cute.

The music hits a slow part, giving me a chance to catch up, just before it ends. His hands go into the air, his score higher than mine. "You will never beat me," he chants, making it really hard not to laugh. This is the most laid back I've ever seen him.

"You're a sore winner. Two out of three."

He readies himself again as Lincoln Park — *Bleed it out* begins. The rhythm on this one I catch on to a lot faster, my fingers never missing the right button. I concentrate, hard, really wanting to cuddle. I think I deserve a cuddle session with all the messed up shit I've had to deal with coming into this. When it ends I mimic my player on the screen in a victory dance.

He's not amused. "Sore loser too?"

"I don't ever lose."

"Score says something different. Take that."

"All right. For round three we're going in blind. Winner takes all."

"Blind how?"

He turns me around to face the opposite direction and then matches me, our backs toward the TV. "You can't see the notes. Just play and highest score wins."

"Competitive much? This is a suicide mission."

"Very. Ready?"

My fingers find the keys. "Yes."

I know the guitar and the voice. "Metallica and Ozzy Osbourne — *Paranoid*. There is no way to master this without memorizing the whole damn game, so I just listen and do the best I can. I chance a glance at him and he has a slight smile on his face. I try harder, because who the hell knows if I'm even hitting the right buttons. I guess we'll soon find out.

Kross

I know I've won before I even turn around. When I don't work I'm usually at home, alone. I never really developed that whole skill of being social with other people; that thing called friends. Most of my childhood was spent alone, so that's the way I usually spend my time off, and in doing that I have to find stuff to occupy my time since I don't prefer to lay around. I could play this game in my sleep. I let her win the second round to make it more fun. "You decided on a spot for my name yet?"

When she realizes I won her shoulders fall. She removes the guitar and hands it back to me. I watch as her entire demeanor changes. I've never understood Females. They're too emotional. And that's something I was stripped of young. I grew up around cold-hearted people and thugs. I was a member of Satan's army for years, getting into gangbanger shit and whatever got me out of that bitch's den, but even I know when excitement turns to dread.

"I'll let you decide," she says. "I'm starting to get sleepy." She hugs me over the guitar lying still at my front, her half-naked body against mine. I flinch at first, like I always do when something touches my bare skin, but shove it aside and try to relax. She's warm. "Thanks for tonight. It was fun. I like hanging out with you when you don't have a stick up your ass. Goodnight, Kross."

Without another glance she starts to walk away. Her panties are only covering half of her ass. I'm not sure whether I love or hate the fact that she's so open with her body. She prefers to go naked or barely clothed. "Just like that, huh?"

She stops and glances back. "What?"

"Giving up so easily?"

"What do you mean? You won."

I take off my guitar and toss it on the couch, before walking toward her and placing my hands against the sides of her neck. "The agreement was winner takes all."

"I thought that's what you were doing."

I shake my head.

"I'm confused."

"Winner takes all. I get both stakes of the bet—yours and mine."

Her smile returns. "You want to cuddle?"

"That's what you chose, isn't it?"

"I thought you weren't a cuddling kind of guy."

"Maybe not, but I never lose. I just alter the rules. I'm going to try something new. I wouldn't wanna be termed a *pussy* or anything." My lips touch hers, instantly backing away. "Besides, you're hot playing a guitar. I'm not sure I'm ready to send you to your room yet."

She breathes out, her hands cautiously going around my neck as I kiss her. I pick her up, her legs instantly wrapping around my waist. She tugs at my bottom lip, rubbing the metal along the front. "I really fucking like that lip ring."

"You're letting me in your room?"

I open my door and walk in, shutting it behind me. The lock clicks into place. "Yes."

"Why are you locking it? It's just us."

"I can't sleep without it."

"Why?"

"Just leave it alone, Delta. I can't go there."

"Okay," she whispers, and kisses me this time, in the hypnotic way that she always does. Between the movement of her lips and her tongue coming in waves it makes you not want to stop. I unhook her bra before lying her down on the bed, following on top of her so that I don't have to.

Her arms and legs wrap around me, pulling me closer. She's already pushing my underwear down my legs. I finish when it's beyond her reach, before repositioning onto my knees and shins. "I like the way your body feels."

"I thought you wanted to cuddle," I say, gripping her panties by the back and pulling them down to her thighs. She moves, allowing me to take them off, before wrapping back around me.

"I do . . . after."

"You want it again already?"

"Yes."

"Why?"

"Because I like it with you."

I align and slowly push inside. Don't ask me fucking why. I've never thought there was much of a point to slow sex. Fast always felt better and made me come sooner. But she's always so damn wet. It's more addictive than any drug ever was. Halfway in I thrust harder, driving all the way to the back. I stop, looking in her eyes, using the neon light that stays plugged in hanging on the wall to see. "I think I want to try something."

"Okay. What?"

"Touch me."

Her hands transition to my back. She's kept away from my front with her hands since I snapped at her. I grab her wrist and place it on my chest. "No. Touch me."

"I don't want you to get upset with me."

"I'm telling you to."

Slowly, she adds the other hand and I release the one I'm holding, letting her touch freely. I pull back slowly and enter her once again, focusing on her face so that I don't get lost in the memories. She finds scar after scar hidden within the ink as her fingertips trace along the designs.

Her feet run down the back of my legs, hers tangling with mine. I like the way this feels—every part of my body touching every part of hers. "You've been hurt before?"

She's breathing hard, a moan slipping each time I go deep. "Yes."

Her legs tighten around mine, pulling me closer. Every muscle in my body tenses when her lips touch to the lighter burn she found last time, as if she remembers exactly where it is. She lightly runs her tongue along the textured skin, making it slightly different from the unscathed. Most people think my chest and neck are covered in ink because I wanted it that way, and every design I chose, but it started out as camouflage.

"You won't be ever again. I promise."

I grip her ass cheek in my hand and slide back into her wet center, never completely leaving it. Fuck, it's so hot in there, wrapped around my dick in a tight fit. I don't remember the inside of a woman ever feeling quite like her. "Some promises can't be kept."

"I can promise I have your back and I'll slowly take away your pain if you'll let me."

My pelvis starts to hit a little harder but no faster. "That's what

I was doing when I moved you in with me." When her feet start to ascend back up to my waist, I grab her calves and move them to shoulders. I lean forward on my fists to lift her bottom half.

"Fuuuuck, you have the best dick."

I thrust hard, hitting deep over and over, close to coming. All I have to do is look at her every time I fuck her and it's enough to get off. When she's turned on it's all over her face.

Her back arches and she starts squeezing around me, giving me permission to nut. I pull her legs down and kiss her as my hips slam between her legs. As soon as I start to come her hands grab my ass and she holds me to her, skin-to-skin. I don't move any part of me but my lips, letting them run down her neck and front until I close around her nipple.

I place my hand on her hip tattoo that runs down the outside of her thigh, guiding it to the one that takes up her entire right side. Suddenly I feel chill bumps on her skin. I look at her. "Are you cold?"

"No. I just like when you touch me like that. You did it the night you gave me my tattoo."

"Touch you like what?"

"Like you're studying my body and memorizing every line, shade, and design."

"Oh."

My hand drops. "No. Don't stop."

"We should get some sleep."

I pull out of her and grab the blanket to pull it down the bed. She crawls up to the head and pulls the comforter to her neck, turning over to face the wall. I'm fighting the shutdown. The cold that I live in is slowly returning. Most of the time before I know it's there I'm already consumed with it. My fist closes so tight that it starts to shake. I told her I would do this. I get under the covers beside her, facing her back. "Delta."

"Yeah?"

"Show me how to cuddle."

She turns over. "You've never cuddled with someone at all? Not even like when you were younger and lost your virginity?"

"No."

"Am I pushing you?"

"I think I need to be pushed."

"Are you comfortable on your back?"

"I can make it work."

She sits up, the blanket falling and revealing her naked chest. Seeing her naked gets me every time just like it did the first time. It makes me a little crazy to be honest. "Come closer."

My mind is moving toward numb. I'm trying to fight the desire to walk out of this room. Solitude is my best friend and worst enemy. I need it, but I also hate it. It's my vice. I move toward the center of the mattress from the edge and turn on my back. She takes my hand. Reflexively I form a fist, but then open it when her fingers close over mine. She was going to adjust instead of asking me to open it. As it loosens her fingers lace between mine and she extends my arm across the bed. She scoots closer, slowly, and then lies back down on her side, placing her head on my chest.

My eyes won't move from the spot on the ceiling they've focused on. This feels weird. I don't know if I like it. Maybe I should just go sleep on the couch. "Kross, breathe."

My chest starts rising and falling with that one word. Her hand hovers over my stomach for a few seconds before she starts to pull away. "Just do it."

"We can try again another night if you want."

"No. I'll work it out. Finish what you were doing."

Her palm lowers to my sternum at the slowest pace, and then her arm settles right after. She starts rubbing up and down my torso, not missing a spot that's free. I feel paralyzed. "It's okay. I won't hurt you. You can relax."

My spine finally curves into the mattress as all of my muscles loosen from their contracted state. "So this is what girls are always bitching about wanting? This is cuddling?"

"Almost."

"What am I doing wrong?"

"Hold me." Hold? We're lying down. I'm not even sure I understand what that means. "Wrap your arm around me."

The lower part of my arm underneath her comes up, bending and hovering over her shoulder. I clench my fist over and over, trying to drive away the urge to pull away. Finally it drops, my palm lying on top of her skin. "Like this?"

"Yes. How does it make you feel?"

"Awkward."

"That's normal."

For the first time I relax in the most complete way, pulling her closer. She has a way of dealing with my fucked-up-ness like no one else likely would. "No, it's not normal, but I'm trying to give it a shot."

"Will you tell me one thing about yourself that I don't know?"

I swallow. That is a disturbing question. I don't talk about myself. Personal information has never been important to me. I wrote off my past the second I left it behind. I don't give a shit about giving it out or getting it. I never have. I talk about things that have a purpose. Guns. Ink. Deals. Money. Those are the things I'm good at talking about. "Maybe. What do you want to know?"

She's still rubbing her soft hand along my skin in the lightest manner, never going past the blanket at my waist. "Promise you won't get mad?"

"I promise not to outwardly show it."

"Is there a story behind the neon lights?"

I freeze. No one has ever asked me that before. "Kross, breathe."

I can feel air in my lungs again. I don't like thinking of my own childhood, much less tell someone else about it. It's always the same fucked up incomplete puzzle. All of the vital pieces are missing. Something like that is extremely personal for me. "Why do you ask?"

"I noticed you have a lot of it."

I remain silent, trying to determine if I'm actually going to go there or just tell her to leave it alone like the door lock. The problem is that I've never openly dealt with my issues. They've just been there for as long as I can remember, but I'm starting to like her in a way that I didn't in the beginning. She's here. And that means I'm not alone. She forces me to open even if it's only a crack. Somehow I need to keep her here. I can't explain the obsession I've had with her from the start, but now it's a little worse. And I'm learning to adjust to the chattiness of another person twenty-four-fucking-seven, when in nature all I want is silence. "If I tell you to stop when I can't go any further will you agree to leave it alone without thinking I'm an asshole."

"Yes."

"It's the only thing I can remember from the time with my mother."

"So she liked them?"

"I don't know. I get blurred flashbacks of them sometimes. Occasionally they're blue, but most of the time pink."

"What happened to her?"

"She abandoned me."

"How old were you?"

"Four, I think."

I try to blink it away, but it grows stronger until it's tormented me a little more.

"Mama! Mama!"

The screams fill the air as they pull me from beneath the bed by my feet. "It's okay. We won't hurt you."

"Mama! I want my mama."

"Calm down. We'll find her."

My tears fall on the shirt of someone I don't know. The crying screams start all over. "Mama!"

"It's okay. We'll find you a good home until we can find your mama. It'll be okay, sweetie."

It was a lie from the time she shoved me under those blue lights. She never found my mama . . .

Lips touch mine. "I'm sorry. I didn't mean to do that to you."

I blink, looking up at her hovering over me. "Do what?"

"Make you zone out like that. You don't move, don't breathe, and your body starts moving as if you're acting out something disturbing in your head. I won't ask you any more questions until you ask me to or tell me first. I think I get it now."

"My hell is not your problem. You have no reason to be sorry."

She kisses me again. "It is whether you pull me in it or not. I'm voluntarily walking in."

"Can we cuddle again?" She turns over and lies down. "Or not."

She laughs, and then grabs my hand, pulling it over her side. "I'm not going to make you sleep like that. You're like a statue. There are different ways to cuddle. This is spooning. Bring me your body." I pull her toward me, my hand against her stomach. "Or vice versa. That works too. This is more comfortable for sleeping."

She laughs again. Laughing puts me into a paranoid rage. "What's so fucking funny?"

"Sleeping, not ass poking. Put that away."

"Your naked ass is on my dick. What do you expect?" I push it down and pull her closer. "Happy now?"

"Yes."

I seal her into the curve of my body, leaving no space. What's left of her perfume becomes more noticeable being so close to her neck. "You smell good. What is that?"

"Ed Hardy."

"Keep wearing it."

"Okay. Goodnight."

"Goodnight."

I situate my lower arm under her pillow, bumping into hers. She loosely connects our hands. All I can do is stare into the back of her ink free neck since she put her hair up earlier. The back of the neck is actually a beautiful place for a tattoo—on a woman at least. It's feminine if done right. I think I know where I'm tattooing my name. That way every fucker trying to stare at her ass will also be graced with a property tag. She just doesn't know my name will be hidden within a design. A brand is tacky. I wouldn't do that to a woman. Names of partners are generally bad luck and rarely done right.

"Kross . . ."

"I thought you were going to sleep."

"I just thought you should know something."

"What?"

"This was my favorite Halloween so far."

"Tell me something about you I don't know?" I ask, repeating her question from earlier.

She tightens our fingers together. "My mother abandoned me in ways too."

"What about your dad?" We ask the same question at the exact same time.

"I never met him," we both say in unison again.

Then the room becomes silent, because right now there is nothing more to say. The world is a fucked up place. Because no good place would leave so many kids as orphans.

CHAPTER TEN

Delta

I open Remington's cabinet to stock it, screaming bloody murder and tossing all of the shit I'm holding as running becomes the only thing on my mind. All three of them start laughing from across the studio. I slip in my attempt to get away in a hurry, losing my balance completely before tumbling to the ground. My head hits the hard floor. "You fucking asshole!"

"Come on, Delta. It's funny."

Remington's womanizing voice is the first one to speak. I grab the clown figurine and throw it at his head. Too bad he ducked at just the right time. "I don't think it's funny at all. Fuck off."

"What happened to the sexy badass that's been walking around the shop for months? Covered in tattoos, hot, and scared of a little clown?"

"Knock it off. This is a fucking business not a playground.

Customers will be here soon." I sit up, my head throbbing a little from the hit on the floor. Kross is standing by his station with a transfer in his hand. He's been in his office downstairs since we got here this morning. It's going to be another busy day. We have back-to-back appointments until 11PM between all of the artists.

That shouldn't surprise me. It's been busy all week, but Kross mentioned there are rush times during the year for tattoos; the people that don't ordinarily have an obsession for ink letting their freak flag fly for a little bit, and since we just came off of Halloween, well, us freaks are the topic of conversation and considered the cool kids of the world.

Things have gone back to a happy medium in the world of Kross and Delta. That one amazing night we shared was short lived, and by amazing I do mean unforgettable. I feel like in ways I finally broke through some of his barriers. But to know that we've both lived without knowing who our fathers are was the starlight in the darkness. It is something we both share, and there are so many questions I have now that I've met someone else like me, but we haven't discussed it since. I'm starting to gather that closing himself off is how he protects himself.

I'm back to sleeping in my own bed, unfortunately, and we haven't had any more personal conversations or cuddle sessions since the whole parent thing happened, but we have hung out more after work, which to me is a plus. His coldness is a little warmer in temperature than it normally is. Instead of solid ice it's freezing cold water. He has yet to give me that tattoo, though, and I'm starting to have Kross fuck session withdrawals, but I don't want to bring it up again, because it's a little depressing to be a young, confident woman and have to do so; so I guess I'll wait until he initiates it and makes me feel like he wants it. I just may combust in the process at this rate of occurrence. It's hard to imagine myself going without sex as long as I did now, but I guess when you see the person you actually want to do it with on a daily basis it makes it all that much harder; especially when they've given you a few tastes here and there.

I start to pick up the stuff I dropped. "You okay?" Kross asks.

"Yeah. I'm fine."

"Nice underwear, Delta," Remington says, slathering his voice with a lustful filter to toy with me . . . or Kross. Us going to the Haunted house has really brought us all together. It was like an icebreaker. Jokes have become regular when Kross isn't around since Monday, now that everyone knows we're seeing each other. Well, assumes. Nothing has been admitted to as to what we actually are. Until lunch it felt like there was an enormous elephant in the room, and then finally, Remington being Remington with all of his open whoredom triumphed and he asked if we were fucking. Talk about uncomfortable. Kross walked downstairs—stormed really— making it that much more obvious, leaving me to answer that awkward question by myself. Test—I kept thinking it was a test. My answer was as vague as I could make it, leaving out any words that would even hint to sex.

Kross' face changes. *Shit.* I forgot I was wearing a skirt.

"Dude, shut the fuck up," Joey whispers.

"What? No one has told me I can't look. Until someone in this place owns up to fucking her she's available in my book. And even then, if a relationship is not fully noted in the form of a disclaimer she's still technically on the market. I've made many girls come and not keep them as mine. I see panties, I think of pussy. Simple as that. Especially when I see the outline of lips."

My head whips toward the three of them, all standing in a

straight line. Wesson looks at Kross and I see him pull Joey back out of the way discretely. Remington has a huge invisible smirk on his face. His lips aren't turned up but the muscles hint a smile.

My eyes widen at the exact same time Remington's does, most likely resembling a Snap Chat filter. His entire body tenses with the sound of the knife striking the wall, opposite of Kross. "I'm fucking her. She's staying with me. Her entire being is mine. If I hear one more word come out of your mouth about it you'll regret it, so remove your fucking eyes from between her legs, close your goddamned mouth for once and mind your own business or anyone else's but mine. Are we clear? Or do you need to pack your shit and get out of my shop?"

His hand goes to his head, rubbing along the top of his Mohawk. It's about two inches shorter along the center, the blue tips completely gone. He's going to have to have that evened out. "You are Papa Smurf no more," I say, unable to help it.

"Delta, go get my knife and come sit down. We're doing your tattoo," he says, an increment of his anger gone.

And like nothing just happened . . .

"Dude, what the actual fuck? You could have killed me."

"If I wanted you dead you would be. You took something personal of mine so I took something of yours. Next time you'll stay out of my business. Get to work."

Remington storms to the stairs, still petting his beloved hair as he disappears out the door. I follow him to the wall beside the door, shaking my head as I pry the buck knife from the wall. It was stuck pretty deep, taking some muscle to work it out, and it's a little scary that he knows how to throw a knife so well that he can give a man a haircut with one throw. At this rate he's going to be fixing a lot of holes in walls with filler.

Cassie opens the door as I turn to walk to Kross' station, letting a client in. "Joey, your nine o'clock is here."

Joey is a metalhead through and through. When he's on piercings all day his music blasts through the walls. His brown head is shaved on the sides and back, all of the length remaining on the top. He keeps it flipped to one side, but it doesn't extend past his ear. Then, you understand the other side of why he's a metalhead. He has earrings like Kross, but he also has two eyebrow rings, a nose ring, and a ring in the corner of his bottom lip like I have in the center. I think him and I both are in the running for the most facial jewelry. He has me beat with the eyebrow rings, though, and that doesn't even include the nipple rings; got a peek at those when he wore a tighter shirt once. He isn't near as big as Kross and he's a good bit shorter than all of them, but his body is defined and sculpted.

The talking between them begins as I hand the knife back to Kross, a smirk in place. "We really need to work on your anger issues."

"I told you I don't like guys looking at you. He pissed me off."

I lean forward, bringing myself closer to him. "There is a huge difference in looking and touching."

"Which is why he's still alive."

"You know, for someone that loathes other people looking at me or touching me you sure as hell don't much. Come tomorrow it'll be a week."

He stares at me. "I don't need it daily to function."

"So, I'm not good enough for you to think of it daily?"

"I said I didn't need it not that I didn't want it. If you knew my daily thoughts you'd be glad you get a break between. On most days I want to fuck you like an animal. Now sit down. We can revisit this conversation when we get home."

My eyes close, trying to calm my raging thoughts. He's so cruel. You don't say that shit to a girl and then expect her to sit down. They open. "If you knew my daily thoughts you'd know I don't want a break, and I'd appreciate getting fucked like an animal if it's coming from you."

The clenching of his glove-covered fists sways my attention, but I keep it to myself. "Where are you putting it?"

"The back of your neck."

Oh, this should be fun . . .

I hike my denim skirt up and throw my leg over the chair. Slowly, I lower into a straddle, pulling my hair up as I do. Right after I secure it with the ponytail on my wrist I can feel his hard body against my back. I turn my head, but his lips are already beside my ear, touching against my cheek as I do. "If this is how you tattoo the back of every girl's neck we may have a problem."

I can hear all three of their guns buzzing in the room; talking in the mix. He grips my inner thighs, his hands sitting at the edge of my panties on each side. "I guess it's a good thing you're the only one I'm obsessed with enough to touch like this then."

"I like you being obsessed. It makes me feel like you want me."

"Why would you ever think otherwise?"

"You haven't asked me to sleep with you since Halloween."

"I wasn't aware I had to invite you."

Fuck, why is this so hard with him? I feel like a child. "So what you're saying is?"

"Knock on my door and I'll let you in."

"Do you want me there? I don't want to push myself on you."

"I told you sometimes I need to be pushed. I'm not wired like you. You'll know when it's too far."

Maybe I need to go at this from a more aggressive angle. I don't really see what it could hurt. I just feel like . . . Fuck it. I'm going to try. "When you're done, I want you to fuck me in your office while you stare at your name on my body."

Without another word I lean forward, placing my forehead against the back of the chair and wrap my arms around it in a hug. He shoves his hips forward, closing any space there was between us. I can feel him against my bottom. He's hard. Thank God. He's finally showing me that I turn him on even when he seems so unaffected. And you know what? It makes me feel like a fucking celebrity.

I can feel the transfer paper against the back of my neck after he cleans the surface. "You trust me?"

"Oddly, yes."

"You want to look at it first or for me to just do it?"

"You trust someone completely or not at all. Do it."

He removes the paper, leaving the damp feeling of the ink in place. I've never been more excited about any tattoo on my body than the ones he's done himself. It's a high in itself, because I know with him he's leaving a part of himself behind. Even if we talk about what I want beforehand I never really know the end result, and every single time it's been better than I expected.

My eyes squint with the first touch of the needle. It's always the worst part, along with continuing after reloading the ink. It feels kind of like broken glass scraping hard against your skin. It's fine as long as he doesn't pick up the needle, but every time it starts back it temporarily cuts off your air for the briefest second before you get used to it again.

Still, even through the pain it's my favorite way to express myself. I can't remember a time that I didn't have a love for tattoos.

I'm not even sure how it started honestly. Since I figured out I *could* draw I've loved it, but there isn't a specific time I remember falling in love with tattoos. It's always just kind of been in the background.

For years I've loved tattoo reality T.V. It's my guilty pleasure I guess. I remember having the biggest fucking crush on Ami James and Chris Nunez from Miami Ink. God, they were so hot. Still are. Ami had that whole bad boy alpha vibe going on that just makes girls wanna fuck his brains out. Chris was the traditional asshole with a good guy side. Kat Von D broke my heart when she left, but the girl is still my idol in the tattoo industry, and LA Ink was also in my top two shows, so I'm just guessing it's something that's built over time.

My favorite tattoo sessions to watch were always cover up pieces; seeing the artist turn something hideous into something beautiful. I know more so now than before that it's not an easy job. It's a skill that takes a lot of talent: having to work with the pre-existing colors, the scar tissue, the deep lines that are hard to cover, and still come out with a design that will take away the regret the client had already. I can only hope one day I'm that good.

At first it was just something I thought was cool from an early age, but also, it's the foundation of one memory I have with my mother that I'll never forget. For my sixteenth birthday we got mother-daughter tattoos. Yeah, a lot of parents or onlookers would have probably thought badly of her signing for me a tattoo at the age of sixteen, but to me, it was one time that she whole-heartedly thought of what I wanted and set aside worldly opinions to give it to me. It was one day she marked out a time slot in her social life to spend with me. We ended up going with a moon and stars on the top of our right foot with shading in the background to create the night sky. It was her version of a promise that she would always look out for me no matter how dark it got; she the moon and me a small star in comparison. Too bad she couldn't actually keep that promise. I suppose it'll always be my fault. My sins drove us apart for good. Not that we were ever close to begin with . . .

After that, tattoos became my obsession. I found ways to get around the no tattoos under eighteen without parental consent law by using someone else's ID and a tattoo artist that turned the other cheek. All he needed was information to keep on file and a payday, and all I needed was another fix.

A moan escapes when he hits a bony place again. One particular spot at the bottom of my neck gets me every time. It feels pretty big. At one point or another I've felt him on just about every part of my neck. My arms are starting to become uncomfortable around this chair back. I allow them to fall, and the first place they go are his thighs. He doesn't flinch nor shake me off. Instead, he allows me to leave them there. That's huge considering Kross is very private about his personal life and not inclined to public displays of affection. Fuck, he doesn't really do affection at all. Moments like these are when I feel like we're a real couple.

The pain is becoming higher and my tolerance getting lower. All of the skin is now sensitive. My eyes start to roll in the back of my head, searching for a state of unconsciousness. The one thing I do best when I'm hurting in any form, emotionally or physically, is sleep. Those are the times that it becomes the easiest. Before I can even register that I'm tired I begin to nod off.

"Where's Mom?"

"Work. So she says . . ."

"Oh . . . But didn't she just get home an hour ago?"

"Yeah, but you know your mother. She can't keep her ass at home long enough to have a family life. It's getting pretty fucking

annoying. Especially since she's older than me. Maybe if she'd act her fucking age she'd get somewhere in life."

"She was supposed to hang out with me today is all. I'll probably just see what Lux is doing."

I start to walk back toward the hall from the living room when his voice sounds again. "It's not your fault, Delta."

I stop, looking at him on the couch in his tee shirt and boxers, his hair disheveled like he just woke up. Really he should be with someone closer to my age than my mother's, only fifteen years my elder. Thirty-two is a good age on a man I think. He's out of that immaturity stage it seems like, but he still is every bit good-looking like a man in his twenties. But I don't understand what she sees in younger men; like she's scared to get old so she keeps dipping into the fountain of youth, because each one gets younger than the last. Him I've always liked though, unlike the ones before. Considering what he does for a living he's a pretty down to earth guy. And why the hell he's still with her is beyond me. They always leave by now, but not him.

"What isn't my fault?"

"That she doesn't love you. If it helps I don't think she loves me either."

"Then why are you still with her?"

"Because of you."

I stare at him, unsure of what to say or how to take that. He stands, walking toward me as I stand frozen in the middle of the small living room of our house. "What do you mean?"

He stops in front of me. "I know she doesn't give you any attention, Delta. I can see it, and if I had to guess it's always been this way. She treats you like you're a burden instead of a blessing. Every time I hear her talk about you she makes it sound like she is stuck with you. That's not how you treat your child. You deserve so much better. The more I recognize her flaws the more I see your beauty. It makes me want to give you what you aren't getting."

"How?"

He rubs his fingers up my arm, leaving chill bumps behind. "Like touching you, for example." He takes another step forward, his hands going around my waist. My breathing becomes erratic. I like the way it feels. "Has anyone ever touched you like this?"

"No," I whisper.

He bunches my tank top in his hands, his fingers grazing my lower back. "Do you want to be touched this way?"

"Yes, but this would be wrong on so many levels."

"Sometimes two wrongs make a right, regardless of what everyone says. I smelt cologne on her when she got home even though she thought I was asleep. The first place she went was to the shower. She'll always be a bar whore, unlike you."

"I don't know . . ."

"Are you attracted to me?"

"Yes."

"Do you want me to stop? If you do I'll never bring it up again."

I try to think. The way I feel is foreign. Every part of me feels like it's on fire. I have that uncomfortable wetness in my panties I get sometimes but ignore. His fingers skim up my back as he looks at me. It feels good, really good actually. I've never gotten close to hooking up with a guy because of everything Lux has gone through at such a young age. It scares the hell out of me, so I just avoid it all together. Before I can stop it the word comes out. "No."

He removes my shirt, leaving me uncomfortably naked since I haven't put on a bra yet. My hands go to my boobs to cover myself, but he removes them. "You're beautiful. I want to see you."

One phrase and all of the stress leaves my body. "Okay."

"I need you to promise me something if we do this."

"What?"

"Promise me you'll never tell. I could get into a lot of trouble since you're just now seventeen. I'll never use you, but I need you to promise you won't use me either."

"I promise it'll never leave my lips."

His lips instantly go to mine, pressing against them so softly I can barely feel them. "I've wanted you for what seems like forever," he says, and picks me up. I wrap my legs around his waist as he leads me to my bedroom and locks the door behind him.

Words like that I never hear. I'm often not wanted. It sucks but it's the life I was given. But he wants me, though, and she obviously doesn't want him either, so I will let him have me instead. It may be wrong, but she has always only cared about herself.

He lays me in the middle of my bed and removes my shorts and panties, baring me completely. His eyes slowly descend my entire body, making me nervous. Does he like what he sees? When he smiles and removes his shirt I relax a little. "Spread your legs for me."

"What? Why?"

"I want to see all of you."

I do as he says. He pushes down his boxers and gets on the bed, his body between my legs. "How many guys have been here?" His fingers brush over my entrance.

"None. I'm still a virgin."

"You haven't had sex at all?"

"You asked me if anyone has touched me. I told you no."

"I thought you meant like cuddled and spent time with you. I guess I just assumed . . . Never mind. You promise you won't regret this?"

"I'm pretty sure I won't."

The tip of his finger starts to rub me. My nerves are making my stomach hurt and I feel nauseous. "Chuck . . ."

"What, beautiful?"

"Can you promise you won't get me pregnant?"

"Yes. I promise. You don't have to worry about that with me. I've had a vasectomy and I followed up to ensure it worked. I don't want kids and I can't afford accidents. I like being in control of who reaps the benefits of my hard earned money."

"What's a vasectomy?"

That word is familiar, but I'm not sure I know what it is.

"I'm shooting blanks. I've been snipped. I'm sterile. When I come it's just semen. No sperm. It would be impossible for me to get you pregnant."

"Okay. Are you going to use a condom? I don't have any."

"Only if you make me. I do with everyone else so I don't end up with something I can't get rid of, but if you've never had sex I know you're clean. I get tested regularly. It's up to you."

"I want you to use one."

"Okay. Be right back."

He walks out of the room, leaving me within my thoughts as I stare at the ceiling. I work to breathe evenly, trying to calm down. I'm seventeen now. Just had a birthday this month. Most of the people my age have done this already. They talk about it at school all the time. People assume I have because I have a few tattoos and a belly button ring, but I never waste the breath to tell them otherwise. People are going to believe what they want anyway.

He returns, already rolling it on his dick. I stare at it in his hand, my nerves only getting worse. "Is it going to hurt?"

I've never had anyone to talk about this kind of stuff with. I don't ask Lux certain things because of the way she lost her virginity, and I don't want to open old wounds for her, so I keep my thoughts to myself. "Probably at first. I'll be easy."

He gets back on top of me, his finger returning, and then he slips one inside of me as he places his mouth on my breast. "That feels good."

He looks at me. "You're so tight. I might like this too much."

"Is this going to be a one-time thing?"

"No. It can be our little secret."

"Okay."

Something touches me. It's bigger than his fingertip. He pushes forward a little. My breathing is embarrassingly out of control, but his hand rests against my cheek. My hands go to his waist. "It's okay to be nervous."

I nod. He kisses my lips, taking my mind off of it as he pushes inside of me all the way, leaving me in a state of confusion. It doesn't hurt like I thought it would. He didn't seem small, leaving me to think that it's me. No girl wants to be considered loose. That I know for sure. But he said I was tight, the questions returning. I wonder if it's because I use tampons.

When I don't make a sound he begins thrusting in and out of me, his groans already starting as he grips my thigh. He looks at me. "Fuck, you feel so good, baby. I can't believe this is what I've been missing. I don't think I'm going to ever be able to stop."

Baby . . . He called me baby. All of the guilt washes away the better it feels. I grow comfortable, wrapping my legs around his solid body and kissing him this time, only harsher. A moan slips through my mouth into his. I like it, regardless of how shitty of a person it makes me.

"Delta!"

I jump at the sound of his voice. "Fuck. What? Is it done?"

I wipe my mouth, ensuring there is nothing embarrassing present . . . like drool. "Damn, Delta. I never took you for a snorer."

I cut my eyes at Wesson, still looking down at the thigh he's tattooing. It's the only gun I hear at the moment. "Shut up. I do not snore."

"Keep telling yourself that. Meanwhile, I believe you're wanted in the boss' office." He looks up, a goofy-ass grin on his face. He's the only one of the three stooges in here. "Didn't anyone tell you that you aren't supposed to sleep in class or on the job? If he comes back without you I'll know you didn't make it."

I glance around, realizing Kross is in fact gone, all of his stuff lying on the tray. I reach behind my neck, feeling the taped disposable cloth in place. Damn. I just heard him. I couldn't have been asleep for that long. Let's be real. I stand. "How long has he been gone?"

"Him hollering your name in a pissed off fashion was his exit call. May the tattoo gods be with you. Never seen boss man so angry. Not even when Remington got a haircut."

"I thought you were my friend. You're going to send me into the lion's den with no backup?"

The girl he's tattooing is staring at us through the entire conversation. He continues talking, looking up when he reloads ink. Nosey-ass client. "I think you can handle it. You are the one banging the boss, after all."

I groan and walk to the door, flipping him off over my shoulder as I open it. "This is how I feel about you right now."

"You know I would've but you gave it to someone else," he calls out as I slam the door shut. This should be fun. Who the hell knows what I did. Or what I may have said in my sleep. I've been known to be a sleep talker, and walker. That dream jars its ugly little head at the worst damn time. Thoughts I have sometimes without even attempting to think of them invade my dreams on occasion; unwelcome little bastards. Fuck my life . . .

Kray

My hands lace in front of my face, fingers resting against my forehead, the anger consuming me whole. I stare down at the grain in the wood of my desk, eyes set between my elbows, trying to calm down. The moans coming from her mouth in a sleep-induced state were totally different than the one before. But that's not the part that pissed me off. What sent rage coursing through every vein inside of me was that one word that exited after: Chuck.

A knock sounds at the door. "Enter."

It starts to open and then she slips inside, treading slowly. "You wanted to see me?"

I sit back in my chair, staring at her, my once hard cock down to a semi. "Tired?"

"About that—"

"Lock the door."

She does as I request. "I'm really sorry. It was just starting to hurt and that's how I deal with pain. I didn't even realize I was—"

"Come sit down."

"Okay . . . Where?"

I have no other chairs in here, because there are never any visitors. I deal with my business in the studio or elsewhere. The rest I deal with alone. "On the desk."

My eyes follow her around the solid piece of oak until she sits on top of it. "Are you going to fire me?"

"Do you think I should?"

"No. Please don't. Dock my pay if you have to or suspend me for a day to think about what I've done. That's far worse punishment. I want to be here. I don't know what came over me, but it won't happen again."

"Okay."

"Okay . . . you're not going to fire me or you're going to dock my pay?"

"Okay you can stay."

"Thank God."

"But for the record I'm not mad you fell asleep. You weren't technically working."

"Seriously? So I just went through all of that shit and you're not even mad?"

"Oh I'm mad."

"Uh. Okay? Can I ask why?"

"One word: Chuck."

"Fuck."

"I'm going to give you one opportunity to tell me fully, without withholding any information, as to why a man's name other than mine came out of your mouth in an orgasmic way when my cock is the one servicing you. If I have to find out myself from someone else it's not going to be good. Unlike most people, I have no conscience. My moral code was long gone before it got started. Even Kaston has more of one than I do. Life and death are parts of existence. Which side a person is on doesn't matter to me."

"I'm not sleeping with someone else if that's what you're asking.

I would never do that. Even if I were that kind of person you scare the hell out of me."

"That wasn't what I asked, was it?"

"He's just someone from my past. Don't you ever have dreams that aren't warranted or wanted?"

I steeple my hands in front of me, my elbows pressing into the arms of the chair. "My patience is wearing thin."

"Fuck, Kross. Are you going to go down the list of your past for me too? What does it matter?"

"I assure you my list is fucking short, and I sure as hell am not moaning their names in my sleep; especially when I'm driving my cock inside of *you* in my pastime, balls deep and ungloved, so I'm going to say this one more time and that's it. If you don't tell me who the fuck he is, why the hell you're dreaming about him, and his history in your life, I'm going to go find him myself for the answers, and you really don't want that outcome. I have a feeling I won't have to go further than that damn strip club, so start talking."

A tear rolls down her cheek, not fazing me at all, but she quickly wipes it away before it gets far. Another follows. "You're right. He is the guy from the strip club. You probably know him as the owner, but he's also the guy I lost my virginity to when I was seventeen. If I tell you more you aren't going to want anything to do with me anymore."

"Try me. I'm a pretty fucked up kind of guy."

"He was my mom's live-in boyfriend."

My blood runs cold. "There is no way in fucking hell you're stopping there."

Her hands start twisting nervously in her lap. Her body is trembling even though I can tell she's trying to stop. "M-My mom was a partier; a social lover. She worked constantly my entire life, overtime anytime she could: part to pay the bills and the other was her play money. She was never around, but it was a life she wanted for herself and was content with. I was the result of an irresponsible weekend out of town, spent drunk. She knows who my father is in the physical sense, but she knows none of his demographics . . . Like at all. He was a soldier in a military town for training and she was always out looking for men fishing holes from what I know. She never wanted me, and often she made that known in many different ways. She rarely stayed home. I had plenty of time to myself; more than what I ever wanted. I've seen an abundance of men come and go in my life. I don't care to even put a number to it. I got to know every boyfriend she ever had pretty close because she left me with them often. To her it was a free babysitter. To them it was easy sex and a goodbye to loneliness. She always knew how to pinpoint the ones that needed a woman. Honestly, a lot of them were more of a parent to me than she was, but the second she started cheating on them like she always did they hit the road . . . Except Chuck, the youngest of all her boyfriends."

She looks at me, pleadingly, tears still falling down her face, but I make no effort to hint this is the end. "Why do you want to know this?"

"I just do."

"It's embarrassing now."

"I don't care."

"He gave me the kind of attention I had never had. Instead of brushing it off I soaked it up. It wasn't something I was familiar with. Lux and I were so used to being on our own or in the middle of shit that it just became part of what we wanted in messed up ways. When he came on to me he said all the right things I guess. We ended up having an ongoing affair behind her back until I graduated high school. He fucked her just enough to stay around for me. Some nights I wondered if she secretly knew, because she made sure I heard them, but I think she just noticed the way he looked at me. And I was okay with it because it was better than the alternative. He wasn't from my hometown. He just stayed there and traveled here for work. He had his own place here, but he pretended with her so he could be with me."

She dips her head, no longer looking at me. The raging fire inside of me hasn't dwindled even a degree. The photographic images developing in my head are making me want to kill. That's never a good thing for people that owe me money. I remain silent as she continues, even though deep down I know I don't need to hear any more. "We snuck around. We did everything a real couple did just under the radar. On nights I worked I lied about why I wasn't coming home and stayed with him here in Atlanta. I fell in love with this city long before Lux and I moved here. It was the one place we could really be 'us'. And because my mom was self-centered and hung up on juggling so many men and a party life the stupid bitch didn't even notice we were always gone at the same time, or that her daughter was fucking her boyfriend. I'm not proud of it, but I don't completely regret it either. He helped make me the person I am today, freeing me from the girl that always wore her heart on her shoulders. Reasoning doesn't really matter when you do something that fucked up in life, but I do have a few. Some of it may have been my own fucked up form of revenge, if I were honest, but some of it was real."

She looks up at me again, her hypnotic green eyes glistening and boring into mine. "I used to be a girl that loved hard. It's ironic given that no one loved me. When someone finally gives a loving person love, she falls hard, and in the beginning I did, regardless of the circumstances. It's easy to think you love someone when he gives you what you need the most. Love doesn't judge, doesn't keep record of wrongdoings, and it doesn't let you choose who you love. It chooses for you. If it did I would have stopped loving my mother a long time ago. As for Chuck. He was good to me. He was genuine. He gave me ways to take care of myself regardless of what others would have thought of the method. And he always told me there would be times that he had to be with my mother sexually for him to stay there . . . with me. With him there I never got lonely. It was never a question of unfaithfulness, but sacrifice, and it wasn't like she wasn't with other men the whole time. We all used each other for something. It probably would have lasted longer, but the day I graduated he came clean to Mom without my consent, thinking that was the key for us to be together openly. I was no longer a minor at that point or in high school. There was nothing stopping us anymore. She did nothing to him besides find someone even younger, but the second we were alone she slapped me so hard I was almost in tears and said things that can never be forgotten. Then, she kicked me out and told me to never come back, so I packed my things and Lux was glad to leave. I haven't been back since. I walked away from both of them that day. Me and Lux went on a road trip. This was a stop. When Lux wanted to stay here I just kept it to myself that his club was here and stayed away. Atlanta is a big place. I left behind a man I had let myself fall for over the course of a year and a job that was making me a lot of money during junior and senior year because my guilt won out. That's it. That's all there is to know. If you want me to leave I will."

"So you loved him?"

Where the fuck that came from I couldn't tell you. My ways of trying to understand things I can't comprehend aren't like everyone else. I'll admit the bitterness is obvious.

She breathes out. "In that 'he's my first love' kind of way. I have attachment issues that I've hidden from you since you're the complete opposite. I was serious about wanting this job, so I've kept it under control. I tend to cling to the people that give me attention, especially if it's someone I want in return."

"Do you still?"

"Love him? No."

"Then why did you go back?"

"I wanted to keep this job and I was willing to do anything. I knew he'd take me back, even with stipulations. It was an income fix like I told you. I had lost my bartending job and then found an eviction notice on my door when I got home. I didn't have many options and I'm not a beggar, so I was going to do something I knew would work, including giving myself to a man I no longer wanted for as long as I had to. I like it here. I've never lied about what I want. I want this. You just happened in the process."

I stand and lean forward, placing my fists on the desk to each side of her thighs. "So you're trying to tell me this shit we've been doing wasn't a premeditated thought? That's bullshit. I'm not that stupid."

"My thoughts in the form of a fantasy and what I know to be real are two different things. I consider myself a realist. After the interview you changed. You seemed disinterested so I took it as a hint. Any hopes I had in an *us* ended with the day."

"When are you going to learn that I don't fit into a fucking category?"

"I guess when you learn you can trust me and stop shutting me out. You expect me to tell you every part of my embarrassing backstory yet you give me very little of yours."

"You wouldn't like what's below the surface."

"Just like you don't like what's below mine?"

My entire chest moves dramatically as the pace of my breathing picks up. "Who said I didn't?"

"No one, so stop assuming you know what I like and what I don't. It works both ways."

"I don't fucking like you thinking of other men, past or present."

She removes her shirt. Fuck. She's not even wearing a damn bra. She doesn't really need to. Her rack isn't that big but it's perfect. Her nipples are my favorite part. "Then make me forget the past. I can't control my dreams, but if you brand yourself to every facet of my mind then that's likely what will become of them. Only you have that power. I can't force you."

I fight to stare into her eyes when mine want to go to her chest. My god. Even I have weak points. What man can easily disregard a hot, naked woman? I'm not that strong willed; not where she's concerned apparently. But still, one point remains unknown to me. "Why do you need me to fuck you to know that I want you? What does that prove? I don't understand this concept at all."

"Because, Kross, I'm a girl. This is the way that makes us feel wanted. Men were designed to be sexual predators in regards to women. We are the prey. When a man wants a woman he wants the sex over and over on a regular basis. A girl shouldn't have to request it. Unless . . ." She zones out, her eyes fixating on something besides mine. "You don't really want it at all. Am I your shamefuck? Like do you just feel sorry for me and have sex with me out of pity or obligation since I live with you?"

A silence occurs. "Oh, God. I'm so stupid."

"That's probably the first accurate thing you've said in a while."

She looks up at me; a little stunned from the expression she's wearing. "Excuse me?"

My arm forms a vise around her waist. I grip her hip and pull her ass to the edge of the desk, before climbing up her leg with my hand and forcing her panties over her ass as I lift her from the hard surface. Her hands grip the edge to keep her body stationary. "You're a pretty stupid woman if that's what you think. You obviously don't know me as well as you think. I don't fuck someone out of shame, guilt, or pity. I don't fuck someone I'm not physically attracted to. I don't fuck someone unless I feel like I'm going to combust. I don't fuck someone that I have to physically try for. And unlike most fucking men, sex doesn't drive me. I don't need it to survive, to function, or for any other reason."

She's breathing heavily. I pull her skirt up her body as her panties fall from her feet to the floor, the elastic waistband stretching as it hits the wider parts. It too hits the floor. My voice is escalating to dangerous in tone, my teeth gritting together between sentences. "You have to endure touching to like sex, and most women can't keep their hands out of the picture. My list is short by choice, not because I lacked the skill to lure women into bed."

I lean forward, pushing her into a lying position on her back. "You want me to trust you with the ugly parts of me? Fine. My entire childhood I was in foster care. None of which were good *parents*. I was an easy paycheck. I was lucky to get one that didn't hurt me, but the one that I was with the longest is the same one that drove me to nightmares. Every time I was touched it was to inflict pain or to torment me, and that's worse than not being touched at all. She locked me in a bedroom by myself with nothing but school books in her attempt to say I was homeschooled. I've lived most of the first half of my life under lock and key, hence the bedroom needing to be locked for me to sleep. If I didn't pass the required tests it was immediate punishment. I was physically forced to pretend she provided a good and comforting place to stay so they wouldn't take me away. I rarely saw the light of day, let alone people."

I stand and remove my shirt, before returning to my body-hovering position, grabbing her hand and holding it to the lighter scar she's already familiar with. I'm angry. I'm trapped in an emotional corner. I don't like discussing my past. I never have and I swore I never would. She stirs things in me that I both loathe and like. And she's hot; so fucking hot my cock is already straining against the denim of my jeans. "Every fucking scar tells a horror story. Hot lighter." I move to each one, stating what they are: belt buckle, old baseboard with a nail spike, whip, cigarette, curling wand, key, fork . . . and that's just the mild ones that are barely noticeable and covered in ink.

She stares at me as I unbuckle my belt and undo my pants, pushing them down with my underwear to my thighs. I lean back over and grip the opposite edge in my hand, then grab her hand again, bringing her fingertips to the deep-set scar beside my dick on my pelvis. "Feel that? I fucking got hard on accident. I don't even remember what I was thinking about or if it was just part of being a boy, but after checking on me she returned with a knife and stabbed me with it in a shallow jab to make it go away. Didn't even get a ride to the doctor and a chance to say it was an accident. Had to try to stitch it up myself with an old sewing kit. Anything sinful was forbidden. Her punishments were barbaric to say the least. 'Spare the rod, spoil the child' was an old Proverb she lived by in the most fucked up ways." I laugh, a sadistic sound coming from my mouth. "But that hard-on was the beginning of more fucked up shit. People like her are why I've never wanted anything to do with that book. My lack of drive is not because I don't want you; it's my own fucked up issues. My mind remains in Hell ninety-nine percent of the time. Every time someone touches me for an extended period of time I fucking lose it. When most people experience touch it's good. Everything I know was bad. I'd rather go without than have to withstand the way I feel when it happens."

Her hand turns and she laces her fingers with mine. It feels weird and is taking focus not to pull away. "But sometimes you let me touch you . . ."

She wraps her legs around me, pulling me between her legs. "That doesn't mean it's easy. Before you, if I wanted to fuck, I made her turn around and bend over with her hands gripping something hard. I've hit a woman for breaking those rules before. I thought for a second she was someone else."

She stares at me long and hard. "You won't hurt me. I can feel it. We both have our own issues. Affection scares you and it's something I need. One day you'll accept that those demons may be in your head but they're no longer here. You never have to be in pain with me and your hard exterior will soften, I hope. It's okay to want me. All you have to say is that you do. I've already given myself to you. And you know what? Over time we will fix us, but nothing beneath your surface is ugly. Scars are beautiful, regardless of the horrible way they got there."

I pull my hand free from hers, the other still clamped tight to the desk. I can see the disappointment on her face immediately. I grab my dick and thrust inside of her, my mouth instantly wrapping around her bare nipple. She's not doing a very good job of smothering her moans, even though they're low. A knock sounds at the door, followed by Cassie's voice. "Kross, your appointment is here."

My eyes set on Delta's. "Take her upstairs. I'll be there in a minute."

I grab both of her hands in both of mine this time, ignoring the weird-ass feeling consuming my body, and bring them above her head to lie on top of the wood surface as I thrust in and out of her. It amazes me how wet she gets; my dick drenched from her. It takes a lot more effort to last. Words sway my thoughts from the way it feels inside of her, so I use them. "If you really want this, you're still going to have to push me; even with sex. I can't just turn it off. Just because you have to tell me what you want doesn't mean I don't want to give it to you in the end. Okay? I'm not programmed to read you like some people can."

She nods, and then squeezes my hands with hers. "Then I want you to kiss me and fuck me slow," she says.

I still inside of her. Fuck. I don't know if I'm capable of slow motion. Coming has always been about speed. I didn't want sex to last long.

She pulls her hands out of mine and they go for my face, touching against my skin slowly. My eyes slam shut on reflex at first, waiting for the brunt of the pain like I always have, but I open them when I remember who's touching me. Her eyes never falter. "Try it with me." She doesn't raise her voice. "Please. Just try it once. If you don't like it you can go back to the way you like it."

I pull back slowly until my head is at the edge. My breathing becomes heavier as I inch back inside. "Like that," she says in a thick, breathy voice that is driving me nuts. She pulls my lips toward hers. "I love sex with you," she adds, in that same damn turned on voice, before going for my lips.

The bottom of her bare feet brush against my ass as I continue at this pace. Her back arches off the wood, pressing her hardened nipples against my chest. She moans into my mouth when I tilt her hips. Her tongue brushes along the roof of my mouth. Fucking hell. If she doesn't stop with those noises . . .

Her head rolls back and her eyes close, her hands lightly brushing down my arms until they end behind her head, gripped on the edge of the desk like mine were earlier. Her neck becomes more pronounced, her veins sticking out from her skin. Every time she tries to mute her voice it only makes it sexier. I've never seen a woman look like this during sex. My heart is racing so fast I feel like I can't breathe. I can see her pulse. I can't stand it anymore. My teeth sink into the front of her neck as I jar my pelvis against the center of her legs.

The scream of a moan that follows I wasn't expecting. "I'm coming," she says in a squeal-like scream. I smother her words with my mouth as I drive inside her one final time.

Yeah . . . Me fucking too.

CHAPTER ELEVEN

I let the phone ring three times. He picks up. "It's been a minute."

"I have a question."

"Always short and to the point. Hit me with it."

I stand at the bottom of the staircase, my back against the wall. "If I hear one fucking comment you're on your own next time you need an order filled."

He laughs. "Let me guess . . . Delta?"

Fucking prick of an assassin. My head falls back against the wall. Just do it. "How the fuck do you date?"

"Kross, you're thirty years old. What the hell kind of a question is that?"

"You're getting close to finding a new dealer."

"I'm going to assume you've fucked her then?"

"What kind of man would I be if I disclosed that kind of information?"

"A fucking man. Period. We discuss these things. I guarantee you if Lux wasn't a damn hermit over school she'd already know about it."

"This shit is your fault. Just answer the damn question."

"I'm working on it."

"Fuck. Yes. My patience is almost gone."

"Well, then your attitude makes perfect sense. Otherwise I was just going to say you are more of a psycho than I thought."

"Like you have fucking room to talk."

"In what context are you referring to when you ask me 'how do you date'? Everyone has dated in some form."

"Not me."

"That's bullshit."

"Goddammit, Kaston. I'm about to hang up and say fuck it and go on about things like I always have. I'm not in the mood for the jokes. I wouldn't have called your pussy-whipped ass if I wasn't serious."

"Shit. Hold on." Muffling comes through the line. "Hey, I gotta talk to Kross about something. I'll be back in a minute."

A door opens and shuts, before silence follows. The legs of a chair scrape against concrete. "Calm your shit. By date do you mean the casual act of existing monogamously with one woman or by date do you mean what kind of stuff do you do when you take her somewhere to prove she's different than a fuck?"

"All of the above."

"Does she know about your side career?"

I glance up the stairs at the closed door. "Yes."

"And she's okay with it all?"

"Getting there, I think."

He takes a deep breath. "Dating in any sense is pretty easy. Consider it like hanging out with your best friend; except she's a girl, she's hot, and you get to fuck her in your spare time."

"I don't have friends."

"Try talking."

"About what? I already talk more than I ever have in my entire life. You know I'm not a talker when it comes to unnecessary shit."

"Fuck, Kross. You may have to change a little. Women like to talk. Sometimes a little too much. Those few times are when you just let it go in one ear and out the other, using common words or phrases like yeah, you don't say, or fuck them. It's almost fail proof. All men do it. Just make sure if she gets silent for more than a few seconds you act like you didn't hear her, because in that case she asked a question and is waiting on an answer."

"Telling her to shut the fuck up for a little while seems like it'd be more honest."

"Then your pussy would be your pussy no more. Look, dating, in general, is about finding balance. We're two different species. Well, everyone but Lux. You know what? Scratch that. Maybe I need to go at this from an angle you understand. When you find a weapon you aren't that familiar with what do you do?"

"I study it, research its history, and use hands on discovery until it's second nature. What else would I do?"

"Exactly. Delta is the new weapon. Right now she's an unfamiliar object for you. You like the way she looks and feels or we wouldn't be having this conversation. And she's piqued your curiosity to the point you want to experience something new. For the most part you just wing it. They're all too different to really place in a category. The stuff most of us do when you don't have to work is watch television together, cook, drink in the Jacuzzi so you can relax and still get to know her. Or just go out somewhere. You don't have to open up all at once."

This is stressing me the fuck out. "And if I take her out?"

"What does she like?"

"Rock. Tattoos. I'm not really sure."

"Figure out her interests through the question game. Then it becomes easy. Take her out to dinner or a concert. Think of stuff that you like to do and she probably will too. I'm pretty sure you two are more alike than you think. If you really want to go all out, take her on a trip. It's always easier to find shit to do when you're on vacation and work isn't part of the equation. If she's like Lux—and I'm going to guess she is since they're almost glued to the hip until recently—she hasn't gotten out much. It's sad really, and when you see if for yourself it tears your walls down."

"What about sleeping together? She brought it up again."

"I'm assuming when she stays over she'll sleep with you. What do you mean?"

"She lives with me."

"What? Since when?"

"The night after our meeting."

"I wasn't expecting you to work that fast."

"Circumstances arose. I dealt with it. Again, you have no fucking room to talk."

"That wasn't a judgmental comment. I was at that crossroads once not all that long ago. I'm just surprised. If she doesn't already sleep with you then where does she sleep now?"

"Her room."

"Do you want to share a room with her?"

"I don't know. Fuck. I've always been by myself. I've never

coexisted with a female. Or really been involved with one for that matter. Does she have to move all her stuff in there and make it girly?"

"Have you not looked at Delta? She's hardly girly. Lux is girly and she hasn't even done that shit. But yes, if you share space with someone your things become mixed in a sense. It's not as bad as it seems."

"Maybe we can just try sharing a bed on a regular basis first."

"You could do that. There are no rules except faithfulness. You can't go shoving your dick in anyone else."

"I get plenty. I don't need or want any more than what she's already giving."

"Want to double?"

"Double what?"

"Date. Seriously? Have you been under a rock your entire life? I know you're kind of the loner, asshole type but everyone at least knows how it all works."

"Something like that," I say. "I'll get back to you on that other. I'll holler at you later."

"Later."

I disconnect the call and set my phone on the small table in front of the stairs. "Fucking wing it. Yeah right."

I stare up the steps. I'm growing a conscience and I don't know that I particularly like it. Yesterday after that completely inappropriate office sex we stayed busy all day. Professionalism has always been something I do well, and the two of us blew that to shit in a hurry. After we closed down the shop she went on a drop with me, so we didn't get home till almost daylight since it was a pretty good stretch of a drive.

Today we're closed. Sundays are by appointment request only

if someone wants to book or if I just decide I'd rather work, which happened often in the past. It was never easy to be alone in my thoughts. There are weekends we all stay in the shop like last weekend, and then there are Sundays I give everyone a life. That would be today. When we got home she walked up the stairs to her room like a zombie. I half expected her to want to come to my room but she didn't even ask, so I didn't either. I've kept to myself all day, trying to work everything out in my head after yesterday. At one point thoughts were running together and repeating until I just couldn't take it anymore, hence the phone call I didn't want to make.

I walk up the stairs and open the door. The bedroom light was on and shining through the bottom crack, so I know she's awake. The only thing visible from beneath the fluffy, white comforter is black hair in a huge messy pile and black fingernails wrapped around the latest copy of *Inked* magazine.

Before I can stop it a smile appears. Well that's a view I wasn't expecting, though I don't know why I'm surprised. The guilt settles. Maybe I do need to give her practice sessions on real skin that won't have a negative outcome if it's messed up.

The magazine slowly lowers. "What's up?"

Yep. I'm breeding a monster. "Who's hot and cold now?"

"The person who's been ignored all day?"

The outside of my fist bangs lightly against the inside frame of the door. "I was trying to work out some things."

"Is that going well for you?"

"No." I grab the top of the frame with both hands. "I had to call Kaston."

"About?"

"Dating advice."

"Who does he think you're interested in?"

"I told him."

Her smile starts to form. I don't think she realizes how much more beautiful it makes her. "You told someone about us on your own free will?"

"Yes. Why haven't you told Lux?"

"You haven't been public about us except in psychotic meltdowns over other men. Lux is busy with culinary school. We go days between talking. And I didn't want to push you too far and risk pushing you away completely."

My hands tighten around the wood. "Delta, you do realize I've never done this before right? I have no fucking idea what kind of stuff is normal. I'm sure I'm going to suck at this couple thing, but for whatever ungodly reason I'm going to give it a shot, because, well, someone else is not going to take my place."

She closes the magazine and sets it on the bed as she pats the mattress on the other side closest to me. "Come in."

I walk inside and sit down beside her, facing the doorway. "Can I ask you a question?"

"Okay." Questions freak me the hell out.

"How short is your list?"

I look at her. "I don't know. Two hand count, maybe more. It wasn't a number I focused on."

"Mine too," she says with a smile. She looks away for a second. "I have another question. I think it would help me to understand the things that actually bother me."

She waits for an answer. "Just ask."

"What's the longest you've ever gone without sex?"

"About a year, I think. Sex is different for me than most. It requires being close to someone in privacy for a length of time. Both of which bring back bad memories. I don't do companionship very well in any form. I was forced to be alone until I wanted it; needed it even. I don't know any different. I was already set in those ways past the point of learning new behavior. Drugs, ammo, guns, those are things that people want with no other expectations. Finding it, stealing it, whatever the fuck it takes to get it, requires very little human interaction. All I have to be is the efficient delivery boy and I get a large payday. Emotions, feelings, and closeness aren't part of it. It's an easy life for me. Tattoos are an outlet for the things inside my head. As for the sex—my hand elicits the same outcome without the stress of the rest."

"You never wanted this with anyone else? Not even an interest?"

"No."

"You said you're thirty, right?"

"Yes." Still, I'm frustrated. "I've always been a pretty smart person, despite having to teach myself everything I know, but I don't know how to do this without looking like a dumbass. I don't like the way this feels. I don't even know where to start. I've always been by myself. I know my own shit. I don't have to tell it to anyone else."

Her grin stretches. "It will get easier. But for starters, why did you come to my room?"

Her eyes are lighter in shade. They usually are when she's laughing or having fun. They get darker when she's angry or upset. "What kind of stuff do you like?"

"The same stuff as you." She laughs. "Will you just forget everything Kaston told you? Talk to me like one of the boys. We can figure this out on our own."

"Thank fuck. I don't think I would be good at anything he said."

Her laugh becomes louder and longer in length, her teeth showing from the way her lips are pulled tight. "Just for the record . . . What did he tell you?"

"To take you to dinner, for one."

Her fingers go to her hair and starts twirling around in the mess. Her focus veers off and hits the comforter instead of me. "Personally, I'm not really fond of dinner dates. They're awkward. You either don't shut up because you're scared of running out of things to talk about or you sit there like a bunch of fucking weirdos in silence. I'm more of an eat cold Chinese takeout straight from the box in my panties and tee shirt kind of girl."

I stare at her, envisioning that view for a moment. A lump suddenly forms in my throat. "I like Chinese food."

She looks up. "I'm not a cook."

"Food is for survival. The less ingredients the better. Those that find it fun seem weird."

Her nose ring reflects the light when she turns to look at me again, her smile back. "I'll refrain from mentioning that to Lux; though to be honest, I kind of agree. I only listen to rock or metal and very seldom anything else."

"Same."

"Any likes in the form of media entertainment I have usually consists of tattoos in some form . . . or action. Gotta love a good action movie once in a while. I throw in horror from time to time. Comedy if it's good enough, but usually it's subjective, so a lot of the time I find it falls short. Fuck romance, though. That shit isn't real. I don't know how all that sweet and mush is supposed to give you the feels. In the movies he's opening doors and dropping you off on the front porch with an innocent kiss and then he calls not even twenty-four hours later telling you he had an amazing time and he hasn't even gotten in your pants yet. Realistically, he's an arrogant asshole that just shows up looking fine, demands for you to shut your own door and fucks you senseless on your vanity when you're trying to work, not even bothering to take you on the date first. Yeah, screw the movies."

I fight against the smirk building as I hear that night from her point of view. "I think we'll get along just fine."

"I'm independent physically. I'm needy emotionally."

"I'm independent and controlling physically. I'm distant emotionally. It's all I know."

"We can find balance. The rest will come naturally."

"Okay."

"I wouldn't have been attracted to you had you not been like me. That whole opposites attract thing is bullshit. Who wants to be around someone they have nothing in common with?"

"Why I'm still single . . . or was, I guess. I was born a breed that doesn't really exist. I don't fit in with most people." A laugh slips out.

"See, we agree." That smile hasn't left. It's contagious usually . . . when I'm not in a bad mood. I've probably smiled more since we met than I have in my entire life. "Why didn't you just come talk to me?"

"It seems childish to be in this predicament."

"I feel like that with you too."

I stand upright and remove my shirt and jeans, before lifting the blanket and getting in bed beside her, not touching at first to prepare myself. She doesn't make any effort to move closer from the middle. Instead, she turns on her side to face me, placing her bottom arm under the pillow. "You look good like this."

"My hair is on top of my head and I have no makeup on. I look like death."

"No. I like you better without all that shit caked on your eyes."

"That's a first . . ."

"You like *Inked* magazine?"

"Yeah. It's my guilty pleasure. I've been subscribed to it forever. I need to make sure they have this address."

"Cancel it."

"I don't want to."

I smile to the mildest degree. "I'm already subscribed. There is no reason for us both to pay for it. We can share."

My hand moves to her barely covered hip and I pull myself a little closer than before. She doesn't move. "Okay. Have you read this issue yet? Ashley Nicole Shelton makes a badass Harley Quinn."

"Yes."

"When?"

"In bed."

"Like me?" Again she smiles.

"Yes. It relaxes me." I stare at her, deciding . . . "I think I want you to move in with me."

"Isn't that question a little late?"

"Your current living arrangements are no longer working. This isn't really your style."

"Wait. Are you asking?"

"Yes. I want you to move into my room."

"Kross, I wasn't trying to be pushy yesterday at the shop. I can stay here and just come occasionally if you want me to. I'm fine."

"No. I think I want you to. I've been thinking about it since you mentioned that I haven't asked you to sleep with me. That's the point. I don't think of things like that until you bring them up. Most nights I lay in bed wondering what you're doing up here anyway."

"Are you sure?"

"Yeah." I pause. "You don't have a secret love for old lady shit like floral and paisley right?"

The laugh comes, and then she grabs her black pillow from behind her head decorated with a girly version of a skull on the front, pointing to it; mostly white with pink here and there like in the bow. "If my comforter would fit this big-ass bed it'd be on here too. Floral sucks, for the record. It should have been left in the eighties or whatever the hell era it came from. It's like a venereal disease. Some asshole started it and the shit won't go away. Paisley patterns remind me of microscopic bacteria. I don't see the appeal to it."

I pull her body against mine. "I knew I liked you for a reason."

I roll on top of her, pushing her on her back. She's staring up at me; breathing hard and gripping my triceps as her legs slowly spread. I gyrate my pelvis between her legs, pushing my erection hard against her center. Her head rolls back and she spreads wider. "I want you."

Just where I want her. I go cold, intentionally this time, and get out of bed. As I make it to the door she speaks, more of a yell really. "You asshole. Where are you going? I thought we were finally getting somewhere."

I don't turn around. "If you want dick you'll have to wait till we're in our bed. For now, we're going to watch a movie. That I can do."

I walk out. Three steps down and I hear a thump against the floor. Following immediately behind is a loud clomping sound along the second floor. It sounds like the house is about to come down. I stop, and just as I'm about to turn around to see what all the commotion is, she jumps on my back and clings to my body like a spider monkey, her arm around my neck with the other gripped in my hair, pulling my head to the side.

I grab her legs locked around my waist, hands clamped onto her shins, already breathing hard and wanting to throw her off. The metal of her lip ring skims up my neck toward my ear, tracing along my strained vein. "Relax, baby," she soothes. "You're too hot to hurt, but if you're going to toy with me then I'm going to toy with you."

I grab her arm and jerk her around to my front, before slamming her back against the wall. My hand grips onto her face, holding it positioned directly at me. "It's not a good idea to do shit like that. My reflexes are deadly." The words grit from my mouth through clenched teeth.

Her middle is against my stomach. She starts pulling her lip ring in and out of her mouth, the metal scraping against her top teeth. "You wouldn't hurt me."

I try to calm down. My hand falls from her face and the fear and anger melt away. That fucking mouth drives me nuts. "Not intentionally."

She removes her shirt, tossing it on the staircase. She remains in nothing but panties. Then her thumb starts brushing over my bottom lip. Her demeanor is serious. Her entire body is beautiful. My fingertips dig into the back of her thighs as I stand here on this staircase, holding my balance and her. "Learn to differentiate when it's me and when it's someone else. Then you'll never make a permanent mistake."

"How do you want me to do that?"

She rubs her hands down the sides of my neck, over my shoulders, and down my arms. "Learn my touch."

She grabs my hair again, tilting my head as she places her neck against the bottom of my nose. "Memorize my smell."

She pushes her bare chest against mine. "Study the way I feel."

She leans forward, her lips so close I can feel her breath against my face each time she speaks. "Never forget my kiss."

Then she kisses me . . . in a way I never will.

Detta

"How's your neck?"

I follow him into his room; arm over chest to cover myself . . . since I kind of left my shirt on the staircase. Talk about the kiss of all kisses. I can still feel the heat on my lips. My entire body is physically thirsting. I want him in the most embarrassing ways. "It's fine. It itches a little, but I'm used to the process by now."

"Sit on the bed. Remote is on the nightstand."

He disappears into his bathroom. "Can I borrow a shirt?" I yell, starting to get a little cold. The bedside lamp is already on. I guess this is where he's been hibernating all evening. Today has been the most boring day I've had in a while, yet still full of daydreaming about one particular man and I can't seem to shut it off.

"I like you with it off," he says, expressionless, returning with a tube in hand as he walks toward the bed.

And then he goes and says shit like that to only make it worse. I swear, I've never been a girl to get all melted and stupid when a hot guy throws out a compliment, but considering his are few and far between I think I'll take it and fist pump inside. Don't ask me why I want him so bad, because still I have no idea.

He sits behind me and pulls my hand from where it's being used as a covering. "You didn't mind showing them to every damn man on the fucking planet for a little cash, so why are you being modest now?"

"Because you make me nervous," I admit, foolishly. "They don't."

He begins rubbing my neck tattoo down with the Aquaphor ointment, not responding. "Are you going to tell me why you went with that particular design now?"

His hand against my skin creates a hypnotic feeling. I feel like a damn dog, ready to roll over and let him rub my belly with my tongue hanging out. Maybe I'm making myself too available, but I can't backtrack. I feel that perseverance will pay off with him; at least I'm hoping. This tattoo will forever hold meaning for me. Not because of what is there, but because it is something that came from him. It's so intricate and beautiful, even with the red coloring. "You haven't figured it out yet?"

His voice slowly dances through my mind, reminding me not to fall asleep. "No, but I'd rather hear your version anyway."

"Tattooing isn't just a job. It's not something you do on a whim—not the talented artists anyway. Anyone that can hold a pencil can hold a gun. It doesn't take a license to buy a kit. All it takes is access to the Internet and a credit card to purchase one. Operating it does not require special skill if you can read a set of instructions. But just because someone *can* tattoo doesn't mean they *should*. There are too many fucking posers out there already, spreading bad tattoos like disease, and then people like me have to figure out a way to fix it to preserve the art of ink. It's not something you master overnight. You don't just come to the shop, do, and go home. It's constant research, learning, and understanding things you wouldn't normally be interested in. It's about respecting different cultures even if you have your own beliefs. You will have people come to you with ideas and no design. They bring you the symbolism or the story and leave it to you to create them a work of art they can live with forever. In one career you become an artist, a historian, and so many other things. You have to want to learn to be the best."

"Okay, so tell me . . . Why the tree?"

"A Birch Tree, in Celtic symbolism, is a symbol of new beginnings. It's said to be highly adaptive and able to sustain harsh conditions. It can grow and start a new life where most other trees can't. It reminded me of you. I was the forest fire that took over your life. I pulled you into conditions that most couldn't put down roots and start over, but you did, and you're slowly earning my trust. To me the tree is most beautiful with vibrant color, and it matches your bold personality, so I went with the red leaves. It's believed to be a sign of renewal, of going where no other will go. I tested you, and despite it being something that scared you, you stayed."

"And the sunlight coming through the leaves?"

"Sunrise is the beginning of a new day. No matter what happened yesterday, it's behind you. You can always start over. I found you at night living like trash. Where you wake is where you start fresh. Know your value, Delta. Just because you had a shitty beginning a few times doesn't mean it's your only. In many things do-overs are possible."

Even in monotone he's anything but calm. He radiates a fierce aura. Always a little terrifying even when he's at peace. He turns my head to look at him. His jaw is working back and forth as he looks into my eyes. "Stripping and selling your body for men to use as a dick flick are for those that have given up hope of a new day ever coming. You're better than that. You're a fighter. Start acting like one. If you don't then history will repeat itself."

"Explain the birds transforming from the top leaves and the flock creating an infinity symbol as they fly toward the sun."

"That's pretty easy. Doves symbolize many different things, one of those being peace. The decisions we make create or destroy it. Flying is possible in any condition, but if your choices in life are wise, you can live in peace forever."

I work to breathe through the emotions consuming my entire body. I'm not a deep thinker. I never have been. I think in the short term, not the long term. Maybe that's why I've made some of the decisions I've made over the years. I don't like feeling naked when I didn't even take my clothes off, so I choose to go with the obvious and the path of least emotional resistance. "I thought you were tattooing your name on my body."

His index finger runs down the center of my neck, even though he's looking at me with my head turned toward my shoulder so that I can see him. I've memorized that tattoo and where everything is. He's skimming his finger down the trunk of the tree. "Learn to read between the lines. The answer is not always laid out in the open for you. My name lies within the bark. People don't have to notice it for it to be there."

He doesn't have to say it for me to get what's being said here. Kross is my new beginning, he's my do-over, he's my life of peace, and he's the path to my forever . . .

My forever.

With every little part of him he lets me see, I need him a little more. I've never actually felt the beginning of forever before, but I'm sure that's what this is. I can feel it in my bones.

I stand from the bed and turn around to face him. He straightens his leg from the bent position on the bed as he repositions his body so that we're eye to eye. I take a few steps in his direction, making my way to stand between his legs, my hands coming together at the back of his neck. His hands immediately find my hips, the calluses leaving chill bumps. He looks up at me, his fingers folding over the band of my panties in a tight hold. I look deep into his eyes, knowing there is no real peace when it comes to Kross. I've only reached his border, but already I know he lives in a state of doom and darkness I may never understand; but that doesn't mean I want anything other than to live in it with him. "Show me peace in warfare. That's where I want to be."

He rips my panties off my body and pulls me on his lap, lifting just enough to push down his briefs before his rough hands take hold on my body. I'm trembling inside, but it's not in fear. My nipples are so hard they're tingling and I can already tell that I'm embarrassingly wet. I push up and grab his dick in my hand. He flinches and grips my wrist so tight it hurts, his breathing labored. Our eyes lock, his holding so much tension. "It's okay. Let me touch you."

His hold loosens slowly, before his hand finally falls away and moves to my back, gliding up toward my shoulders as I align him at my center and push down onto him. The hand on my thigh tightens when I seat myself completely, leaving no space between us. I start to ride, slowly, wanting to draw it out as long as possible, pulling every little grunt and growl out of him that I can.

I place my hand on the side of his neck as I kiss him, tugging on his bottom lip. The texture of his skin changes from smooth to a raised patch. I never stop kissing him. I never allow my body to completely disconnect from his; just rhythmically pump up and down in various ways, trying not to come already. I follow the scar I've never noticed since he has a large neck tattoo.

This scar is bigger than the others, dense in width, but there is no doubt what it is. As my hand reaches the end his hand laces over mine, his lips pulling away. "Why is there a cross carved into your neck?" I whisper, almost inaudibly, a sinking feeling in my gut. "Tell me who would do that to you."

His eyes search mine for a moment, softening, before they zone out once again and I notice the change in him instantly.

Cold.

Dark.

Stoic.

He rolls us over and forces me to turn around, standing on all fours. He says nothing. His hands grip onto my ass and he rams himself inside me. That's when I know I've lost him. It's going to be rough from here on out. It always is.

CHAPTER TWELVE

Detta

"**D**ude, that's fucking wicked."

I lean over Remington's shoulder as he reloads ink, looking at the shoulder piece he's doing on the bearded man in leather—a skull with some badass shading and huge spiders crawling out of the eye sockets, the front legs and eyes of one peaking over the clients shoulder from the front. The skeletal hands are crossed under the head holding a pair of daggers. A black flag flies behind it, only half the club name and logo visible. Every detail is perfect down to the hair on the spider. It looks so real it's scary. A chill runs down my spine, imagining something that size crawling on me, and I'm not even afraid of them. "Am I allowed to talk to you now?" he asks, a little bite coming through his words. "Because if blades are going to go flying I'm going to have to ask you to leave my station. You're dangerous, princess."

A laugh slips out. Fucking princess . . . A princess would take one look at me, and turn around, all judgy and shit. I shove his shoulder at precisely the exact moment 'moaner' over there starts in Kross' chair. It's like fucking clockwork. If looks could kill she'd have been dead long ago. Every five minutes or so she starts again, sending out her mating call. The sad part is Kross isn't even paying her a lick of attention. It's obvious. Desperate whores make my blood boil.

I tousle his much shorter laid down Mohawk. "I told you I was sorry like a thousand times, even though technically it wasn't my fault. Be my friend," I whine sarcastically. I sigh, playing the defeated girl. "Come on. This is me asking really nicely. I need session hours under my belt. I want to watch the good shit. Wesson is doing a fucking flower and Joey a butterfly. That's like the fourth one this week. I just can't. It's so cliché. Plus, it's an overload of estrogen over there. Way more than I can handle."

"You really are a rare breed of female," he says, with a smile under his breath. He goes back to working on the skull, adding a little bit more evil to something that's already scary as hell. "What about boss man?" He smirks. "He's doing a pretty sick religious piece over there."

The disgusted look is all over my face, I know. I can't help it. That's what happens when you mark a particular dick as yours. You become possessive over it. "Hell no. The first time I see her try to rub her nasty ass on him I will cut that bitch. Probably not good for business." I put my hands together and bat my heavily mascara-coated eyelashes. "Please."

"Let me pierce your nipples and we'll call it even."

That came out way too loud; making it obvious that it was intended to be heard. I clear my throat, caught off guard, my mouth running dry. "Uh . . . I mean . . . I've thought about it several times, but I always chicken out. I haven't trusted anyone that much yet. It's like entrusting someone with a knife and your dick for circumcision when you're old enough to know that a blade is coming at something you hold dearly. It's not to be taken lightly. You fuck that shit up— it's permanent."

He never looks up as the needle pulses against the skin. It's a hypnotic thing to watch. "I would never fuck up something I love so much. Your nips would be in the best of care."

"Keep talking and next time it'll be a body part," Kross' voice booms across the room, causing us both to look up. He's still hunched over, his glove-covered hands splayed over her hip bone, working on the bottom of the very large cross ending on her pelvis; her shorts pulled down so low you can tell she's freshly shaven.

"See, princess? Dangerous. Boss man has his hooks in that sexy little body."

The bitch under him pushes her shorts down another centimeter or two, a sound coming out of her mouth that doesn't reflect pain or the words to form a sentence. A jealous surge overcomes me and I can feel my mouth losing control. The underlying motive may play a part in whatever is trying to plot in my head. "What's the big deal, Kross? You just pierced a set this morning. It's no different."

"Part of the job."

"If it's part of the job, then I'm just a client."

"No, you're not. Drop it."

"It's my body."

"We'll discuss it later."

"There's nothing to discuss. It's my decision."

"I said no."

"Why is this an issue? You look at tits, clits, and asses on the regular and I don't freak the fuck out. If he's seen one set he's seen a hundred. It's business. Like you said. And I've wanted them done for a while."

He's still tattooing like his responses are programmed instead of thought out. "I'm done with this conversation."

Deep down I know I wouldn't let anyone but Kross pierce them. Never even crossed my mind. And I should shut the hell up, because his voice could pierce steel, but I've always been stubborn with a mouth that gets me in trouble. It's who I am. There is no sense in changing now. Sometimes I just like to push him. It reminds me that he's not a robot and this thing between us isn't a dream. "Good. It's happening."

He looks at me, his expression scary as hell—eyes black, muscles tense, anger vibrating through every vein. I'm almost positive that's the look a serial killer wears during a kill. He looks possessed. "Try." The finality of that one word slams into me, and my brain took the hint.

She moans again, my aggravation spiraling out of control. "Bitch, would you shut the fuck up? He's not interested in case you can't tell. A whore usually knows her place, and it isn't here."

"Delta," he snaps. Her mouth is gaping, his neck is straining. "Outside. Now."

"Fuck this."

I walk to the empty station and open the drawer, grabbing the pack of cigarettes I hide in there, before walking through the small break room and shove open the back door, revealing the metal staircase leading to the employee parking lot.

I quickly descend, my back hitting the brick of the building as I light up. My head falls back as the smoke enters my lungs, releasing so much bad energy, my mind finally working again. With every replay of what just happened, I'm reminded that he is technically my boss, despite the fact that we're fucking. I'm not sure how that all escalated so quickly, but since the little dart throwing practice with knives occurred, the guys are totally different around me when Kross is in the office. I was kind of one of them before. Now interaction is too serious unless he's gone. It sucks.

With each exhale I pull on the filter again, burning down the paper. Kross thinks I quit, but mostly I sneak them when he's not in the studio. I've cut back, but quitting completely isn't possible having to deal with his damn mood swings. I just blew my secret to shit now, though, and all that body spray and mouth wash was wasted effort.

The door flies open. I don't even look. I know it's him by the lack of sound. Normal people make noise. Kross is like a ghost. It's fucking creepy. I drop the filter when he lines up in front of me, putting it out with my shoe as his eyes bore into mine. His palms go to the brick to each side of my head. I try to turn my head to blow out the smoke, but he grips my cheeks in his hand, holding me to him. The smoke billows around his face instead. He doesn't cough, he doesn't look away, and he doesn't stop breathing. He's completely unfazed. "What the fuck was that? I just let a five hundred dollar tattoo walk out the door."

"The bitch was trying her best to show you what she looks like when she comes. I just thought she should know promoting her services wasn't appropriate in a tattoo shop."

"You can't talk to customers like that. I don't care if she's trying to shove her tits in my mouth. I know how to adjust. This is a fucking business. My business. And if I didn't believe in word of mouth I wouldn't have so much goddamn money. I don't run a charity. Ink doesn't leave my shop unpaid for, and I don't lose money. You lost it; you pay it back. That's the way this works."

Anxiety builds inside. "Are you fucking serious? You just tried to tell me what to do with my own body *in front of clients* like you don't see racks and pussy all the time. I was proving a point. How is that fair? What's next, are you going to tell me I can't pierce below the belt on males."

"You're damn right."

My mouth falls. "That's bullshit."

"I think you're forgetting this is my company. I can do whatever I want."

My eyes sting with anger, moistening along the rims. "You're an asshole. You talk about professionalism but how unprofessional is it to take a walk-in and then pawn it off on someone else upon finding out what they're in for; all because my boyfriend thinks it's okay for him to touch all over girls for 'business' yet I have to turn down work instead of learning from it. The male *genitalia* or for better word *cock* is a complex muscle. If you can perfect the art of piercing that without getting it hard, in my book you're a damn pro."

He grips my jaw in his hand. "In case you haven't noticed, only one female fazes me. Only one rack gets me hard. Only one clit makes my hand twitch, and only one pussy appeals to me. Not one other motherfucker is touching a body with that kind of power. When I know you can hold another man's dick and not flinch or blush, look at it with no uncontrollable thoughts, and shove a needle through it with no remorse, then and only then, will I let you look at anyone else's dick but mine."

My mouth is watering. Heat begins to rise from my feet. I grip the front of his shirt in my fist, pulling him closer. His lips are so close when his hand runs up the inside of my thigh, his fingertips slipping under my panties until they brush over my lips. "Fuck."

My legs reflexively spread, asking for them to enter me. Just as the tip goes in a horn goes off, scaring the shit out of me. His hand disappears with the sound of her voice. "You dirty bitch. You have a lot of explaining to do. Get your ass in the car. Our friendship is on the line."

I fight the smile with the sound of her voice. One look at Kross and it becomes easy. I glance at her. Time and love hasn't changed her much. She's still sitting mighty comfortable in that gorgeous yellow supercar with a hefty value, dressed to the nines, showing off a smile only a villain wears with the window down. "Lux, I'm on the clock. It'll have to wait till after work."

"Bullshit. I'm taking your deceitful, lying ass to lunch. Besides, Kross is going to be busy for a while. Lover boy has an appointment. He's waiting upstairs."

I glance at Kross. He's staring at me. "You have two hours before I come hunting." His hands drop. When they come back in sight one is holding a hundred dollar bill, handing it to me. "No girl of mine is eating on Kaston's dime. Here."

"I'm not taking that."

"It wasn't optional."

By the look on his face I know if I don't accept it he'll force it somewhere. I take it and start to walk off. He grabs my neck before I can pass, pulling me to him. "You still owe me five hundred dollars."

"What? Then why are you handing this to me? Where is it going to come from, my paycheck? I won't have much left."

His thumb brushes my lips in a way that alters my balance. "Better be figuring out how to give a five hundred dollar blowjob. I've thought about these lips wrapped around my cock. When the last person leaves, we're going to find out if they can pay off your debt."

A shiver runs from my neck to the base of my spine. Before I can respond he's already walking back up the stairs. My feet hesitantly move toward the car as the door slams, the disappointment settling that he didn't even kiss me.

I get in the car, waiting for her to speak. I know it's coming. I've kept Lux in the dark about everything, and for good reason. I don't need her pity. I don't need her to teach me her way of life. I don't need her worry or handouts. She's finally living a full life, and I knew if I told her about the apartment or the job she'd try to give me money. It's what I would do if the roles were reversed. It's always been her and I, and when all you have in this world is your best friend you tend to watch each other's backs, but I'm the type of person that I'll make it on my own somehow or another.

I pull on my seatbelt, looking straight ahead. I can see her staring at me from the corner of my eye, her wrist resting on the top of the steering wheel. Her engagement ring is catching just enough light to draw attention to it, my eyes following the sparkle. I never thought it would be her before me, but I will never let that statement leave my lips. "Just for the record, I've decided to take the high road instead of being pissed at you for keeping secrets from me since my busy schedule has caused me to be a shitty friend."

I glance at the entrance to the shop, wishing I were back in there when I should be focused on the fact that I haven't seen Lux in so long. A girl date is way overdue. "I'm not the only one keeping secrets."

She picks up a section of my long, black hair, combing her fingers through it in a motherly way, like she always has in a serious conversation that was geared toward me, her bangles clanging together as her wrist moves. "Fair enough. It's funny how men bring out a loyalty so fierce that we hide from the ones we've always been closest to; keep secrets from the ones we've always shared everything with. But I think with you and Kross being a thing now Kaston will understand. Never again?"

I look at her, my green eyes meeting her blue ones. Lux has always been the more beautiful one in my opinion. She has that model look about her, and the older we get the more different we seem. On the exterior she looks so put together, with her large barrel waves and pristine makeup, her outfit screaming hot, high-class trophy wife. But below the surface she's always had it hard. She had to grow up a hell of a lot faster than me, so she's always been like the mother hen of the two of us.

I think back to the conversation between Kross and I about trust. "I'm not sure if I can make that promise, but I'll certainly try."

She gives me a knowing smile, before it evens back out into her previous seriousness. "I know that look. You better start talking."

I take a deep breath. "Yeah. Let's go to Joe's. That's what it's gonna take for me to explain that man and me; if it can even be explained at all."

CHAPTER THIRTEEN

Detta

We walk into the hole-in-the-wall bar we found right after we moved here. It's old school, with a large U-shaped bar in the middle and high-top tables surrounding it. There are a few old arcade games in the corners and a built-on room for pool, TVs ornamenting the walls. It's dimly lit inside, the glass entryway door and the windows blacked out with tint, *no entry under twenty-one* decorating the glass. It smells of stale cigarettes. It's never packed; a few blue-collar workingmen seated at the bar.

Regulars for sure.

The snobby people can't stomach the old bar stench to eat lunch. And men in suits don't want to be caught dead walking out of a bar of this class. They tend to migrate to a martini spot Lux used to frequent sometimes. But Lux and I found this place when we were a couple of high school graduates with little money and empty stomachs. It's cheap. We walked in and never got carded. I guess they expect you to obey the sign on the door. The fact that it's there keeps cops off their radar. Twenty minutes in we discovered the food was good, the people were better, and we've been coming here ever since. It's our place. We don't share it with anyone in fear the best kept secret of Atlanta will be discovered and we'll no longer be able to just walk in anytime we want for a quick, low-key meal.

"Marie hasn't forced you into retirement yet, old man?" I smile as Joe turns around from wiping down the bar, no doubt already recognizing Lux's voice. He always did have a soft spot for her outspoken, no-shit-giving attitude and lack of filter for the elderly.

The lower half of his face is turned up in a smile. His white hair is combed over in a part like it always is. And his uniform never changes: polo with the 'Joe's' logo on the pocket over the left breast and a pair of relaxed khakis. He's pushing seventy, but you'd never know it with his stocky build and too-young-to-quit personality. And for his age he's a stubborn fuck. Still working and doesn't take shit off anyone. They say this life ages a person well beyond their years, but I'd say with Joe it's quite the opposite. This bar keeps him young.

I follow Lux to the bar and pull out a stool, taking a seat as he meets us on the other side. "Never. She likes her bingo and lunch dates at the country club far too much for me to sit at home and hold her back. Besides, I have forever to get old. And golf is too damn boring to me. I get more action cutting someone off after too many drinks than watching a ball fly. What brings my two favorite trouble makers in on this lovely day?"

He glances between Lux and I with his arms crossed, forearms down on the bar, leaning onto them for support and waiting for one of us to speak. I nod toward Lux, the smile already reaching my eyes. "Thing one here is getting hitched, Joe. Can you believe it? She finally found someone to put up with her shit forever."

His face transforms into one of joy, his cheeks hinting a rosy shade. "That's wonderful. Who's the lucky sap?" he winks.

"Oh, just some guy that fell into my trap and was too stupid to run," she teases. "I tried to talk him out of it, Joe, really I did. Ain't no man got any business marrying a girl like me, but he seems sure of himself, so I guess I'll stick around to torment him forever."

He grabs two beers from the cooler, removing the caps and setting them before us. He always had this weird rule about no hard alcohol till five o'clock in his bar. So before five, beer it is. "I'd say he's a pretty smart man. I knew one would come along one of these days and never let you go. Both of you. The right one knows when to hold on." He smiles. "So, when is the big day? I'll be expecting an invitation hand delivered."

"Eh, you know me, Joe. Can't commit to too much all at once. For now he should be happy I said yes. When a date calls to me I'll take it, until then, it's yet to be determined. Plus, at the moment I'm just trying not to kill one of my culinary instructors. My attitude really doesn't like taking orders. It's a constant struggle."

I turn up the beer bottle at my lips, letting her words run in one ear and out the other, trying to calm my raging nerves still in a mess from Kross. She places her arm around me, pulling me into her. "Besides, that's not even the real reason we're here. I'm not the only one that has a male counterpart lingering around these days. Your favorite little villain here has been the busy one: training to be a tattoo artist not far away, ditching her BFF, banging the boss . . ."

My beer decides to spray across the bar with force, a cough following behind. Joe is like an adopted grandfather. And who the fuck tells their grandfather they're banging anyone, let alone their boss! No-fucking-body. "Lux, would you shut up!"

Joe starts laughing and straightens his posture, holding his hands up in surrender. "I'm going to take that as my cue to go to the kitchen. The usual?"

I nod, mortified, and Joe turns to leave the bar. I smack her on the side of the tit, hard, drawing a laughing whine out of her. I may not give a shit about a lot, but I still have a little meter inside that tells me when to keep things to myself and when to speak. Lux lacks that trait. And I had obviously forgotten. "Do you know how bad I want to torture you with a needle right now?"

She takes a sip of her beer, an evil grin covering her face. "How else did you want me to get rid of him? I love him, but he can be a bit of a talker. My time with you is limited."

"You really have no shame. You don't discuss who we're banging with innocent old men! It's fucking weird. And personal."

"Oh . . . I forgot you're the one that likes to keep who you bang a secret from everyone, including me."

I squint my eyes and flip her off. "Bitch, I will cut you."

She grabs my face in both hands and plants her plump, red lips on mine. When she pulls away, she makes the kissing sound. "My baby is back."

I wipe my lips and look around, hoping to hell no one is still in here. A couple of guys are eying us in the back corner. I place my elbow on the table and use my hand as a visor to hide my face. "The way we greet each other is a personal thing, Lux. In privacy it's fine, but in public we look like lesbians," I whisper.

"I'm sorry, did you think that was an invite? Look away, asshole." I close my eyes and shake my head. I think I've been around broody too long. Usually I find her extroverted ways refreshing, but today,

I want to put a cork in her mouth. She leans in, mimicking my low tone. "I hate to break it to you, love bug, but we've kind of already won that title in ways. A certain someone's birthday not all that long ago seems to ring a bell. Tell me, who gives you the better orgasm? The sexy, alpha tattoo God that has you blushing like a damn school girl or yours truly." She winks to drive her point home.

I clear my throat, shoving away the memory. That was also the night before my interview with Kross. So much has happened since then. "Our relationship would never make sense to anyone but us. Labels have no place in it."

Her smile grows. "He doesn't know, does he?"

"There is no reason for him to have that knowledge. It's our secret."

". . . And Kaston's," she says casually, taking another gulp of her beer. My mouth falls.

Joe returns, setting down two fried shrimp salads, before quickly fixing us two glasses of water. "It's on the house, girls. I've got to stock the bar. I'll leave you two to chat. Don't leave without saying goodbye, you hear?"

"Sure, Joe. Thanks," I reply, before stabbing my fork into the poor undeserving shrimp and pointing it at her. "Why the fuck does he know that, Lux? Is he going to tell Kross?"

She doctors her salad by cutting up the boiled egg and adding the ranch dressing. "Shit happens. It was a while ago. The details of why are hazy. I wouldn't think he'd say anything, but I can't make any promises. What would it matter if he did? It was before you and Kross. It was actually kind of humorous seeing Kaston get jealous over a GIRL."

I sigh. "He's more judgmental than you think."

Her lips turn up in a sarcastic confusion. "Uh, Delta, are we talking about the same guy? You know, the one covered in tattoos that probably cusses like a sailor." She lowers her voice. "The same one that is my fiancé's arms dealer. Do you know how stupid a judgmental gunslinger sounds?"

My shoulders drop. There is no easy way to go about this. We will be here all day if I don't stop dancing around explanations. So, the best way to deal with this is honesty . . . on both sides. I lay my fork down, take a sip of water, and square my shoulders toward her. "He caught me stripping."

Her confusion deepens. I hold out my hand, stopping her mouth from opening. "I'll explain everything. Just give me a few minutes. It started when I got cut from my job at the bar. Well, let me backtrack. Kross had me working a bunch of weird shifts, never the same hours, so it was impossible to try and work out a schedule. I started arriving for my bartending shifts late, calling in some, not showing up even. You know how bartending is. You rely on tips. Work one good night on the weekend and you could be sitting comfortably for a few weeks, but everyone fights over weekends and we were already on a rotation between early and late, weekends and weeknights. He started punishing me slowly at first by cutting the best shifts and giving them to other bartenders. I figured I would do my time with shitty shifts and figure out a way to work it out with Kross once I proved myself, only it got worse, not better. I'm barely making over minimum wage with Kross, and still have to pay for shit like electricity, food, my cell phone and gas, so my rent got behind. The night my boss finally pushed me to PRN till I proved I still wanted to take my bartending job seriously I came home to a fucking eviction notice. I didn't know what else to do. I can't live in my car, even though sometimes I like to pretend that's an option. We both know that's a recipe for rape and brutal murder in the ATL, so I did the only thing I could think of. I called Chuck."

"Fuck, Delta," she interrupts. "Why didn't you call me? I would have given you the money. I told you when you finally walked away from that sleezeball to never go back. We would do whatever the fuck we needed to in order to survive. I would have even been okay with it, if that was the final option, at another strip club! But that's the point. That's not the final option!"

"I know you would have. That's exactly why I *didn't* call you. I didn't want any handouts. I sure as hell wasn't taking any of Kaston's money. I get it, you're pissed at me, but you should know better. I've never taken money from you and I'm not going to start now. Anyway, I went in and asked for my job back."

"What did the motherfucker want from you to give it back?"

"Things are not without sacrifice."

"You slept with him, didn't you? After all this time?"

"I had no choice."

"We always have a choice, Delta. At least since we left. Even then you had a choice, but I get it. But here and now, you don't have to be that girl anymore. We promised we would never let that life control us again."

"Why are you being so high and mighty? It's not all that different than you with all those men before Kaston."

"It's completely different," she argues. "Those men I chose. I picked them out of a roomful based on a checklist and I never strayed. Suits, shoes, jewelry, cars, money. They served a purpose to better my life, not bring me down. He manipulates you to get his fucking rocks off. I never loved those men. In some fucking twisted way he made you love him. He knows how to tell you the right things to keep you hanging on. You were finally past that. I'm really upset that you would fall back into his trap so easily. I would have much rather you came to me instead. I have money saved from before Kaston."

"Do you want to hear the rest or are you going to tell me shit I already know?"

She breathes out and turns toward me, grabbing my hand in hers. "I'm sorry. I'm just disappointed that you feel like you have to chase your past to avoid asking me for help. You're my best friend, Delta. We walked out of Hell together. I'll die before either of us go back."

I squeeze her hand. "Well, then you would have loved to have seen the way Kross put him on the floor my second night . . . after he mysteriously appeared in my dressing room before the end of my set and then pretty much fucked me like a whore. He just took it. Didn't even ask. It was like nothing I've ever experienced before. It was hot. And this is coming from the girl that gave a try to the whole cuff and riding crop thing once."

And then the Cheshire cat grin comes out to play. "It's been way too long since I've had sexy details from you. Please tell me that man has an enormous cock and the stamina of the Energizer bunny. I've wondered it . . . He also looks like he would be a little on the abusive side in bed."

I think on that for a moment—our private life. The way sex with Kross is more difficult yet more satisfying than any man I've ever experienced in the past. A small part of me wants to tell her everything, to get her advice on how to go about a man like Kross since she has more experience than me, but a bigger part of me wants to keep it all to myself. "I'll put it to you like this: biggest, thickest, best, roughest, and so fucking good."

"God, I've missed our talks. You didn't tell me how you ended up being bunk mates, though."

"He asked me in a very serious manner 'what the fuck I was doing there'. I tried to explain even though it embarrassed me. He took my eviction threat reasoning and tossed it out the window apparently. He was pretty simple about it. Just said he couldn't be unfair at work and pay me more till I earned it, but he sure as hell wasn't going to let me strip, for whatever reason, so I was informed I was moving in with him, and well, would you turn *that* down? No, because you didn't with Kaston."

She glances around the room, bringing her voice to a whisper. "So, I know you're a little more morale than me, even though in the physical sense most would say the opposite based on first impression, but are you sure you can handle his . . . *hobbies*?"

My heart starts to race. I can barely breathe from all of the adrenaline running through my system. It's the first time I've really been able to talk about my feelings with it all, but I still fear I'll say too much and upset him or betray his trust in me. I don't want him upset with me. I begin turning the diamond stud in the corner of my lip; a nervous habit I have. My voice is barely audible. "At first I wasn't. He took me on a delivery. I was terrified. I had no warning on what I was going into. Those men scared me. I had to do things I wouldn't normally do, and I've done a lot in my life that most would deem bad. For a moment I actually was scared I might not make it out of there alive . . ."

I remember exactly what happened, step by step. I let the memory invade my thoughts; something I've suppressed until now. With every second I linger on it, it strengthens. A face I've become familiar with assaults me; warm eyes I can't seem to forget, and a man I'm starting to trust. The way he looked that night, standing there with those men, so calm and collected, no fear present; before was a vague thought. Everything happened so fast. It didn't take long for the drugs I've never tried to take effect. It's strange how they can alter the point of view in which you experience things.

Because then, I didn't notice how he looked at me.

But now—I see it so clearly.

"One thing I know for sure, he will never let someone hurt me. That knowledge makes accepting it a lot easier." I pause, letting myself view it a little longer, before it disappears back into the file my mind houses it in. I quiver under his scrutiny, even though it's only in my mind. He radiates just as much power when he isn't present as when he is. Then his face slowly slips away, my mind unable to bear it any longer. The whispers return. "I've never been a criminal; never even considered breaking the law aside from underage drinking and smoking. I slept with a grown man as a minor for an extended period of time. But nothing I could do time for. But I'm almost positive I'd do anything that man asked me to do."

She looks at me, studying me. "I've been living in this world of secrets for a little while now. I've seen things, heard things, even done things, but more importantly I know things to be true. It's a life of cover-up. A constant disguise. Once you're in it you don't just get out. That's been made very clear to me. I need to make you completely aware of this situation before you get caught up in it. If he wants you in the way that Kaston wants me, he's not going to let you go without a fight, and that's if he does at all. You won't be able to leave once you're involved. You will be his partner in every aspect of the word. If he gets busted, are you willing to go down with him? Like I said earlier, I know this look. I've seen it on you before, just diluted. Only this time, there is something else there that wasn't last time. Fascination. Addiction maybe. All those months ago on your birthday, when you first took me in for that tattoo, I knew there was something to him that sets him apart from any other guy to you. Whether you've figured it out or not yet, you're in love with him. Can you do the time if it comes to it? For him?"

Love? I would hardly call this thing between us love. I'm not sure what Kaston is involved in yet, or why he would ever need a dealer for weapons. I always thought a couple were plenty for one person, but even so, I can see how he is with Lux. I've seen the way he looks at her. She completes him. He loves her more than himself, and he isn't afraid to show it. I don't think that would ever happen with Kross.

To love someone you have to know without a doubt that living without that person would alter your life in a big way. If he ditched me today, tomorrow, or a year from now, I believe with every part of me his life would resume just like I had never came into it. That saddens me, because I find myself already wanting him forever in whatever way I can have him, and that fact answers the question on the table. I know, that even if I end up behind bars staring at a small cell for many years, the amount of time I got to be by his side, work beneath him, learning what makes him the way he is, and experiencing him in a way that not many get to experience him will all be worth it. Every time he pushes inside of me, touches me, and kisses me, my mind jumbles and my body completely alters in state.

It doesn't matter what he does to me, what situation I end up in, or what he forces me to do, I only want him more with every passing second. The asshole in him appeals to me. I want to know what's beneath his surface in the worst possible way. I want to be the one that shows him affection, teaches him the act of love, and witnesses him experience it all for the first time. Could I be in love with him?

Fuck.

"Delta?"

The haze clears from my eyes and Lux is still staring at me, waiting on me to answer patiently in the motherly voice she only shows me; always has. She would have been a good mom, even so young. "For him I would do or withstand anything," I whisper, my insecurities starting to arise. "Problem is, no man like that ever wants forever with a girl that falls this easily. They want the chase. I knew I was needy emotionally, expected it and forewarned him, but love I was trying to avoid. I wasn't aware I was that obvious. Now I'm scared I may push him away without knowing it. Why can't I be like you? Turned off by love, by commitment. The female equivalent to men like him and Kaston. You're the girl every man wants to keep. You aren't predictable. I'm the girl that appeals to a man outwardly but the second they discover the person beneath the ink is just like every other girl they can have so easily, I'm no longer interesting. Nothing sets me apart like you."

Her eyes soften. "Delta, that's not true. Every alpha wants a beta. That's just the way it is; always has been. Me—I'm fucked up in plenty of ways. Kaston forces my beta to surface when he needs it. You and me—we're both betas, regardless of what anyone thinks. It's why we found each other when we needed each other the most. We're the same. If I were really an alpha I would have told my mother no. I would have told him no. I would have gone to the police when I buried my daughter. My beta just learned to disguise itself as an alpha to survive. It adapted."

She reaches down and touches her finger to the first tattoo that was ever stained on my skin; the one that matches the woman's that gave birth to me. "You want to know the real reason I moved out? What I told you was a lie."

My brows furrow. "Yes. I don't like you keeping secrets from me."

"Even though we both had shit for mothers, I've always felt like you needed one more than me. Mine loved me; she just couldn't leave the drugs alone long enough to show it except in glimpses over the years. They ruled her every waking moment, drove her decisions, and a lot of the time I was the cost. I became her bargaining tool when there was nothing else. But still, she loved me, and that made everything I went through bearable. Yours, however, deserves to be hung like the witch she is. She's never loved you, and she wasn't scared to make your life miserable by reminding you every fucking day. Your kind soul, so full of love, deserves someone to love you in return—a loving mother. Our entire lives I've secretly tried to be that for you, since the moment I met your mother. I tried to replace her. Mothers are supposed to be strong for their children. They don't break down. When I'm alone. When the memories overwhelm me. When I can't handle the scars another second. And when my heart tries to stop beating over the loss of my daughter, that's what I do. I break down. But no matter how hard it gets for me, there is still you. You need me to be the Lux you know. The alpha version of myself. And I can't have you seeing that side of me. Ever."

My chest becomes heavy, constricting with each command to breathe that won't come. Feelings I've pushed away for so long come flooding to the surface, drowning me. And for the first time in a long time—aside from the few minor tears with Kross lately—I cry.

I cry for never noticing she was putting behind her own issues for me.

I cry for never being that for her.

I cry knowing that she's right . . . about everything.

She grabs my face in both hands and wipes away my tears with her thumbs. "Stop it. I haven't seen you cry in a very long time. I didn't tell you so that you would get upset. I know what you're doing inside and I don't need that from you. I've always been strong enough to fight off my own demons. I only told you because my hopes for you are that you let a man deserving of such a pure heart love you the way you need. I think Kross is that man for you. I feel it in my bones."

I grab her hands in my own, holding them to my face. "I don't think he'll ever love me. I don't think that he can."

She smiles, as if she has some knowledge that no one else has. "If I can fall in love, anyone can. Sometimes we just need someone to put forth the effort and have a little patience. I'll tell you a secret if you keep it between us."

I smile. "Always."

"Kaston and I have talked about you two several times. He said he's known Kross a while and never seen him publicly interested in someone. He said he's seen a change in him since you started working at the shop, and one night he made a few mindless prods to Kross about you, before the two of you started. The funny part— right after is when Kross started pursuing you. If a man like that didn't think you were 'different from the rest' he certainly wouldn't be calling up my fiancé for dating advice. He may not know exactly what he wants with you yet, but he definitely doesn't want anyone else to have you. Give him time, Delta, and I think you'll be shocked at what he's capable of. Criminals love too."

"I love you."

"I know. The feelings have always been mutual, even when it seems like life is driving us apart. I know I've been busy with Kaston for some time now, and I know I seem distant with culinary school, but I still think of you even when we go days without speaking. You're the reason I'm working toward my dream. You believed in me enough to send in that application just like I believed in you enough to run my mouth that night about your portfolio. We can both have our dreams. I still want to be the one you tell your secrets to. I'm always here if you need me, no matter what it is. I'm only a phone call and a car ride away. You'll always be my best friend. You'll always be my person; the one I loved first. I'm going to say this and then I can't say any more. It's too much emotionally for me to handle, but Kaston is teaching me how to filter my feelings so that from time to time I can express them; something I've never done. You may have needed a mother for lack of having one, but I needed a daughter. In ways, even though we're best friends, we also gave each other exactly what the other needed. We complement each other. We're each other's dark to light, fire to water, and negative to positive. We are each other's balance. Yin and Yang."

My eyes well up again. "Is he that person for you?"

She looks at me, confused. "What person?"

"The one that breaks with you when you break down. The one that holds you when you can't stand; catches you when you fall. The one that loves you when you can't love yourself. The one I haven't been for you."

The tear falls, meeting the tip of her thumb. I feel like the shittiest friend. Everything I've been numb to for years is crashing down around me. I wasn't there with her when her mom died like I was with Sophie. In ways I felt like it was Kaston's place and not mine. Like she wanted him there over me. I didn't want to overstep. I should have seen that things from our childhood have continuously eaten at her over the years, regardless of how put together she always seems. I should have known there were things with Kaston she wasn't telling me. I should have prodded more when her Porsche was suddenly absent after the breakup with Callum. More than that—it should have been me at the airport trying to make her stay when Kaston didn't know she was leaving. I don't deserve her. Her strength over her battles makes me look like a pussy, and yet she's still such a beautiful person.

She smiles bigger than I quite possibly have ever seen her. "Yes, and that's why despite my fears I'm going to marry him when he least expects it. When he's not asking me to choose a date. I would give that man anything, he just doesn't have to know." Her smile falls some. "But Delta, you have been that for me. We were just too young for you to realize it. When I lost Sophie times were dark. I didn't understand things that were happening to me, or feelings I was having. You helped me sort those things out even though you didn't fully understand them yourself. You have a pure heart and a kindred spirit for someone who had no guide to be that way. Your soul is clean even though you think it's tarnished. What happened with Chuck isn't on you. You were a fucking kid, Delta. A teenager. A girl with emotional issues. You were vulnerable. He used that to get to you. He was a grown-ass man. *They* were. They knew better. We didn't deserve what happened to us just because we consented to them. Stop letting that dictate what kind of person you think you are. You are good."

I force her into a hug. "I've missed you so much. Yin and Yang. I like that. It should be permanent. Will you get a tattoo with me? Please. Now that you've broken your tattoo cherry."

She laughs in my ear. "I've missed you too. You have no idea." She breaks the hug and glances at her ring, before looking at me with a smile on her face. "Tattoo huh? I guess I owe you that much.

If it weren't for you dragging my ass in that tattoo shop neither of us would be here. You got a deal, if you draw it yourself and tattoo mine."

Excitement rushes through my body. "Deal!"

"Now, eat up, because Kaston sent me a text on the way here that you were on a strict time allotment and threatened me if I broke it. Apparently your lover boy has you on a tight leash." She smirks. "And Kaston said by the look on his face and the tone in his voice he was not to be fucked with. There is one more thing we have to discuss to clear the air. But not here."

The heaviness between us lifts and nervous energy swirls in my belly. What I wouldn't give to be a fly on the wall when he walked back in that shop. A smile appears before I can stop it. I glance down at my phone and press the lock button to turn on the screen. A text I didn't know I had is displayed on the lock screen from ten minutes ago.

Kross: You are down to one hour.

I glance up and Lux is staring down at the screen, before returning the grin I know I'm displaying. "Alpha always wants a beta," she repeats, and for the first time in a long time, relief washes over me, and suddenly I'm starving.

CHAPTER FOURTEEN

Kross

I walk out of my office from going over financials and inventory as Cassie turns off the open sign and locks the front door. Remington hands me the bank deposit bag lying beside her purse from her seat he's sitting in behind the counter. "What are you still doing here? Your last appointment was wrapping up an hour ago."

"Waiting on Cassie to close. We're going out."

Cassie looks at me, unsure. "Unless there was something else you needed me to do, of course. Register is counted and closed down. Appointments have been confirmed for tomorrow. Everything is clean and tidy down here and phones are set for voicemail. I just locked up."

I look between the two of them as I take the bank bag to lock in the safe. "Don't make me enforce a no fraternization policy

The two of you are fucking adults. You know he's a whore. I better not come into my shop to post-fucking drama between the two of you when he decides to stick his dick in one of the customers after hours. Got it?"

She points between the two of them. "The two of us aren't—"

"I don't give a shit what you are or aren't. It's my only warning."

He stands as she grabs her purse, rolling the chair under the desk. "Noted. Does that go for you and Delta too, boss man?"

My eyes lock on his. "I wouldn't go there."

"Kidding. We like Delta and don't want to see her go. I was just wondering."

"You don't control your mouth you'll be the one to go."

"Got it. See you in the morning, Kross."

He grabs her hand and pulls her toward the stairs. "Cassie, I need you to open in the morning. Delta can close and take your next morning shift. She has something to do early."

"Okay. Works out better for me. I had something tomorrow night with family anyway. Goodnight."

I walk into my office and insert the bag into the safe's slot, letting it drop down into the locked bottom before shutting off the lights and securing my office. The door to the stairs is open and Cassie and Remington are already out of sight. I check behind her like I always do, ensuring nothing was left undone. The building is quiet. The way I personally like it.

Before Delta, when it was like this, I used to tattoo myself to relax before going on a job. It was an easy way for me to transition from one way of life to another. Lately, I find myself just wanting to go home when the day comes to an end, whether a job is following or not. Solitude is usually a type of therapy for me just as much as it is a curse, until the bad memories begin, but today when she went to lunch with Lux I didn't like it. The entire fucking time all I could think about was where she was and what the hell she was doing.

The need for a GPS searchable phone actually crossed my mind. I'm not above controlling, psychotic, irrational behavior. I tend to thrive on it. I'm a patient man. I have to be to do the things that I do, but that was the longest two hours of my life. It didn't help when Kaston looked at me and laughed as I glanced at the door and the clock, then told me with those two I actually have a reason to be jealous, and then explained why. Yet I'm supposed to just get used to the thoughts consuming my damn mind because they're inseparable.

Fuck. That. Shit.

I never thought rage would engulf me from a girl that wasn't my own. I wanted to pull her out of that damn car by the hair when she dropped Delta off and had her arms around her, hugging her. If she hadn't been wearing his ring I might have let myself react to it, but I know Kaston, and I know that girl would be six feet under if she cheated on him, male or female.

I walk up the stairs, closing the door behind me, arriving at the top within a few seconds. When I open the second door the studio is quiet, dimly lit, and smells of disinfectant cleaner from where she mopped the floor and cleaned the stations. Everything is orderly and the trash cans empty. Everything is exactly the way I like it, the way I physically need it. I can't handle filth. I lived in it for too fucking long.

I glance around, looking for her. I spot her at the empty station on her hands and knees, ass in the air with her head buried in the cabinet. Her black skirt is sitting on her ass, the lace panties peeking out. My feet continue forward, my eyes glued to the areas that should be covered. I stop, crossing my arms over my chest.

She's looking through the various large bottles of ink colors being stored in there for convenience since it's currently a vacant station. My guess is she's refilling the smaller bottles at each one. I've said a million times I needed to fill that spot. The truth is we need another artist at minimum. I never like to start big in a new place. I'd rather expand once I know the money is in the location. Every day we were overbooked I stared at it, knowing a stack of applications was sitting on my desk and slowly increasing. I never seemed to actually want to fill it for whatever the reason. I think it was just meant to be hers.

I'm not a religious person. Too much bad shit has happened in my life to believe someone is looking out for me. It's easier to believe there isn't a God at all than to think he plays favorites, giving some people a leisurely walk through life while the rest of us run from the fucking fire. Reincarnation is even harder to stomach, because if my childhood was payment for a previous life I was one sick fucker. The list of why I don't fit into any spiritual category could go on and on. I don't believe in much of anything, but if I were to ever put any amount of thought or faith into something I would say *survival of the fittest* is the closest thing to making sense. That's what this life is about: surviving. Some of us just do it better than others.

But, now that she's here, it's hard not to wonder if there is some higher power up there, grouping us shitty individuals together for a greater cause. She fits in. She belongs here. And I'm starting to think that station has been waiting for her. I've been waiting for her, in whatever way that is. "So I'm supposed to be okay with you hanging out with someone that's had her tongue all up in your cunt? Please, explain to me how that's going to work, because if a dick was involved it sure as fuck wouldn't happen."

She jumps at the sound of my voice, hitting her head on the wood.

"Ow. Shit," she whines, backing out of the cabinet and jumping to her feet. Her cheeks are a fresh shade of pink, her eyes wide. Her fingers go to her earrings, twirling over the gauged out hole as she looks at me. "Um, it's not like you think. We don't like each other. I mean, we do, but not like that. It just sort of happened. Fuck. It's complicated."

"Explain it to me. This is something I need to physically understand unless you want supervised play dates."

"You wouldn't—"

"Wanna bet?"

"Have you known this whole time?"

"Start talking. That shit doesn't 'sort of happen.' You don't see me getting Kaston to suck me off just because we're friends, if that's what you want to call us."

She plops down in the tattoo chair, her shoulders drooping. "It's happened twice."

"Two times too many."

She narrows her eyes. "I expected judgment from you, but this is bullshit. It was way before you. Well, the first time."

She glances at my crotch, her tongue slipping over her bottom lip. "I control that too. Not until I get an explanation."

She huffs. "Why the fuck I want you so bad I have no idea. Fine, if you must know. The first time was our senior trip. We were in Cancun, Mexico. Shit happens with tequila and being away from home. Have you ever eaten the worm at the bottom of the bottle? We were trashed. I didn't want to end up on the news like previous girls and the guys in our class weren't doing it for me. Plus, my need for loyalty meant I had a ping of guilt that I was supposed to be in a relationship even though he was probably at home fucking my mother. It came up in conversation. We were curious. Alcohol was talking. I didn't think it was that big of a deal, because if he asked about men I didn't have to lie. The second time was the night before my interview. I was worked up over you, nervous, I hadn't been with a man in way too long, and had not had a real orgasm in even longer. Also, it was my birthday. I guess I seemed needy and she was giving. It had already happened once and never became anything. We aren't lesbians. We both like dick way too much to even consider that route. And I can't say that I regret it, because it chilled me the fuck out from the anxious state you had me in. It was just body parts. My mind was not on her."

As if she realized she said too much she shuts up. I move toward her, leaning over her as my fists go to the seat. Her head falls back until the back of the chair stops her, our lips barely apart, eyes locked together. "What was it on then?"

Her breathing hitches. "Nothing."

"Lying to me isn't a good idea. We've already been down this road."

Her eyes close. "You. It's been on you since I met you."

I straddle the chair, standing before her. The tip of my finger touches under her chin, pushing her downcast face upward. She opens her eyes. Her lips separate, creating a small opening. "Unbuckle me."

Her hands slowly rise until she's gripping my belt buckle. Her eyes never leave mine as she unbuckles it and then unfastens my jeans, her hands slightly shaking. She stares at my boxer briefs, not moving, not saying anything. "Speak."

"I've never been scared to give head before."

"Why now? All dicks work exactly the same."

"But the owners behind them don't. If I'm not any good I don't want you to stop wanting me."

Her vulnerability turns me on. Her weaknesses fuel my need for power. Her desire to please me drives my want to keep her. The rest is a bonus. I push my hand down the front of my underwear, pulling my dick out. "It'd take more than a lousy blowjob to make me not want you. Open."

She tilts her head back slightly, her eyes never leaving mine. "Then collect what's due." She opens her mouth, wide, pushing her tongue forward.

Delta

He grips my hair in his fist. holding my head still. I keep my hands in my lap, wringing them around each other in my attempt to calm down. I've thought about this since he mentioned me sucking his dick this morning after the incident with the client. It's plagued my mind all day. My heart is pounding, my nerves are unsettled, and I'm trying with every ounce of control to keep from shaking. If I gag I will forever hate myself.

I've given head; through self-teaching and listening to step-by-step instructions from Chuck. He wasn't afraid to tell me exactly how to do things. The age difference kept me from questioning it. Due to the fact I haven't had a relationship since then my experience with blowjobs is little. The idea of disease freaks me out and I refuse to suck latex. It's disgusting. So for me, I tend to experiment more in the category of penetration than oral, where I can hide behind a condom. I prefer random hook ups to strum the chord rather than use their tongues on me.

But with him, everything is a yearning I can't control. There is nothing I want to avoid, regardless of the consequences. He places the tip on my tongue, rubbing it up and down in a short burst. As if it's a silent command, I close my mouth around his head and hold still. Before I can prepare myself he thrusts forward, the tip hitting the back of my throat. My throat contracts, trying to purge what's blocking it.

I breathe through my nose, my eyes welling up from the unexpected invasion. His face is relaxed, his body still, his words absent. Our eyes burn into each other's. He pushes deeper, testing me, but this time I've relaxed my throat some and evened my breathing. He smirks, and with that one movement of muscle I relax completely. He's making this a game. Only a guy like Kross can control everything down to his own dick.

He starts to fuck my mouth, speed increasing with every thrust. His dick comes out a little wetter with every stroke. He's rough, not caring in the least if I'm uncomfortable. He's using me as a tool for his own pleasure. The lust in his eyes spurs my reflexes, my instincts. I create a tight suction, my tongue sweeping along the undercarriage of his cock, the metal of my lip ring massaging his skin. His neck is corded, deep grunts slipping through his lips.

My panties are drenched at the sight of him, knowing I'm the one turning him on. My reservation slips away. My fear leaves. The only thing that remains is the lust running rampant through every vein in my body. His eyes veer as my hand begins to move, traveling beneath my skirt where my fingers move my panties aside.

I circle my fingertips in my wetness, before moving for my clit, stroking myself to the same rhythm he's using. A sound I've never heard from him occurs—a deep, masculine melody without his mouth even opening. It doesn't take long before I'm at the edge, rounding the peak of the orgasmic coaster and so close to falling.

My throat vibrates from the unintentional moans and my eyes start to close.

Just before I orgasm my mouth becomes vacant and I'm lifted and turned like a rag doll, my body taking stance on my knees on the chair. "Jesus, Delta." I hug the back of the chair as he rips my panties down my legs and rams his cock inside of me before I can keep up. He strokes my clit as he pounds inside of me, my body heating, and perspiration coming through my pores. My eyes close without effort, my mouth unable to from the loud screams being drawn out by every hard hit to my backside. My hair is sticking to my face, a strand falling in my mouth. He grips my chin in his palm, tilting my head. His lips touch the edge of my ear as the orgasm begins to tear through my body. "I'll fucking kill you before I let someone else have you."

And as those final words settle in my mind, my pussy locks around him as he pulses inside of me. "No one else wants me," I whisper.

"Good, because anyone that tries is a dead man. I've buried bodies for less."

A tingle runs up my spine, as if a warning. The scary part isn't that I believe it, but the fact that it makes me feel alive.

CHAPTER FIFTEEN

Kross

I catch the 9mm he tosses at me, staring at it. He requires all runners to wear one and he changes them out regularly, even though I've never had to use it. "I need you to take care of it. No runner steals from me and gets away with it. His three days to bring me my fucking cut is gone. I'm done."

I pull back the slide to see if it's already loaded. It is. I run my hand along the barrel, letting my fingers caress the metal, the pattern causing me to close my eyes, to memorize it just like I do with each one. I've dreamed almost every night since I moved up to his personal distributor from small time selling on the streets of putting a bullet between her eyes. I want so bad to watch the blood drain from her body, beat by beat. I've thought up so many different ways to do it. How I would dispose of her body.

Patience. The state worker sticks her nose in too often to do it right now. I have to wait. Wait until I'm out of the fucking system. My day is coming. And when it does, I'm sending that bitch to Hell and then I'm going to play in her blood.

"Kross, did you hear me?"

I glance at Damien, sitting comfortable in his large leather chair, his suit pressed and clean. The smoke from the Cuban cigar billows around his tan cheeks and silky black hair. "You want his head?"

An evil grin spreads along his face. He puts down his cigar in the ashtray and stands, one hand twisting the gold ring on the other. He walks forward, resting his hand on my shoulder. I flinch. He retracts instantly. "We'll save that for your second kill. This time, just bring me those gold teeth my money paid for. That's proof enough. I trust that you don't want to betray me and take his place. Do you want to know why I chose you, Kross?"

I holster the gun in the waistband of my jeans and pull my shirt over it. "Why?"

"When he brought you along to pick up his supply, you had that crazy look in your eyes for something darker. I knew you were better than running dime bags on the streets. You belong at the top. Why let others control you when you can control everyone else? Look at this," he says, holding out his hands to everything around him. "You could have all this. All you have to do is put in your time with me. When the day comes for you to leave, it's up to me whether I let you go. If you do right by me, learn what I'm willing to teach, then you'll walk away a king. You may be just a kid, but I think you were meant for this. Some walk in the light. Others rule the shadows."

My soul is blazing. My skin is crawling in ways I've never experienced. My mouth is watering at the thought of stealing a *final breath, stopping a beating heart. "He's running. How do you want me to find him?"*

He turns and walks to his desk, placing his cigar between his lips. He grabs a folder from a drawer and drops it on his desk. "My PI has enclosed all of the details on where you can find him. I don't care how you do it; I just want it done. I have a reputation to uphold."

I stare at the folder. "Okay."

His grin returns as I step forward to pick it up. "If you make it slow and painful, there will be a hefty bonus waiting on you when you bring what I asked for."

I grab it and start for the door when his voice halts me. "I'll only warn you once, boy. Don't get caught. And if you do, I don't exist. Name, face, location, information—it's forgotten. You know nothing. Second chances aren't given. And I choose people that won't be missed."

My teeth clench together. I nod once and leave the room. My moment for revenge has come. And I'm going to enjoy every brutal second.

It took me three days to decide how I wanted to do it. I mapped out where he was at what time. I watched him, and I waited. His stupid ass is at the drop house. The one place I wouldn't be caught dead if there was a hit out on my head.

I peek through the window. He looks around, before pulling a duffel bag through the floor, returning the floorboards to their place. He unzips it, pulling a stack of cash wrapped in a rubber band out, and then putting it back. I slip through the window. His head snaps up, a flashlight shining on me. "Fuck, Kross. You know better than to sneak up on someone in the dark. What are you doing here?"

"I could ask you the same question."

"Look, Man, I'm relocating. You're going to have to find another supplier."

He grabs the duffel bag as he stands, turning his back on me. I blink, letting his shoulder become her face as I pull out my knife. I focus like I've done a thousand times; targeting the place I want. As he arrives at the door I throw, the blade of my knife slicing through his shoulder. His knees buckle, but he stands back up before hitting the ground. My eyes become transfixed on him as the blood runs in lines down his back, staining his shirt in red, his arm immobile. I'm pulled back to the present when he turns, the end of the barrel staring at me. "What the fuck?"

My adrenaline spikes when most people would probably fear. I'm not scared of dying. Dying would probably be a peaceful alternative to the life I live. But I sure as fuck am not going down by a smalltime dealer that can't even aim a gun at a kid without it shaking uncontrollably.

I withdraw mine and pull the trigger before giving him an answer, the bullet blowing through the front of his working shoulder, sending his gun flying out of his hand. "I've already found another supplier—the same one we've been using this entire time—and it looks like you've pissed him off."

His eyes go wide. "Damien sent you? He doesn't deal directly with runners."

I shrug. "I guess it's good to know who you're stealing from."

He turns and tries to run, but I storm forward and rip the knife from his shoulder, grabbing his shirt and jerking him back. "Look, kid, let me go and we'll split what's in the bag. He never has to know. I was just going to borrow it for someone and put it back. I wasn't stealing."

I spin him around and push him against the wooden door, stabbing my knife through his shoulder and the wood, holding him to it. He screams out. "If you didn't borrow it with his permission it's stealing motherfucker."

I grab my backup knife from my boot and stab it through the other shoulder, pinning him to the door. "Fuck! Please! Let me go."

I laugh, seething through every word as rage takes over. "It's too bad for you I've been waiting a long time for this." I pull the pliers from my back pocket, looking at them. "If people were smart they would think about shit before they do it. Everything has a consequence."

He looks down at them. "What are you going to do with those?"

"A few things have been requested." I shove open his mouth, my hand gripped on the handles of the pliers, the teeth clamped down on the correct one. Without hesitation I pull, ripping the gold tooth out by the root. He screams through it, calming the constant hatred that suckles from my soul. One by one I remove the ones of value, feeling a little more relieved with each. Blood pools in his mouth, spilling over like a waterfall.

His head slumps over from the constant groans of pain. He begins to cry as the stench of shit burns my nose. "Just do it. I can't take any more. To just be a kid you're a fucking demon."

I grab my gun and shove the barrel against his cheek. "Is this what you want?"

He nods, but instead of giving him what he asked for I remove one knife from his body and slice down his front, ripping him open. "Guns are noisy, and messy. A bit impersonal for me. I prefer to watch you die."

I rear back and drive the knife through his gut. A once breathing body becomes lifeless. I watch his eyes change as it does. It's something I'll never forget. I pull the knife out and stare at it under the dim light of the flashlight on the floor. For the first time in my life I feel powerful, relieved, and all of the control is finally mine. I'm not the one in pain, but the one inflicting it. It's intoxicating.

I collect my knives and wipe them on his shirt, sheathing them on my body. I secure the payment and grab the duffel bag, along with the flashlight. I squat before him after pulling the lighter from my pocket and strike it, holding the flame to the hem of his shirt. I watch it slowly burn up his front, picking up with every breath of oxygen it takes, the heat blanketing my face. I memorize the way he looks burning, the smells wafting through my nose, and with every second that passes I know this may be my first kill, but it won't be my last. With the rise of the flame up the door I know that I can't stay anymore, so I stand, slowly backing away before hightailing it out of the house quietly.

As I walk through the field a smile pulls from each corner of my mouth, and for a moment everything within me is at peace. There is no pain, no fear, no loneliness, and no memories haunting me. Everything is silent. And even if it doesn't last, the temporary break from madness makes it all worth it.

I open my eyes to an empty bed. I sit up, looking around my room for her. The sound of water splashing filters in the room from the bathroom. My hands wipe down my face, trying to pull me from the grogginess.

The clock only reads 6AM, but it feels later. My head is pounding. My body is tired. My mouth feels as if it's been swabbed with a cotton ball. I feel like I have a hangover without drinking a drop of alcohol. The bitch sucked me dry at the shop. I'm positive I've never had sex more than once in a given week, let alone a day, until her.

I've never been a big drinker of anything, but at the moment I feel like I need to consume a gallon of water. The need to hydrate has never been so strong. Last night. Fuck, I don't know what last night was. I've never been as fucking horny in my life as I was last night. Watching my dick disappear in her mouth drove me wild. Every time my head hit against the back of her throat I wanted to nut. The way her tongue swept along the bottom while she sucked me hard was my undoing. But what made me snap was her moaning around my dick while she masturbated. I've never witnessed anything like that and I've been on this earth for a long time.

My hand runs through my hair while my feet hit the ground. Right now my head wants no part of sex, but the hard member attached to my pelvis says that's a lie. I make my way across the room and open the door to the bathroom. It's not locked.

I lean against the doorframe, crossing my arms over my chest. She's staring at me from the bathtub, bubbles covering everything but her head. "What are you doing?"

She smirks, one brow rising. "I thought that was obvious."

"Get out. I have something to show you."

She rolls her eyes. "Kross, I just got in. I physically need to soak. Can it wait?"

"No."

She glances at my dick, the corner of her lip slipping between her teeth. I push it down, my boxer briefs doing little to keep it hidden; pissed it's still hard. "Jesus. It's not sex. Last night never happens. I need to refuel. And I wouldn't have changed the schedule for that anyway. I don't work like that."

She makes no movement to get out, my irritation growing. "We have shit to do. Come on."

"Are you going to shut the door so I can get out?"

"So you can lay there? Not a chance in Hell."

"Oh my god, you're ridiculous," she says, before standing in the tub, water sloshing around the inside. Her body is covered in bubbles, but before she steps out she rakes her hands down her breasts, baring her nipples, eyes locked with mine. I clamp my jaw shut, physically forcing myself not to look, but able to see anyway.

She grabs the towel in her hand and steps onto the rug, wiping her face as she makes her way toward me—body bare, glistening from being wet. She turns to the side and steps through the door, her hard nipples brushing against my arm, one by one.

Before she gets too far I grab her arm and pull her back, slamming my lips against hers. Breaths heavy, hearts pounding, thoughts racing, I force her back to the bed, pushing her down. She works my briefs down as I roughly fall on top of her, her legs instantly wrapping around me. I push inside of her. "I fucking hate what you're doing to me."

I pound into her, letting my aggression out. I can't deal with bottled up anger. It makes me want to kill; like I once did so often, and since I started working for myself I don't allow myself to take a life unless someone fucks me over. Bodies turning up are an unnecessary risk I'm not going to take without a cause. I have too much to lose.

Her head rolls back against the mattress, her fingers pulling at my hair. "Well, I fucking love what you're doing to me," she says, and then as my eyes meet hers, my heart slows, and my thoughts die down. My movements become deeper and more controlled, my abs slowly contracting with each roll— everything becoming less erratic. Everything inside of me feels foreign, unpredictable. I'm not sure what that means.

My thumb traces along her bottom lip as I grind against her, massaging deep inside of her. Her palms are shelved on my tense shoulder blades, her feet propped against the back of my thighs, holding me close. "Hell, yeah," she whispers. "Don't stop."

"My control is slipping. That's not good for you. I need it."

She pulls my lips close to hers, brushing her bottom one up both of mine. "What do you need from me?"

I blink, trying to clear the haze from my head. The way she looks at me is too much. It causes me physical pain. Every scar is burning, feeling like they're slowly being ripped open. Anger, control, hatred—all those I can sort through. But this. This intimacy. This constant fucking need to be in her. This obsession with wanting her in my sight nonstop. All of those things I'm having trouble grasping. It's slowly destroying my sanity.

I grip her ankles, pushing her legs back to angle her toward me, and then I finish what I started. She arches into me, and the second she clamps that tight pussy around me I blow, my chest heaving.

I pull out, trying to get up, but she meets me on her knees, holding my face in her hands. I don't flinch at her touch anymore, but I'm still not used to it or to the point that I welcome it. Touch is something I've only ever had in pain. It's reflex to stay away from it. Since I'm grown I'm not sure I'll ever want it. "Kross," she says in a short tone. "Tell me what you need. I want to understand."

My eyes scan hers. My fists pump within my palms. Everything screaming at me is to close off, to shut up, and to keep her out. She's an outsider. I begin to pull back, but she follows me, her voice softening. "Please."

And then something happens that never does. I want to let her in. And I have no idea how. "I need to take a job. I've cut back since you freak out at each drop. I haven't taken any new clients. I've postponed meetings. You act like I don't notice, but I notice everything. No detail slips by me. Study, silence, it's what I've done my entire life. I need to work. It's a part of me. It keeps me balanced. But I can't—"

My mouth shuts. "You can't what?"

"I can't leave you behind," I admit; a confession that is going to fuck me over at some point. I know it.

She closes her eyes. I stare at her, unsure of what exactly she's doing. I don't understand women. People fear me. I know this. I have the reputation that I do because I'm thorough, never back down, and keep to myself. I also serve as my own justice system when needed. I don't hire people like Kaston to do my dirty work. I dirty my own hands. But learning how to interact with people is something I've never done. I have reflexes and instincts. I don't have emotional understanding. Body language is one I don't speak and I speak many.

She opens them and stares into my eyes, taking a deep breath. "Then take me with you. I'm ready. I know you won't let anyone hurt me. I trust you."

Every muscle in my body relaxes. The back of my hand runs down her chest, my fingertips brushing over her erect nipple. "Do you still want these pierced?"

Her breathing becomes labored. "Yes."

"Tonight after work. Right now, I have something to show you. Follow me."

Then, I turn and walk out of the room, underwear in hand, leaving her there, on my bed, naked and flushed. I need space. Because I'm about to do something I've never done with anyone else. I'm going to teach her everything I know . . .

Starting with a gift.

CHAPTER SIXTEEN

Delta

I take off running in a sprint, trying to catch up. The soreness between my legs doesn't go unnoticed, which was the reason for the bath. With every rub of my thighs I feel a zing of pain, and with every ache I'm reminded of the hottest night of my life. There likely isn't a spot in the studio that wasn't christened. I didn't even mind having to stay longer to re-sanitize everything when he finally grabbed his clothes and took off for his office after round two, shutting down.

Disappointed in the sudden coldness after something so heated, I stared at his retreating form after he demanded I clean up and disappeared. Thirty minutes went by, lots of thoughts, replaying everything that happened, and I finally went down and knocked on the door.

"Kross," I call out, knocking on the door. Shuffling sounds occur *and the door opens.*

He looks angry. I'm not sure why. "You done?"

"Yes. Everything is clean and germ free."

He pushes past me, heading for the stairs. I rush after him, grabbing the back of his shirt. "Wait. What's wrong? Did I do something?"

He turns around, his hands going to each side of the doorframe. His jaw is working back and forth, his eyes piercing something deep within me, making me nervous. "Do you service all men this well?"

My mouth falls, not expecting the harsh words, hating the sudden hatred spewing with his tone. "What's that supposed to mean?"

"Oh, I don't know, maybe that any girl who can ride me like a damn whore, make me come more than once in a two hour period, and suck my cock like I've never experienced usually is one. Who trained you, Delta? What else was going on at that strip club? Because that shit up there was porn. The average girl doesn't fuck like that."

I draw back as if he slapped me. I narrow my eyes. "You're an asshole. You started it! For fuck's sake, I've never heard of a guy complaining about being 'fucked too good'." The anger takes control of my mouth. There is no stopping me at this point. "Or have all of yours just laid there like a corpse and spread their legs for you?"

"I prefer one I can control like a puppet on a string. Makes it easier to never look back once it's over."

Don't ask me why, but something clicks in the short amount of time his eyes stare into mine. Thank God for peripheral vision. Or maybe I'm just finally really starting to understand him; how he works. I smother the smirk trying to form and take a step toward him. Before he can open his mouth I grab his dick through his jeans—his hard *dick. "Or are you just pissed that I do this to you and you can no longer control every situation?"*

He grabs my neck, hauling me backward until my back is pressed against the cool glass. His neck snakes toward me, his lips skimming over mine so softly they barely touch. He's teasing me. Wetness pools in my already damp panties, but I keep my palms against the glass. "If I've got to be in this hell so are you. Prepare to be sore, because you're going to drain me, bitch."

A shiver runs down my spine as I make my way through the house, remembering that promise. What a promise it was. I file in behind him, pulling the black *Metallica* tee shirt I grabbed from his drawer over my head, a pair of his boxers already in place. I still haven't moved my things into his room. I sleep there, but the rest is exactly how I came into it. Call me crazy, but I wanted to make sure he was serious and not pressured before making it so . . . final. I can live with separate spaces for a little while longer.

And he hasn't asked why my stuff is absent, seeming content just that I'm there, so I figured that was even more reason to wait. The longer I'm around him the more I realize that sudden anything is bad for Kross. He needs an adjustment period. Me—the part I need I'm getting. Where my stuff is stored doesn't matter to me.

He stops at a door tucked away at the back of the house and shoves a key in the lock. It's a door I've noticed familiarizing myself with the house, but the second I realized it stayed locked up I left it alone. I haven't even asked him about it at the risk of being an intruder in a house that isn't mine. Plundering never was my thing. Everyone needs privacy of their own.

When the door swings open a dark staircase comes into view.

Dark, as in, I can only see the first two steps dark. I halt at his back, a nervous tick occurring low in my belly. "This isn't the part where I become the main character in a horror movie is it? I don't want to walk down there and find tools to become lawn fertilizer."

He glances at me. "Your imagination is too colorful."

I raise one brow. "Is that really dramatic, though . . . considering everything? Serial killers and sociopaths are never the obvious."

He remains facing the stairs, his head turned toward me, but tilts his head slightly, his jaw upturning toward me. "Not all serial killers enjoy killing women," he says, and then he makes his way down the stairs without another word, leaving me speechless, mouth gaping with sudden chill bumps as my blood runs cold.

Utterly fucked.

And the scary part—I don't give a damn.

He turns on a light at the bottom as I make my way down, hands to each side of me on the wall so that I don't trip. It's a basement from what I can tell. I come into the room and halt, my eyes scanning everywhere, overwhelmed. It's a large finished basement all right, but every wall is ornamented with weapons of different size and make: assault rifles, shotguns, handguns, knives, swords, and everything in between. Each has an exact place, as if it was a precise thought or measurement on where it was hung or stored.

Instead of furniture it has metal safes, cabinets, counters, and workbenches; built in shelving for storage. It's like an assassins lair. And at the moment I feel like Angelina Jolie in *Mr. & Mrs. Smith.* "What is this place?"

I chance a glance at Kross. He's studying every piece from where he stands, a reverent look on his face. "My personal collection," he replies, still not looking at me.

"Personal collection?" I scoff. "It's a fucking arsenal. Why do you need this much?"

He glances at me, no crack of a smile. "We live on a planet filled with violence, hungry for war, and every being fighting for power and territory. If it's ever brought to my door, I won't be caught with my pants down. This life is ugly, Delta. You don't dance in the shadows without being a master of the art."

I look at him. Really study him. I can't help it. Everything he says or does I'm drawn to like a bug to light. On the exterior he's hard, a little terrifying, and sexy as hell. Just beneath the surface he's angry, awkward, controlling, and just a tad bit, or a-lot-a-bit psycho. But at his core, and I mean deep down in a place that isn't reachable with ease, I think he's a broken little boy that never experienced love and a shattered man that's scared of becoming that same little boy again if he were to get it now.

Maybe Lux was right. Do I love him? Or is it wishful hoping over something I have always wanted in return. Then it slams into me. The knowledge that if I could change his childhood for him I would in a heartbeat; even if it altered his life so much that I didn't have him now. And I probably don't even know half of what he's been through.

I think buried six feet under his surface is a beautiful soul. Every once in a while, when he doesn't even realize it, I get a glimpse of him unarmed, and it makes me want more. That's why I'm here, isn't it? I'm willing to become a criminal for him. I'm willing to risk jail to stay. And death is a very real possibility if I don't leave.

But even so, I want him. I want all of him. Regardless of how long I have to dig. I grab the nape of his neck and kiss him, nothing else on my mind but his lips. Our tongues tangle, falling into a familiar dance. One hand combs through my hair, locking into a fist at my crown, the other slipping around my waist.

My arms circle behind his head, no sound except our heavy breathing. He lifts enough for me to take the hint, my legs circling around his waist. I don't know how long we've stayed like this— kissing, groping, breathing—when we finally break. His eyes are clear, when so often they're haunted. "I didn't mean what I said last night. I was a dick to say that shit to you. You just make me fucking crazy. I don't deal with things like normal people."

I smile, remembering it again. I'm one of those girls that don't let words bother me. Well, from everyone except one person. I know I'm not a whore. I was with one man until I left him. I had some wild phases after. Did some experimenting. Played the casual sex game. But a true whore doesn't go for any lengthy amount of time without fucking someone or multiple people. And before that night with Chuck I had been on a pretty long stretch for someone that's been sexually active for years. "You did mean to say it. You're not a man that says things without premeditation. You're an arrogant, controlling, psychotic bastard most days. But I'm choosing to take it as a compliment. And it's about fucking time you broke from this ridiculous game of controlling when we have sex and how often. Most men want their dicks in something almost constantly. Regularly. It's okay. I'd rather stay sore than think I don't turn you on enough to want it to the point of madness." I kiss between his eyes, softening my agitated tone. "But you're also *my* arrogant, controlling, psychotic bastard. I don't want you any other way."

For dramatic effect I rub my center up and down his hard length, my voice thick with lust. "Besides, I like servicing your dick on the regular. It's the best one yet." He grunts. My eyes drop to his lips and back up again. "What's the point in having sex with someone that doesn't bring out the porn star in you?"

Kross

I swallow, my eyes falling to her hard nipples showing through my shirt. I lower her to her feet, trying to put some distance between us. As much as I want her right now—in spite of what my brain says is logical—I've got to find balance again. With her I constantly switch between Dr. Jekyll to Mr. Hyde and it makes me fucking crazy.

I pinch the front of the shirt. "This looks better on you than me. Keep it."

She smiles. Fuck, the girl has a beautiful smile. It's one of those that makes you hone in on her the second she uses it. She has multiple I've noticed, depending on what she's smiling for. Witty sarcasm has one. Playful banter another. But this one is my favorite. It's the one she radiates when I notice something about her aloud or tell her something about myself without her prying. Most often when she's caught by surprise in general. It's not only the act of the mouth being upturned, but her cheeks change in hue from skin tone to pink and her eyes alter in shape slightly and give off a glassy shine. "Are you giving out compliments today?"

"Just stating the facts."

"Oh," she says, her voice sounding different than usual. She steps toward me, her palms going to my stomach. My abs clench at first touch, catching me off guard, but then I relax as she rubs up my front. Her fingers touch the balls of my nipple piercing. "Does it hurt?"

"No more than anything else."

She slides the barbell side to side. "I would have never let anyone else do it, you know."

"Then what was that shit in the studio with Remington?"

She sighs, her shoulders drooping some. "It's always to feel you out, Kross. To get your attention. To see if it gets a rise out of you at all. Sometimes I feel like when it comes to me you're just indifferent. Maybe because I've had a thing for you since the beginning. Then that girl you were tattooing was moaning and trying to move her shorts so low you could almost see everything. You didn't stop her, tell her to cool it, or mention you were seeing someone so her efforts were wasted. You just . . . sat there." She takes a deep breath. "Never mind."

"You've had my attention since you dropped off your design with Cassie."

Her head snaps up to mine, our eyes meeting. "You saw me? Before the night of my tattoo?"

My finger slips under the section of hair lying over her breast. "Yes. I was on my way in for my first appointment. I saw you walking across the parking lot. I sat in my truck and watched you the entire time. When you left I asked Cassie about it. Six weeks and five days you sat on a waiting list for two spots with me to open. It would have been longer if not for Kaston. He's one of the few that I work in on short notice. When I knew the slots were added I had Cassie call you. I knew who you were when you walked in with Lux that night."

Her face flushes. "Why haven't you mentioned it?"

"When was it ever relevant? In case you haven't picked up on it, I'm more of an internal person. That likely won't ever change. When I tattoo, everything else fades away, except you. Always has. Since the day I laid eyes on you I've never been able to tune you out.

I can feel your presence. I can be lost in a design, the gun going, and still I know your every move. When it's necessary for someone to know I'm seeing someone, they will. There is no damn reason to have that conversation with a client I'm not even paying attention to when you're in the room. I've never fucked a client in the past and I don't intend to start."

"I'm glad we had this conversation."

I grab her hand and pull her toward the closed door in the back. "Good. Now get your ass over here. We don't have all day. I'm booked solid till close."

Detta

He opens the door, revealing a small tattoo setup I didn't know existed in this house. It's fully stocked with everything, only a private version of each station at the studio, enclosed in a single room instead of out in the open. I look at him, a grin on my face. "You have your own personal tattoo studio? You would . . ."

He migrates to the walk-in closet and disappears inside. Moments later he returns, extending a big box toward me. I stare at the words on the front. *Tattooist: Tattoo Kit.* My heart starts pounding. "What's this for?"

"It's a *Verge Duet Kit*. It has everything you need to get started. I have plenty of ink and supplies here. I set it up just like the shop. All you have to do is familiarize yourself with where everything is. Use it. There is a huge difference in your comfort level with your own gun versus someone else's. I moved mine to the cabinet. You can customize and pick your own foot switches, clip cords, and machines once that station has your name over it. I'll even buy it."

I'm trying to listen through the shock.

"The space is yours to practice. I'll still teach you things at the shop, but the best way to learn is hands on practice. We can work here when we're home. As a business owner I can't let you practice freely on clients until I know you have a basic understanding and have seen you do it enough. It's a liability. What you need is practice hours. It's no different than a pilot needing so many flight hours before he can get a job in commercial. Vinny was a long-time client that I knew wouldn't mind because he knew I wouldn't let him walk out with a shit piece. I have a few clients like that I'll let you do things on from time to time. For now, there is enough practice skin in the drawer that you shouldn't run out for a while even if you used one to two a day."

My nails go to my mouth as I stare at the box. My eyes gloss over, blurring my vision. I've gone from never crying to almost crying all the time. But this—he'll never know what this means to me. I've been looking at tattoo equipment for years, dreaming of the day when I had my own. The truth is, you can get a basic kit for as little as fifty bucks, the average around a hundred, but I know that particular kit is not one the average amateur can afford. "That's about a four hundred dollar kit. I can't take that. You've done enough already."

He pulls me by the shirt and forces me to sit in the tattoo chair, placing the box in my lap. He bends forward, our eyes the same height. "You're not a damn charity case, Delta. I took you on as an apprentice. I wasn't thinking with my fucking dick when I made that decision. I'll absorb the training costs just like any other company would. I don't have a spotless reputation for nothing. My artists fuck up they get fucked, because I only employ the best.

"The shit you do around the shop—the bullshit maid work—you have to start from the bottom, doing the stuff no one wants to do. With tattoos becoming popular too many people up and decide on a whim they want to be an artist. I needed to know you were serious before I vested time in you. I'll give you lessons, homework, and tests—which will be timed according to design and size. You don't have to ask me to come down here. I'll give you a key, but it has to stay locked up."

Before I can stop them the tears cross over the threshold and push over the edge, then continue rolling down my cheeks. I wrap my arms around his neck, pulling him into a tight hug, hoping he didn't notice. No one has ever done something like this for me, and I never in a million years thought when it happened that it'd be Kross. "Thank you. You'll never understand how much this means to me."

He pulls back, looking at me before I can attempt to wipe my eyes. He has a curious expression on his face. The backs of his fingers then trail down my cheek, ridding them of the tears. I can barely breathe the way he's touching me; so soft, so caring, the total opposite of anything that is Kross. But he doesn't say anything about it. "I have a few calls to make before we go to the shop. Why don't you set up and get a feel for it and then we'll work on it when we get home tonight."

"Okay," I whisper, fighting to keep my emotions under control. His lips press against mine, his hand on the side of my face, pushing my hair out of the way. Then, he releases me, and walks out of the room, shutting the door behind him. "I love you, Kross," I say, the words tumbling out of my mouth, as if they needed to be said to make me believe something I've been denying all along.

I love you, Kross."

I sit at my desk with my burner phone clenched in my hand, dazed and confused as I stare at the video feed from all of my shops on the computer; yet to make any calls. I heard it. I shouldn't have heard it. For once it pisses me off that I have such good hearing, because now I have no idea what to do with that knowledge. I don't want it or need it lingering around in my head. I have enough unwanted shit up there. Like the memories with no attachment. The past that haunts me. A man like me is incapable of such feelings.

Love.

I don't understand the concept nor do I feel a fucking thing.

I'm numb.

I've always been numb.

But my pulse is pounding.

My heart is racing.

Thoughts are spinning so fast I feel dizzy.

Memories are attacking me so hard it's difficult to catch my breath.

The door slings open, the knob hitting the wall. I clench the comforter tighter, my eyes squeezing hard in hopes she'll go away.

"Where were you today, boy?"

I try to remain calm, praying she'll think I'm asleep for once. My stomach rumbles, making me silently plea inside that somehow I can fly away from here, from her. Maybe they'll come get me and take me to another new house. I'm used to it by now. Anything has to be better than this place; the place I've been the longest.

She pulls the cover off my body, the leather belt slamming against my back. "Get up!" she roars. "I'm not going to be disrespected by a bastard kid."

I glance at her—her eyes black, the color absent. I don't speak. I've learned it's easier when I keep quiet. She slings the belt again, the buckle digging into my skin. "Where were you?"

I'll never tell her where I've been. I don't care what she does to me. Sneaking out, learning my place in this God-forsaken world away from her is my only form of sanity. I'm just waiting for the right moment for my revenge. Another strike. My teeth clench. Everything inside of me wants to scream, to fight back, to run away. But I'm not old enough in the eyes of the state. If I did it's only a matter of time before a cop brings me back. "Were you out looking for a little tramp to make you feel good?"

She takes my silence for agreement. "You know, my Winston used to do that. When he said he was working late while I was home playing the perfect little housewife, he was really in some rundown motel with the first whore that would remind him he wasn't too old. Time after time, they got younger and younger. Maybe it's time I treat you sorry little bastards a lesson. Turn over, boy."

I do as she says, preparing for whatever is coming this time. Her eyes scan my fifteen-year-old body, giving me chills. My blood runs ice cold when she says, "You know, to some people forty-nine isn't old at all. Maybe I should have married someone my age all that long ago instead of someone twenty years older always looking for a younger model. I was a good wife. Always teaching my Christian values. I still paid for his sins. I guess you'd have to find out for yourself, though, to understand. Strip."

My breathing accelerates, not moving. She rears back and strikes me again in the pelvis. "I said strip!"

I push down my boxers, baring myself. She removes her silk nightgown, no clothes underneath. A wave of nausea hits me as she climbs on the bed. She gropes me, my dick hardening against my will. I try to push up the bed. "Get the fuck off me," I scream, but the second my mouth opens the leather of the belt pushes into the opening. She presses down, causing me to bite down on the leather.

In a different life I suppose she was probably a pretty lady, but her bitterness, the smoking, and the loneliness has made her seem way older than the age she gives.

I grip her wrists, preparing to push her off. "Do it and I'll make your life worse than it already is. I know you sneak off in the middle of the night. Fight me and I'll make it physically impossible for you to leave this room."

My hands loosen. Leaving here, even if for only a few hours at a time is the only way I mentally survive. I need it like I need air, more than I need food or water. I'll do anything, withstand anything, and be anything to keep doing it.

She grinds herself against me, leaving wetness on my skin. "Hold it up," she says, lifting off me just a little.

I do as she says, grabbing the base of my dick the way I do sometimes when thoughts fill my head and I can't get rid of them except to stroke myself. When I feel her touch down on me, I clench my eyes shut, trying to picture the girls in the magazines that I keep between the mattresses.

Then, moments later, my teeth bite into the leather and I scream out at the feeling of being inside her warm and wet body. I scream *because I hate it and because I like the way it feels. And then, everything inside of me that ever felt anything goes completely numb as she starts to ride my body and writhe against me. "This is all you'll ever be good for. No one will ever love you."*

The last thing ever said to me before everything that existed inside of me died, along with my virginity.

Three words and the Hell I live in is back full force. This is me. She may need me, but there is no way a girl like that can love me. Criminals are unlovable. This is the man I am. It's best for those three words to be forgotten, as if they never existed. All the more reason to confirm a job meeting.

Unknown number: Three days. Midnight. Salsa club on Canary Street. Wait for my text.

I stand, making my way out of my office, locking it up behind me. I need distractions and I need them now.

CHAPTER SEVENTEEN

Detta

I stand by the truck, duffle bag sitting on the ground as I wait for Kross, wondering where the weird-as-fuck text came from that said to get ready and pack a bag for a couple of days. Then he disappeared for about an hour. I only know he returned by the slam of the front door and the blur of sweaty, inked muscle that passed by me to go to the shower. I've racked my brain wondering where he went or what he was doing. Or who. Then I internally slap myself at that absurd train of thought. *We're exclusive*, I repeat to myself. He wouldn't do that to me. Would he?

I've never been a jealous person. Hell, I knew Chuck wasn't only with me and I was perfectly fine with it, given the circumstances. But right now I want to chain smoke and ask questions, even though I know it's none of my business. Just because we're having sex on the regular, living together, and together nonstop doesn't mean he isn't still having a side life that I know nothing about. Even though we claim to be exclusive, he doesn't technically owe me anything as much as he's already done for me. I did come to him first . . .

Sex, speaking of.

I open my purse and dig through it, looking for my pills. After moments of scrounging with no luck, I turn and rest it on the hood to free up both hands, taking out my wallet to make more room. Still, to no avail. Fuck, where are they? I check the last possible place they could be—my small makeup bag for touch ups. Not there either. "I can't already be out."

I think back, trying to remember how many I've taken. The more I think about it, the more it seems I've been popping them like candy almost. That's likely not what they were designed for. I'll just have to make him stop by a pharmacy. I really need to figure out a way to schedule a doctor's appointment to get back on birth control. I internally sigh. That shit isn't cheap. This is where insurance comes in handy. Something I don't have.

My pack of cigarettes is lying on top of my wallet from where I dug them out. I grab it, shoving the rest back in, before lighting one. On exhale I turn around, leaning against the side of the truck, attempting to calm my nerves. My eyes close, letting the nicotine fill my lungs. I've got to figure out an alternative method here. This isn't going to work. He's keeping me too occupied all the damn time. What is alone time anymore? Regardless, something has to change.

Maybe we should have the discussion about him pulling out. I reflect back on the first night, the way he took me without question, no care in the world to what I wanted, and suddenly I don't think those kinds of talks work with a man like Kross. He takes what he wants. But I'm pretty sure that's what drew me to him in the first place. And somehow it makes me feel different to him that he doesn't pull out, regardless of whatever the truth is. I am a little scared to open up the floor for that conversation. I like living in my little bubble of self-created facts in regards to Kross and me.

Before I can open my eyes my cigarette is ripped from my lips. When they do there is one very angry hot man standing in front of me. There is no sense in someone smelling and looking that good. "What the fuck did I tell you about this shit?"

"What? I was smoking outside of the tattoo shop before Lux showed up and you said nothing. I thought that was our peace treaty."

He tosses a perfectly good cigarette down and digs it into the ground with his boot. "No, it wasn't. I was having an internal battle on whether I should be pissed about your jealous outburst or not when in contrast to what you may think, I liked it. The responsible business owner won out and shoved the boyfriend aside."

Boyfriend.

My heart melts a little. Then it's shot to Hell and back with, "Give me the fucking cigarettes."

I stomp my foot into the ground like a defiant toddler, crossing my arms over my chest. "Kross, I'm a grown woman. You can't boss me around outside of the shop. You can ordain it a smoke free campus and demand that I never touch them inside of your house and even your truck like on Halloween, but outside it is no man's land. I can do whatever the fuck I want."

His palms go to the metal, his face leans in, and if looks could kill I'd already be gone. My insides quiver a little in fear, but outside, I stand my ground. Even when his voice booms like thunder, sending every brazen cell in my body running to hide. "Let me tell you one goddamned thing. If I backed down every time someone told me no

I'd still be working for someone else, probably living in some shit apartment to stay low-key, and scared of fucking daylight in fear of running into the cunt of a foster mom that took my virginity, abused me in whatever way she could find, tormented me mentally, and continued to ride my cock until I killed the bitch. Cigarettes bring back fucking memories. They remind me of her smell, her leather skin, and the discoloring of her teeth. It is a hard limit. Now give me the fucking cigarettes—every last damn one—and the lighter too. This conversation is over."

Words lunge in my throat.

Air backs up into my lungs.

Tears threaten to spill from my eyes.

Every muscle falls in mourning.

My heart breaks in two, like it did so many times with Lux.

Then, robotically, I hand him the pack and the lighter, as commanded. For the first time since I was sixteen, nausea engulfs me at the thought of smoking. My mouth opens to speak, but he cuts me off. "I don't need or want your pity. Get in the truck."

I do as he says. This conversation isn't over. But one thing I learned from Lux is that an outburst confession in anger isn't the place to talk about someone's demons. It's merely a way of feeling someone important out before letting them in. She suffered alone for a long time before she told me what was going on. So for now I'll wait. I'll wait for him to offer me more, because something told him he could trust me with it in the first place or I would have never known. Even those drowning in hurtful secrets only reveals them at the exact moment they want to, to whom they want to. The thing about secrets—they'll torment your soul forever before they'll slip to the wrong person.

He opens the back door and tosses two bags on the seat, before rounding the back of the truck heading for the driver's side. When he gets in his entire body is tense, his muscles rigid and hard. I wonder just how burned he is inside. Regardless, he's the most beautiful man to me, and I only want to know more. "I'll never tell," I say, looking at his profile. "But I'll take some of the burden if you'll let me. You and Lux aren't all that different, yet you are." I reach over and place my palm on his cheek. "I can be your safe haven, Kross. All you have to do is let me in."

His entire body falls, and he suddenly looks exhausted, as if a kingdom weighs on his shoulders. He places his palm on mine, grabbing my hand, and then pulls it down but doesn't release it. "I need . . . I need to check in on one of my shops." My shoulders slump. He's shutting down again. Like he always does when he gives me a small glimpse of what's inside. I go to agree when he speaks again. "I need some time with you. Away from the fucking shop. Away from here. Just us. I think that's what I need. Then, maybe I can face it enough to tell you more."

What small part of me that was still put together shatters. I nod, quickly turning toward the window in just enough time to wipe the tear as it falls. His hand releases mine and he starts the truck, pulling away from the house. And after years of living in silence, I pray.

I look out the window. staring at the unfamiliar territory. It feels strange being in a different time zone. It seems simpleminded, but I've only left the state of Georgia once, and that was to go to Cancun, Mexico on my senior trip. The continental U.S. is an unexplored place for me. I've longed for the chance to visit many places, especially those of several iconic tattoo artists, but I learned long ago that some dreams will never come true and are better left forgotten.

That was until today, when boarding an airplane was as simple as a credit card and a man I call my boss, my lover, and maybe in some ways my best friend. The flight was short but seemed longer with the silence lingering between us. He seemed . . . distant. Me, well, I'm still reeling from back at the house when my heart broke for a man for the first time.

So often when we think of rape it comes to men raping women, or men raping kids, boys included. It just becomes the obvious that men can be cruel, vicious creatures. It's never something anyone wants to consider, but it's a harsh reality of this world that likely will never totally go away, no matter what we do in an effort to prevent it. But never do I imagine a woman raping a boy. I'm not sure any of us do. It's said that women are emotional beings, born with a motherly nature that God engrained in us. We're supposed to protect children, not abuse them. It's time, though, that I realize just as many women are ugly in this world—doers of evil. I know this by example of the woman that I call Mom, and even she's not *that* bad. She may have hurt me in a lot of ways, but physical aside from slaps across the cheek or sexual abuse wasn't one of them.

When I think of him being a victim of something so demonic, so heartbreaking, something dark begins to brew inside of me that I don't understand, and feelings occur that I've never allowed the chance to roam in my mind. Like violence. The need to protect him no matter what. I'm not sure if it's normal, or what it means, but I can't wrap my mind around someone wanting to hurt him.

Now, here I sit, looking up at the skyscrapers that paint such a beautiful place. I've traded one city for another. Two vast places. A sea of people in each. Similar in ways, yet so very different. His door opens, drawing my attention from the view. Am I being rude? I should say something. I just don't know what to say in fear of offending him or asking the wrong thing. He hasn't opened things up for conversation yet. Words have been few since we left.

He rounds the SUV rental, opening my door. His hands go to the top of the doorframe and he leans inside. "Why do I get the feeling you haven't traveled much?"

"Gut feelings are usually accurate."

"How many states have you visited?"

"The one I currently call home."

An aggravated sigh falls from his lips. "I was warned."

"What?"

"Nothing. Let's go."

"Can I ask you a question?"

"What?"

"Why Chicago?"

He studies me for what seems like forever. "It's the shop I haven't visited in the longest. Illinois is where I used to call home. The place I was born."

My eyes widen and my heart begins pounding against my ribcage. He's slowly letting me in. And releasing a little of the mystery one fact at a time. "So this is where you grew up?"

"The outskirts." He tugs at the front of my shirt. "Come on. There is something I want to show you."

My nerves tangle in my stomach as I inch out of the vehicle and walk by his side through the lot to the storefront. Tattoo signs hang in the window along with a lit up open sign. Vinyl decorates the door. A familiar business name graces the glass. It looks smaller than the one back home, sharing a huge building with other occupants.

He pulls open the door and lets me enter first. The lobby is laid out much the same as back home. Clients are waiting in chairs, reading magazines, and a young brunette is sitting behind the counter, looking at a computer screen with the phone to her ear. Her hair hangs in long, thick, silky sections over her shoulders. The only tattoo visible from this angle is a pair of angel wings on the inside of her wrist, only showing because of the way she's holding the phone. She too wears a uniform. We have got to discuss the girls he hires. The contrast between them and me are like night and day.

She glances up after the door chimes. "I'll be right with . . ." Her face freezes, her dark eyes lingering on Kross in a way that makes me uncomfortable, before she begins speaking into the phone. "Can you hold please?"

The handheld phone piece slowly descends from her ear. "Kross. Johnny didn't tell me you were coming today."

He walks around the counter, stopping beside her. "I didn't tell him," he says coldly, and then starts doing something on the computer. She stares at him in a way I've never seen Cassie look at him. Want. Need. Or something in between.

She inches her body closer to him. I'm starting to feel like an intruder. She's pretty, but heavier on the makeup than Cassie. And she's making me like Cassie a whole lot more at the moment than I already did. I rest my hands on the counter and she looks at me. "Can I help you?"

"I'm just . . ." My brows dip. My train of thought goes completely blank. What am I supposed to say? She is staring at me in a deadpan manner, making me feel stupid.

"She's with me, Veronica," Kross says, still occupied with whatever he's doing on the computer. "But if this is the attitude you have with clients you better fix it. The passive-aggressive bitchiness won't last very long."

Her eyes never leave mine. "With you . . . as in?"

"As in, the rest is none of your fucking business." He releases the mouse and heads for me, still looking at her. "Where's Johnny?"

"My apologies, Kross. It's just a surprise after all this time." *After all this time?* "If he's finished with his last session he's in the office."

I want to laugh at her half-hearted 'apology'. It's not even believable, and only leaves me with more questions as he takes off for the door to the back of the building while I'm still standing here, narrowed eyes at her as she gives me a damn evil smirk. "Delta," he snaps, causing me to take off behind him.

I catch up. "Uh, were y'all?" I couldn't help it. The question was digging its sharp claws into me.

"You're the first," is the only answer I get, but somehow it's enough to make me relax. Moments later, as we come through the short hall to the back that opens into a large room, all is temporarily forgotten.

My heart begins to pitter-patter at the sight.

My mouth waters.

So much excitement rushes through my body it's hard to stand still.

Masculine laughter along with the buzzing of tattoo guns fills the room.

I count to myself. Ten chairs. Eight artists present. Each one busy with a client, in lax conversation amongst each other. God, I want this so bad. "Look who it is, boys. The fucking king decided to check on his kingdom."

I'm pulled out of my internal kid-in-a-toy-store moment as

Kross hauls me across the room toward one of the empty chairs. "Colter" labels the top just as every station is back home, with the exception of the open one, only here it's a different color scheme: neon blue and black. I glance at the one who's talking; Blaze it says, tattooing a shin with a grin on his face. His large muscles are covered in a long sleeve, ink extending up his neck and down his hands. Half of his head is bald and completely marked, skin barely visible, his dark hair lying over on one side from the large section on the top. "We were starting to think you forgot about us," he continues, never looking away from the piece he's doing.

"I prefer random drop-ins. I dislike predictability," Kross responds blandly as he sits in the tattoo chair. "Better way to catch people doing shit they aren't supposed to," he says with a grin, as if that's the least thing he expects to happen.

Blaze finally glances at me as he reloads ink, his eyes roaming all over my body, the smile still present. "Don't I know it. Who's the chic?"

I work to calm myself down. That feeling you get when someone is watching you . . . That feeling is multiplied by about ten right now. I can feel every eye on me, and this is so much worse than being naked under the eyes of horny, drunk men at a strip club. I stand awkwardly by the head of the chair, suddenly feeling underdressed in my skinny jeans and midriff-baring long sleeve. This is covered for me, but it doesn't feel like it. It feels revealing. The weather here caught me by surprise. Down south we rarely need jackets before January. Right now I want to put on the jacket I took off at the door when I walked into a heated building. I had to dig these clothes out of my stowed away winter clothes at the request of Kross. I thought he was crazy when he told me to pack warm. I've never in my life been modest before today. I like showing off my tattoos. Go fucking figure.

"Blaze, Delta. She's my apprentice. Delta, this is my first artist—Blaze. He's been with me the longest." Kross' hand snakes around my waist and grips my hip, before reeling me toward him where I'm dumped in his lap. My ass is on his crotch . . .

With my cheeks heating Blaze smiles bigger at me, his eyes focused on the sitting position Kross chose when there is plenty of room on the chair for me to sit beside him. He then looks at Kross again, before going back to the tattoo he is working on. The tattoo lover in me has already looked at it. It's a Halloween piece. What looks like an old haunted house with an aged white picket fence. Jack-O-lanterns and bats litter the scene, a full moon in the background with the silhouette of a werewolf howling in the middle of it. "Your apprentice, huh?"

"Don't give me shit, Blaze."

Did I catch teasing in Kross' voice? Surprisingly, I feel rigid in this position and his body seems relaxed, when usually it would be the opposite. There is also a room full of people that I'm too afraid to look at right this moment. He seems so different with this guy versus the guys back home. "When did someone become worthy enough to apprentice under you, a girl, nonetheless?"

"What are you blind? Have you seen her? I'd want her in the shop every day too." My head turns at the same time as Kross'. It's a built guy with shoulder length dark hair and a short beard to match, walking across the room, a right dimple on display. He only appears to have one. He's sexy in that Harley owner kind of way. "I thought I heard your demanding ass out here." He grabs my hand and softly pulls me out of Kross' lap, bringing me into a hug. "Name's Johnny, sweetheart. Business manager and artist, so that asshole over there can take off when business gets good and leave his tattoo seed everywhere. And you are?"

"Delta," I say, a smile tugging on my face. He has a softer personality. If I had to guess I'd say he's mid-thirties.

He moves me to his side instead of returning me to the seat I was enjoying, his arm wrapped around my shoulders, palm resting against my arm. He smells of smoke and manly musk. "Why don't you save everyone the hassle of asking one by one what they're all wondering and go ahead and tell us. Where did you find this one? It doesn't seem easy to get your attention." He smirks. "At least not since I've known you, and we both know that's been a while."

My eyes lock with Kross'. His stare is blank. If anyone has perfected the poker face it's Kross. I wish I knew what was going through his head right now. I'm sure any minute he's going to shut down, just like he does every time things get too personal, too intimate. He grips the edge of the seat with his hands, his triceps becoming more noticeable through his Henley. "Pretty simple. She and a friend walked into my shop for a tattoo. The other one started talking her tattoo dreams up. I decided it wasn't time to let her go. She's got skill."

"And since when do you bring an apprentice on business trips and seat them on your lap?" He squeezes me closer. There is definitely prodding going on. "Or let that temper come out when someone else becomes acquainted with said apprentice?" Kross' fingers look like they're digging into the seat, close to breaking through the material. He's watching Johnny's hand. I take a step forward, not wanting to push him, but Johnny holds me still. "I've known him longer," he says under his breath.

"Jesus, Johnny, I'm a fucking man. I wanted her. Give me my girl before the nostalgia goes away and I beat your ass."

And just like that he softly pushes me toward Kross, an obvious playful expression on his face. "Gladly. I just wanted to hear you say it. Welcome back. It hasn't been the same without your grumpy ass around here." He turns around and walks off. "I'll be back. I have some errands to run."

Kross positions me back in his lap. *My girl.* Any girl that can hear that from a man like him and not become a puddle isn't normal. I relax into him, content, less nervous. "So, are we working on your sleeve while you're here?" Blaze asks.

"Maybe."

"You must be the best," I cut in, growing more comfortable with every passing moment. "He told me once only the privileged get to add to those.

One side of his mouth pulls up, and then he glances at me as he puts his gun down and picks up the plastic wash bottle of soapy water and paper towels. "Who do you think he apprenticed under? Some may think he was born with a tattoo gun in his hand, but I can promise you when his ass came to me he was no more skilled than you. He hasn't always been this arrogant."

I turn my head to the side, his lips almost touching my cheek he's so close. "It's true. I trained under him for three years. And I bribed him with damn good money to leave that hole-in-the-wall shit studio in the ghetto to work for me. Even offered him Johnny's job first, but he didn't want it."

It warms my heart to know he had someone he could look up to after everything he's been through. And his constant raging mood simmered down the second we walked in here. I can tell he respects them. And now that I look at Blaze in a new light, I can see the age lines on his face that Kross doesn't wear, showing he's a good bit older in years. My belly fizzles when his palm presses against it, his other arm pointing out, my eyes following. One by one he goes through the stations, even though the name labels each one. "Blaze, as you know, Johnny, and Donovan—all of the originals." He moves to the next one, continuing. "Monte, AJ, Colter, and Frankie were added next. Colter is off today. His band plays local gigs so he works his schedule around that. Then when I left Leo took my station. We added two more stations last year. Alec and Andre are the newest members of the tribe."

Each raises a hand or gun as he calls out their names, with the exception of the missing 'Colter'. Kross seems happy here, so the question lingers as to why he would leave. I say my hellos to each guy, all seeming so different, but most not as chatty as the first two. "Did any others start out as an apprentice?"

"No. I told you before I only hired seasoned artists. Everyone here came from previous shops with years of experience under their belts."

I continue to look around, mesmerized by his success. He came from such a harsh background and look at how he's turned his life around. It's more than I can say about myself. Honestly, right now I feel so inadequate compared to him. My self-esteem is taking a nosedive. I can only hope to one day have a tenth of the success Kross does. He and I rarely discuss personal details. Getting information out of him comes in small waves. But when he admitted to recognizing me the night of my appointment, I was too embarrassed to confess anything about myself.

The night of my birthday when I dragged Lux into that tattoo shop, the only thing she knew was that I had been on the waiting list for months. It was the one detail I knew I could reveal to get her to agree—a guilt trip of sorts so she wouldn't deny me. I couldn't stand the thought of going to see him alone. I'm a pussy really.

But never did she ask me why in the hell I would even be on a waiting list for a tattoo when there is a tattoo shop on every fucking corner. That's the beauty of Lux. She doesn't need a lengthy explanation from me when something seems odd. She's my ride for life partner. I could probably kill someone and call her and she would come help me drag the body across the floor, not even bothering to ask who it was or why he was dead.

My body before had been an artist's playground. A lot of hands have touched me with ink. I was never picky when I wanted another tattoo. I've even gotten free ink from agreeing to go out with the artist that did it. It never went beyond one time or a few exchanges via text.

But the truth is: I read an article in one of my tattoo magazines months before he opened up shop in Atlanta. They did a 'who you should know' artist spotlight on rising tattoo owners and Kross was the feature that month for his Vegas shop. I had never heard of him before that moment, even though I made him seem famous to Lux. Something about him stood out in the words. I know every public detail about him: how many shops, where they're located, years of trade, age of start, etc. It's almost creepy if I really allow myself to think about it. I memorized the entire thing.

Then I saw his photo. The one taken in front of the shop. And something inside of me wanted to know him, as crazy as that sounds. He was hot; by far the sexiest man I had ever seen, even still, to this day, but he was also more. Mysterious, dark, domineering. I don't know. I can't explain it. I've never had such a strong connection to someone I've never met or seen in person before.

After scouring social media in hopes to learn more, I made myself forget about him in an effort to not be a stalker. Tried to at least. My mind wasn't so easily swayed. But one morning I walked into a privately owned coffee shop I frequented about a block from the shop and his new shop was included in the coming soon section of the 'Coffee News' flyer that is left as reading material at the counter week after week; community news I guess you could say. I'm almost positive that's the first time I've ever spilled the contents of my purse before.

Embarrassed to no end, I picked up my belongings, took the flyer and my coffee and left before I recognized someone. I stared at that damn piece of paper for three weeks, my stomach in knots, before I could work up the nerve to call the number for an appointment only to be told that they were in the beginning stages and still in the process of staffing. I put my name on the wait list they were compiling and followed instructions of bringing my design idea by.

My birthday.

I received the call the night before my birthday. It was like a present from the universe. As hard as my heart was hammering against my chest during the telephone call I knew I couldn't meet him alone. If he knew, I'm positive I would be less appealing to him. He can never know it was anything more than coincidence, because the apprenticeship was not part of the plan. I don't want to lose it by looking like some crazy girl chasing a made up crush.

"What's bothering you?" he asks against my ear, startling me. I didn't even realize I was zoned out.

Lie.

I know he won't buy the whole 'nothing' response. I turn sideways, my ass moving to one thigh, my legs falling between his so that I can look at him. "I was just thinking . . . How about those nipple piercings now?"

He clenches the inside of my thigh, the blacks of his eyes growing and consuming the brown. "Here?"

"Yes. Here."

And without another word he lifts me, standing behind me. And like a girl in love, I follow.

CHAPTER EIGHTEEN

Detta

He kills the engine in the parking garage, sitting silently. Today has been the most relaxing day I've had in a while. Well, I don't know if the word I would use in describing a piercing would be relaxing, especially where Kross is concerned. I can name one single occurrence when I've been turned on while enduring pain inflicted by a needle and that would be today. I wasn't sure that whole *pain is pleasure* thing was anything more than a crock of shit until I saw the way he was looking at my nipples, meticulously thinking of every touch, every action. He acted way more professional than I wish he had, but there was no doubt what I saw in his eyes was heat and the protrusion of his jeans was the result of a silent thought.

But everything after was laid back. He let me watch various styles being permanently etched on skin. I got to know most of the guys on more than a first name basis, and Kross didn't even seem agitated when one offered to let me pull up a stool and watch like he would have if I sat with Remington, Wesson, or Joey. He even had pizza delivered for all the artists in the break room; something I've never seen Kross do. He's just . . . different here. Calmer. At least in the shop he is.

There is one thing, though, that I'll never forget about this trip. The part that consumed most of our day. I let it play in my mind one more time, because it'll forever be special to me.

"You know what you want?" Blaze asks as Kross removes his shirt and straddles his chair. "You're running out of room down the arms but there is some space across your shoulder blade and the top of the arm free."

"Delta," he commands, pulling me out of my stare down with his partially naked, fine-as-fuck body. Gets me every damn time. Makes me stupid.

I walk forward. "What?"

"Wanna draw it?"

Apparently I can't hear either. "I'm sorry, but what?"

He glances at Blaze, but I can't see the expression on his face with him facing away from me. Blaze pulls open a drawer and follows through by handing me a marker. He laughs at whatever expression I'm wearing. "He wants you to design it, beautiful. Have a seat."

I stand here, holding this marker like a damn idiot, shaking. "Kross?"

He breathes out, still not looking at me. "Come here, Delta."

I do as he says, his eyes meeting mine. "I don't think I'm ready," I whisper. "If you don't like it, you can't just wash it off."

His fingers hook over the front button of my low-rise jeans, his fingertips brushing against my smooth skin. He pulls me toward him. The pain from my newly pierced nipples slashes through me with the feel of his touch turning me on. "I've seen you draw. You aren't an amateur. Stop bullshitting and tell me what's really bothering you about it. You need to practice freehand on skin more than paper. A body isn't two-dimensional and flat. You have to work with the natural curves and contours."

"Because it's you. Not some friend that can be pissed at me if it sucks."

"You're in my bed, on my cock, and my roommate. I'm pretty sure that qualifies for any and all of the above. How is this different?"

I glance up; surprised he'd mention our sexual relationship aloud, even in hushed tones. The room is mostly vacant, only a couple artists still working at the moment. The rest are on break. At some point Blaze put ear buds in and started prepping. "I've never seen someone with so much beautiful ink. Everything works together as if it belongs. I may not be an amateur with sketching in a notebook, but I am an amateur at this. I don't want to mess it up. You're important to me."

I regret the last thing that slipped. It wasn't intentional. But then he smiles. God, that smile doesn't come out often but it's blinding. My panties become a puddle of hot need. "Sit your ass down and stop overthinking it. We have to learn to trust each other at some point. If it sucks I'll just take it out on you later."

He tugs me closer to the chair, forcing me to straddle it behind him. I can't argue with that outcome. Defeated, I sit, studying his back. I don't get to see it like this very often, up close and personal in plenty of light. Every scar stands out to me even though it's hidden in the ink. My heart re-crumbles every time I see one, reminding me that he's been through so much more than I can even comprehend.

My hands rub up his body softly, my fingers gliding along every taut muscle, memorizing what he has already, learning his style. My heart smiles when goose bumps appear. Then, marker in hand, I think of something that would remind me of Kross. Not the slightly psychotic hot tattoo artist, but the beautifully broken, wicked, protective man that I'm falling for. I just hope I don't end up so far down the rabbit hole that I can't come back.

"Are you sure you don't want to do something? I'm not trying to keep you a secret, Delta. You don't owe me anything. Here I'm not your boss. We can do things if you want. I just may be shit at suggestions, but we do have to eat."

I look at him, sitting over in the driver's seat, hand on wheel, opposite forearm resting on the center console. I desperately want to hold his hand. But I fight against it. He's not that kind of guy. I would like to do things like a normal couple, but the part he doesn't realize—the reason I'd rather be alone with him—is because he gives me more of him in privacy. It's selfish really. I'd rather sit at home and do random shit like play Guitar Hero with him any day than to go out in public and him clam up. So I lie. "I know. I'm just over stimulated and tired. Flying really kicked my ass. We still have tomorrow right? I'm totally fine with hanging out tonight and exploring then." I glance out the window at the dim parking garage to drive my point home. "This looks like a fancy building anyway. I want to see your digs, because I was totally expecting a hotel."

He gets out and grabs our bags from the back, locking the doors as he leads the way. I follow behind the entire way to his door, standing patiently, observant of just how fancy it really seems inside. When the elevators are top notch you know you should be scared of what's waiting.

He opens the numbered door and we walk inside. I halt, backing against the door as it shuts. It's a fucking penthouse. An ungodly oversized, open layout, completely upgraded penthouse. How many of these does he have? I was joking downstairs, thinking it was a small apartment since he is obviously rarely here.

My nervousness spikes. I'm not Lux. I don't know how to be a player in that game. I can't compete with money, exotic cars, or money-hungry trophy girls. It's a world I don't belong in. I think for Lux it gives her a sense of security; a peace in knowing she'll never return to the life she came from.

But for me, money is a reminder of what my mother neglected me for. For a single parent she did okay for herself, but it was never good enough. She wanted the life she never got because of me. Money could make that happen. A man with lots of it is a ticket to a happy life. Money is a form of power. She made me think she loved me by handing it out in small amounts here and there, but only enough to keep me fed and clothed. I swore I'd never be her. I'd never be with a man because of what appeared to be in his bank account.

Money was also the reason I sold my innocence in the strip club. Dancing underage should have never been my life. Chuck hyped it up to win me over. It was a way to make a lot of money in a short amount of time. For me, I saw departure in my near future and needed a cushion to make it happen. Mom certainly wasn't going to pay for college or help me find my way, and I never liked school enough to go past senior year. Too many times I saw that money could make girls do things they wouldn't otherwise.

I also know that women searching for sugar daddies take husbands away from wives. Mom wasn't above seducing a married man. And they were in the strip club regularly, shining their rings as if they meant nothing. People get hurt. They get cheated on. Money in large amounts isn't for me. It destroys everything in its path. I'm a simple girl. And simple is good enough for me.

My back presses against the smooth wood in rolling waves. "Delta," he says, caution in his voice. "Why do you look like a deer caught in headlights?"

"Are you rich?" The shameful question leaps from my lips in a fearful whisper.

"On paper, no, but I'm not hurting either. My tattoo shops bring in a profit that I could live off of and not want for anything. I'd be sitting comfortable with the rest if I never worked another day again. I can't exactly claim arms dealing to the government on my taxes. And the riskier the job the more it costs."

I slide down the door until my bottom hits the cold tile, my chest heaving in the beginning stage of a panic onset. He slowly walks toward me and squats to my level. "I don't think I can do this. Arm candy is something I'll never be. Money makes people different."

His arm extends, gripping my chin in his thumb and forefinger. "I've been 'rich' longer than you've been an adult. I prefer to invest my money in charities and programs like homes for orphaned kids and abuse help for victims instead of cars and worthless materials." He rubs just beneath my lip ring, his eyes burning into mine. "If arm candy is something I wanted I certainly wouldn't be with you."

My heart explodes into a million pieces and the remaining sparks rain down into the pool that is my stomach. A feeling I've had every time my mother told me how 'different' I was compared to normal girls—the girls that men wanted to publicly keep instead of playing with in the closet. My self-esteem burned out every time she told me the way I look embarrassed her. Somehow through the blurry vision the words find a way out. "What am I then?"

"You're more."

With no other words he stands and turns, taking our bags further inside. It doesn't take long before his retreating form disappears. As if I was holding myself together, I break, and the tears fall. I'm not sure why. I feel like a silly little girl. But he brings forward every emotion I've worked years to block out, to bury. And for the first time in a long time, the insecure girl I used to be takes over, causing me to cry. Silently in my hands, against the door of a man that overwhelms me and scares me all the same.

Finally, the words slam into me: *You're more.* And I pull myself together. I breathe deeply, wiping my eyes in an effort to look less like I've been crying, hoping like hell my eyes aren't red. I stand, grabbing my purse to go find him.

It's cute, though, you thought you had a choice.

I walk into the large bedroom to him sitting at the foot of the king sized bed, his dark jeans blending next to the navy bedding. The room is decorated to impress, unlike his house. I highly doubt he decorated it. Expensive looking art decorates the walls, a large area rug tying in the colors of navy and cream accents the floor. There is a gas fireplace mounted in the wall and reading chairs in the extra space to finish the look. By the lack of dressers I'm guessing the closet must be massive. It's very clean and orderly. Surprisingly, it seems very impersonal.

"I rent it out for additional income," he says, looking down at his hands, fingertips pressed together. "Had it professionally decorated to appeal to tourists. Property is never a bad investment, but it's useless if it doesn't turn a profit." He finally looks up at me, eyes locked and, emotional? "I guess when you grew up without a place to actually call home, you can't help but need more than one."

The tears fall in rapid succession, leaving no time to even ward them off. I lick the salty drops from my lips, forcing my lungs to work. Why is he explaining himself? "Money may change some people, but for others it's a vital part of life needed to function. It's something I must have or I go to a dark place that's hard to come back from. I do things that are hard to stomach there. Having money is a balance for me. My equilibrium between a place I barely escaped from and what most call normalcy. I'm not selfish with it. I give back more than what I keep. You can call me fucking Robin Hood if you want, but it keeps me sane. I work my ass off to make sure I have it."

I can barely see through the salty sea spilling from my eyes. "Kross—" The words lodge in my throat at the young boy sitting in front of me replacing the man I know; scared, bruised and battered, beaten. I try to blink him away and fail. When he looks at me his dark eyes are hollow, his innocence stolen. Blood begins pouring from the cross that is slashed in his neck. Each scar I've memorized appears one by one, fresh.

His mouth opens, and with one phrase shatters my soul. "Save me, Delta."

I reach for him. "I'll save you, Kross. I'll find a way."

"Delta," his voice rings out, his hands holding my face. Kross is standing before me, his stance warning high alert, eyes scanning mine, searching for something within their depths. Every muscle feels heavy, defeated, as I stand under his hold.

My hands wrap around his wrists, emotionally drained, cheeks soaked. It's too late to be embarrassed at this point. "What?"

"I can't be saved."

"I can try," I whisper.

His lips crush against mine, feeling more like lead than a

feather. My core floods with need. My breasts become heavy. His rough hands rub up my bare sides, gripping the bottom hem of my top. Our lips part so that he can remove it. My bra falls before I can register it's unhooked. The nursing pads protecting my new piercings from my bra go with it, reminding me I need a shower from the fresh wounds.

"I need to shower first," I say, winded, as he unbuttons my jeans and sends everything traveling to my feet with one push of his hands. A single veer of his eyes to my chest and his hand finds its way between my legs, two large fingers pushing inside of my wet opening. Every logical thought runs into a back corner, leaving me unable to speak. Suddenly his shirt is being tossed on the floor and my hands are working his jeans over his ass.

I drop to my knees, forcing his fingers out of me, and take his long length into my mouth, moaning down every inch as I quickly suck through each pump of my neck as my lips become a vise. Thank God for a strong jaw with a girth like his, making it harder to comfortably suck and control teeth. His thighs clench before the tiny, teasing bead of salty pre-cum is released. I lap it up, my hand gently squeezing around his balls.

He fists a handful of my hair and he jerks me to my feet, not letting me finish, before pulling me toward the bed where I'm tossed on top. My legs are pried open to the point of pain and his tongue flattens over my pussy, causing a fresh wave of moisture to rush forward. He shovels through my folds and presses the hard tip against my clit. My bottom surges upward, my heart pounding, nerves sparking like sparklers. I grip his hair, trying to stop him with little success, my brain at war with my limbs. "Shower. Please. I reek of airports, planes, and sweat."

He bites into my skin, his bottom teeth skimming against my

clit, causing me to scream out in the most embarrassing cry. Then he raises his body to an upright position. "Demanding little bitch today," he says, before flipping me over as if I weigh no more than a piece of meat, disregarding my request. He grips my hips and pulls my ass into the air, the force pushing my head into the mattress, my face covered in a mass of black hair. The sting of his hand striking against my pussy sends my hands clenching firmly around the bedding. "It's too bad I'm not the following orders kind."

Then, as if teaching me a lesson, his mouth clamps over my clit, his nose closer to my most intimate place than before, the tip pressing inside. His oral assault is more than I can bear, and within seconds I'm coming hard, my center being forced against him by the rest of my body as my orgasm tears through me.

When his mouth is no longer pressed against me I roll over, spent, not able to move. I don't have to. He lifts me off the bed and throws me over his shoulder, drawing a squeal, and giving me a bird's-eye view of one fine, hard ass, free of any markings or ink. Hair swaying, I grip his hips as he previously did to me, and pull my lips against one cheek, before kissing the opposite.

He rewards me with a corkscrew motion as he slides a pair of fingers inside of me for the second time. "Fuck." My breath catches. When he slips out of me my feet make contact with the pebbled floor of a shower. My hair sticks to my face as the water rains down on me from above in a steady, constant drizzle, hardly giving me a chance to catch my breath with water spraying from multiple angles.

He pushes me against a wall, his forearms pinning me in. His eyes look haunted, his body tense, the tension rolling off him with the water. "What happens when you fail?"

"What?" I ask, caught off guard.

"When you find out something lost this long can't be saved."

"We live with one foot in the fire . . . together."

Then he kisses me in a way he never has: hungry, needy, trusting. His large body hovers over me, towering over my small size. He lifts me up, my arms and legs instinctively wrapping around him. I'm preparing for him to take me hard and heavy, but am surprised when he pushes into me in one precise movement. Instead of the pounding I'm awaiting he rocks into me over and over. Every blissful invasion is a ripple effect as he pours his trust into me. He stills inside of me, releasing his orgasm as I tighten around him through my own, the emotional breakdown drawing it out sooner than normal.

He pushes his forehead against my chest, not speaking, and not making an effort to move right away. "Kross," I say, the words on my tongue. He looks at me, and already I can tell he's shutting back down, his eyes different.

I love you.

In my head I was brave. I told him how I felt unlike the coward that I am. Because in my head there is no fear of him not feeling the same. It's a two-sided truth. In my head he says it back, when in the real world I'm not sure he would. So instead I say, "Thank you for letting me in."

And before he can say anything I softly kiss him, letting my lips say what my tongue can't.

CHAPTER NINETEEN

Kross

He slides the folder across the small table of the back corner we're occupying at the salsa club in an old part of town. Lower class residents are all that call this place home now. The crime rate is too great for the people that can afford to live in a safer place. Gangs roam the streets around here after dark, looking for anyone stupid enough to be wandering around outside, unarmed, and away from public eyes. The rougher the area the better for me. I find owners that keep their eyes turned and mouths shut if you sling a few hundreds their way. "Four million dollars will be wired to your offshore account if you can get us the nuclear missile. Half when you send me the photos that you have it in your possession and the other half at transfer. Details and location are here."

I stiffen as his thick accent coats every facet of my mind. He reeks of communism and hatred, foreign money, but I'm not in this business to ask questions. I do this for one reason: security through stacks of cash. I pick it up and open it, studying the details of the missile, where it's currently being stored, and who's guarding it. Delta is clenching onto my shirt beside me, not making a sound and looking off at the sweaty bodies on the dance floor.

I grip the back of her neck and pull her closer. She glances at me, the fear so thick I can smell it. That's not good in these situations. It shows weakness. "Get up and go to the bar," I whisper. "Find the woman in the tight red dress and heels. Her name is Selena. Tell her I said to show you a good time and I'll come find you." She nods and goes to stand, but I stop her. "Do not go with anyone but her. Do you understand?"

"Okay," she says, and I finally release her, watching her the entire way.

I turn back to him. He's studying her in a way that I don't like, making me uneasy. "What makes you think I can get something with this kind of clearance?" I ask, getting his attention once again.

"We have several contacts that pointed us to you. Each one of them said if anyone can get it that it's you. We're willing to pay to ensure it's ours."

"And if I'm not interested in the risk?"

He glances at the men flanking each side, then back at me. "We'll just have to make sure the reward is worth the risk, Mr. Brannon. If time is what you need, you shall have it. I'm a patient man when it comes to something I want." He opens the lapel of his jacket, pulling out a small flip phone. He lays it in front of me. "The number you need is already programmed. I trust that you'll make the right decision. Price is negotiable. Present me the details and we'll go from there. I'll be waiting for your call."

He stands, seconds before his guards, and then they leave together. I lean forward, grabbing it, and holster it in my pocket, every flag going off in my head. For the first time in my life I'm dreading a job offer, and I've done some fucked up shit for a buck. The question on the table: will I listen to the chill running down my spine and turn down that big of a payout for the first time or will I risk everything and take it?

Three weeks. It's been three weeks since that meeting and my mind is no closer to a decision than it was when I left that night. I haven't even started recon to see if I want to commit to the job. Something is causing me to stall. I never stall. My rules are simple: seal the deal, plan the job, secure the product and make it untraceable, deliver the order, receive the payout. Then, forget the job ever existed. That's it. No questions, no thinking, no fucking talking, and no judging the client. My guys know the rules. Anyone breaks them they don't get a slap on the wrist. They die. What the client does with the product after I've been paid is none of my business.

I stare at the coordinates on the computer for the tenth time in the last week. I pull up the file that wipes itself and the entire drive if this computer loses its power source. The cursor hovers over my Russian contact. If I reach out I can't back out of this job. I'm not a patriotic man, but I certainly don't hate my country either. It just turns a blind eye to a lot of people doing fucked up shit to good people and kids. Four mill isn't worth something that could be termed as treason should I get caught. Being labeled a criminal and a terrorist are two very different things.

I put the screen on hibernate when a knock sounds at the door, opening at the same time. Delta peeks her head inside, her long, dark hair that I love falling in the open space. "Kross, can I come in?"

I glance up. When I do she walks further inside. I sit back in my chair, my elbow resting on the arm as I take in the black, silky nightgown that hits her thighs—way too long for home, but way too short for anywhere else. I wave her in. My eyes hone in on the outline of the nipple rings protruding from the thin material. Her cleavage seems overwhelming, bulging out of the top. Either she's gaining weight in only her tits or that's a smaller version of the nightgown I've seen several times. "You just take a bath?"

She blushes. "Yes. You weren't in the living room when I got out."

"You do something different?"

She crosses her arms over her chest, her shoulders folding in as if she's cold. Her tits round even more at the top. Any higher and they're going to pop out. Everything about her stance shows insecurity. "What do you mean?"

"Your skin looks different. Shiny, maybe, but different."

"I'm not wearing makeup."

"This is different. I see you without makeup every night."

She slumps. "Do you notice everything?"

"Yes."

She breathes out. "Do I look bad? You're making me nervous."

"Just different." My eyes go to her distracting tits again.

"Kross, you're starting to shut me out again. Chicago happened, and it was . . . unforgettable. You're different there. Which is surprising since that's where . . . Never mind. Since that weird meeting in the club you've been slowly shutting me out. Have I done something wrong? I thought we were finally getting somewhere."

Those tits again. I bury my eyes in my hand, trying to get a fucking grip. She's been in here all of two minutes and my cock is throbbing, thoughts running full speed in a different direction than what's been occupying them for weeks. For years it was obedient; hated me, albeit, but obedient, and now suddenly it's an asshole that can't stay dry.

When I look at her she's wearing unshed tears. I don't understand these fucking emotional outbursts she has. "Come here, Delta."

She rounds my desk, cautiously, before stopping beside my chair. I spin toward her, knees spreading apart as an invite. She walks between them when I tug the fabric that covers her navel. My palms lightly touch down on the backs of her thighs, skating along the smooth, clean-shaven skin until they're clamped around her hips, above the strings of her panties. She shivers. "I've had a lot on my mind. I've always been this way. Why would you think you've done something wrong?"

"We were having sex more, and now you're backing off like before. Over time it's becoming more scattered. It's been a week. It makes me paranoid. Guys don't backtrack . . . unless . . ."

"They're fucking someone else?"

Her posture falls. "Yes."

I pull her on my lap, her legs straddling mine. I slide my fingers under one strap, pulling it off her shoulder. "Is that why you're wearing this instead of your normal pajamas? Even if I wanted to fuck someone else—I don't—there's no time. We're always together."

"I just thought maybe I'm getting too comfortable for you."

"So you bought this?"

"No, I've had it."

Before I can stop myself her pierced tits are staring at me, my hand already wrapped around one, a hiss slipping through her lips. They're heavier too. "Your tits are bigger."

"We've been eating out more. Maybe that's why."

"It doesn't show in your ass."

"I don't know, Kross, why are you so observant?"

"I have to be."

She grips my shirt and removes it. "Why don't you want me as much?"

"I was giving your body time to heal. I can't keep my hands off them every time I see them."

"It doesn't matter. They're still sore. I'd rather deal with it and know you want me. Had I known it would take this long to heal I might have rethought getting them so soon. No other piercing has healed this slow."

My brows dip as I look at them. "They look exactly the way they're supposed to look. They shouldn't still be sore." There is no crust at the puncture site. I turn one to ensure it doesn't catch. It slides through with ease, but the clench of her hand on my shoulder is concerning. I drop my hand.

She masks the pain and grinds her middle against me, placing both of my hands on her breasts. "It's probably just girl stuff then. All the more reason not to stop. I want you to touch me."

I squeeze softly, before pulling her toward me, my mouth pressing against the warm, round globe, careful not to touch her nipples yet when what I want to do is bite the rings and tug. I've pierced a lot of nipples, but none have ever appealed to me like hers, and she doesn't even have the barbell yet. One hand falls as my lips travel to hers, finding its way between her legs. I tug her panties aside and shove two fingers inside. They're hugging her walls without even spreading.

When my knuckles press against her skin she gyrates against me, riding my fingers, her kiss becoming rough. Everything is liquid heat and swollen. What the fuck is going on with her body?

She breaks. "Please fuck me. It's not enough." The combination of everything is sending me into overdrive in a matter of seconds. And I snap.

My hand surges upward, sending her body higher, long enough to pull my sweats down in the front. When she comes back down I've already got my fingers out and my cock ready. It disappears inside, and with the sound she makes you'd think I just gave her a line of blow. I meet every rock with a thrust, her tits bouncing in ways they never have, making me fucking nuts.

I grab a ring in each thumb and forefinger and pull just enough for her to feel it. She cries out, but the result is her riding my cock so hard it feels like it's seconds from breaking. The comforting, tight hold her pussy has on me causes me to blow. I grip her hips and hold her center against me, grinding her so hard her clit rubs against my pelvis until that beautiful face morphs into the one that makes me a little more psycho than I already am.

As everything stills she looks at me, the words spilling from my lips as my mind works to figure out the fucking puzzle. "I don't know what's different, but I like it."

She smiles and pushes off of me, fixing her panties back in place and pulling up her nightgown. Then she stands. "Happy Thanksgiving, Kross. I ordered a traditional meal since neither of us cook or have families to celebrate with. It was delivered before I came in here. I'll be in the kitchen if you want to eat with me."

And then she walks out.

Thanksgiving? Then I remember. One of those holidays normal people hype up that makes the rest of us cringe because I'm forced to close or I'm chalked up as being an extra cruel asshole. Not that I care, but I could do without all the whining from employees that they are missing out on seeing their family that they don't care to see any other time. It arrived without me even noticing. Normally I'm prepared. This one is the worst one, because what in the fuck have I ever had to be thankful for? Not a damn thing, that's for sure.

I pull my gray sweatpants back into place and stand. But I do have something I don't want to lose. Maybe that's the same thing.

CHAPTER TWENTY

Detta

I park my old Beetle in Kaston's driveway, preparing myself. I've been working myself up about this all week. It's not that easy to get away from Kross. The lack of space is probably why I'm in this pickle in the first place. You can't keep secrets from him without it going unnoticed. So as much as I didn't want to I had to outright lie. I'm supposed to be helping Lux study. I'm still not sure he believed it. Cook, study, be here. What the hell is the difference? The way he looked at me as he sipped his death coffee gave me the hint that he just went along with it because I was trying so damn hard.

I glance out the window at them. Lux is tangled in white Christmas lights and Kaston is on a ladder propped against the house, tugging at her for slack with a staple gun in his opposite hand, attaching the strands along the edging of the roofline. They look awfully domesticated for someone of his classification. I've tried to block out what Kaston does in my mind, because Lux seems very much okay with it, but it's still hard to digest.

Kaston glances my way, and seconds later Lux turns around. She waves me over, her arms the center of a mess of tangles. I grab the pharmacy bag and get out, slamming the door behind me. It's cool today; the air chilled enough for a long sleeve and light jacket. We can thank the cold front coming through. And for once it actually feels like the start of winter instead of December disguised as July, like it was a mere three days ago. Damn bipolar weather.

My feet crunch against the fallen brown leaves as I make my way toward them. "What's up, Delta? It's been a minute," Kaston says, just before the staple gun goes off again. He climbs down to move the ladder, his reach extended.

"Yeah, Kross keeps me busy."

He repositions the ladder where he wants it, a smirk on his face. "Figured as much."

I glance down the house, over half of it already done. "This is very . . . normal of you, Lux. Are you into the whole Christmas tree and candy baking thing now? Because if I remember correctly, you make fun of my little tree every year."

I smile, unable to stop myself. She narrows her eyes at me, before her shoulders fall in the dramatic Lux fashion. Her hair and loose shirt tail blows as the breeze picks up, her perfume mixing with the air. "Do I look like a festive bitch? This was not my idea. I'm just here for moral support, because, well, he puts a roof over my head." She rolls her eyes. "Although, the baking I might consider. But I draw the line at Christmas music. It makes me want to gouge my eyes out."

Kaston stomps up the ladder again in his jeans and flannel shirt, boots making noise against the metal. "I guarantee by next year you'll love Christmas music. Just wait. I've already started Christmas shopping," he retorts. "You know you love gifts."

I stare at him in awe. The way he looks at her there is no doubt he's completely in love with her, and I love him a little more for it. All I can hope is that one-day I have someone that loves me like that. "Um, babe, do you really need me? I think I need some Delta time. I promise I'll be your Christmas tree slave later."

"Get out of here," he says, no irritation in his tone. He turns back toward the ladder, grabbing the strand of lights that's hanging and runs it along the wood so that he can continue outlining the house. Lux loops her arm in mine and tows me toward the house until the door is shut and I'm gaping at the house as big or bigger than Kross'. Touches of Lux all over the house are obvious. But it's massive and beautiful, the staircase a sight in itself. It's definitely no bachelor pad. What the hell does it mean when criminals make this much money?

"Delta." I turn around at the calling of my name. "As glad as I am that you're here, what's wrong? You've never come all the way out here before. You always want to meet in the city when we hang out."

"I think I'm pregnant." As if my tears were waiting for me to admit it aloud, they fall, and once they do the floodgates follow.

Lux

I slump against the bathroom wall, staring at the closed door, my head spinning from the Deja vu. Memories start assaulting me. I breathe deeply. In. Out. In. Out. Just like Kaston taught me. "Pull yourself together. She needs a friend."

The toilet flushes and the door opens, making it easier. She walks out, shutting the door behind her, her back mirroring mine against the door. "It's done."

"What did it say?"

"I don't know yet. It said it takes a minute or so. I'm scared to look." Her voice cracks. "I'm sorry, Lux. I didn't know who else to turn to."

My brows furrow. "Why are you sorry? I'd be pissed if you didn't come to me. You're my best friend. My soul sister."

"You know, because of . . ."

"Sophie?" I breathe out. "It's okay. It's easier to deal with saying her name than to try and avoid it. She should be remembered. I'm good."

"Are you, though? We never talk about her."

One, two, three, four, five, six, seven, eight, nine, ten.

I shove the memories back. "Delta, we both knew at some point—maybe not this soon, but at some point—in life this would happen. You can't tiptoe around my issues. I know for years it controlled your decisions. You're the most loyal friend a girl could have, but you're finally living freely, irresponsibly, and erratically in love. I haven't seen you this happy ever. God knows all of us need that phase a time or two. Some days I'm not so good, but today I'm okay. Right now you need me. Let's face this together."

I can tell she's not telling me what's going on in her head. Delta has always held everything in, but she wears her emotions on her face. She hides behind a thin armor. "How long have you suspected it?"

"Since right after Thanksgiving. We were together that night. He kept saying I was different, repeatedly." She breathes out. "Kross is very different from any guy I've ever known. He's observant.

He picks up on everything and doesn't miss a single detail. I love that about him and I also hate it. I think some of it is his way of understanding change."

Her eyes well up. "You and he have similar backgrounds, ya know. At least from the stuff I know. It feels wrong to tell you without him knowing, so I'm just going to leave it at that. I'm still earning his trust. That night my skin looked 'healthier' I suppose and my boobs were magically the only things bigger on my body. My nipples were sore. Having recently had them pierced I just attributed it to swelling and part of the process. But then he acted like it was completely crazy after that amount of time to assume it should still be painful. I wrote it off to being time for my period. You know I've always been irregular, unlike you. There was no real way to calculate it. But then a few mornings later he was brewing his coffee and a wave of nausea hit. I've been watching ever since. I've never had premenstrual symptoms longer than a week. I've got the bloating without the blood. Still, there is no period, but the symptoms haven't left. Yesterday, my banana nut muffin sent me to the toilet in a run. Either my mind is powerful or I'm pregnant."

"Did your birth control fail?"

Guilt is all over her face. "You remember when I told you I stopped having sex?"

"Yes."

"I also stopped taking my pills. It was a useless expense at the time. I cut it. I didn't think they were necessary, so I just kept Plan B stocked. The problem with that method is that when you start popping them like candy because you're in a relationship you start forgetting that you didn't take them here and there until there aren't any left because you can't find time to get away."

Something doesn't add up. "Was he wearing condoms or is he

like Kaston and suddenly they don't exist?"

"He never wore one and never pulled out. Save the speech. It was stupid of me, I know, and this has never been an issue prior to him, but you don't know Kross like I do. He gets what he wants and I wasn't really against it for some ungodly reason."

"Did you at least discuss the fact that you weren't on birth control? Or what about STDs?"

"No," she cries out, tears rapidly falling. "He's going to be pissed at me. I was going to get more pills and forgot when he unexpectedly took me to Chicago. Fuck, Lux. What am I going to do?"

My brows rise up toward my hairline, surprise settling in. I walk forward, grabbing the door handle. "Well, for starters, let's just get it over with before we get in over our heads and it be negative. You or me?"

She moves to the side. "You. I don't think I can."

I walk in and grab the stick off the back of the toilet, my eyes veering down at it. "Pregnant: 3+ weeks. Definitely pregnant," I say, bumping into a chest that is definitely not Delta's.

I glance up to a man that looks entirely too happy for someone hanging Christmas lights. I remember the pregnancy test is in my hand. I shove it behind my back. "You're pregnant?" he asks, with a big-ass grin on his face.

My face contorts into a mortified expression. "Boy, I'm fixed. Get out of here with that."

His smile falls more than I wish I had noticed. He glances at Delta leaned against the wall, hands behind her back. She has those puppy dog eyes, sad and pleading. "Please don't tell Kross."

"Oh, fuck."

I slap him on the back of the shoulder when she starts crying again, cutting my eyes at him. "Not helping. Out."

He holds up his hands. "Fine. I know when I'm not wanted." He stops in front of her on his way through the door. "In all seriousness, though, don't take his first reaction seriously." He winces a little. "Eh, I've known Kross for a lot longer than it seems. He's going to have to come around. But there's something about you. Always has been." Then he rubs her shoulder in a brotherly way and leaves, taking a little more of my heart as he goes. Damn him.

"What do we do now?"

"Now, we need to call a doctor."

Delta

"I can't afford a doctor. Lux. Why don't we go find a free clinic."

She passes me the clipboard and pen from the receptionist. "You're not going to a fucking free clinic, Delta. I got a doctor to work you in. You're going to see him and I'm going to pay. You're going to let me and not say a damn word. We can try to get you on that government insurance later if you're that hell bent on doing it on your own. We'll figure out the details when all this is done."

I grab it and sit in the closest chair, dropping my purse beside me, before hurrying through each line of the questionnaire with messy handwriting. Lux takes it as I finish and walks back to the check-in, handing it to the receptionist. I glance around; trying to pretend I didn't see her pull out a credit card, round bellies everywhere. A couple exits through the door from the exam room area, smiles on their faces as they look at the strip of ultrasound photos, pointing at various places.

You're never going to have that.

Lux sits back down beside me, dropping her purse on her lap. "What if he breaks it off? He's not Kaston, Lux. I saw the way he looked when he thought it was you. He was happy. That's not going to be the ending for me. I can feel it. Then what am I going to do?"

She turns, taking my hand. "I think you've always been hard on yourself, because of your mom. You don't really think that other people can love you in spite of everything. Kross may not seem like the type of guy that can fall in love, but I have this feeling you'll be surprised, even if it takes a while. The two of you are intense in the same room. It's hard to explain, really. Like a high voltage electrical current swarming around the two of you. It's a little weighted and uncomfortable for the rest of us. I don't think either of you realize it. But if I'm wrong and he turns out to be a douche bag that can nut in you and not man up, then we'll do this together . . . again. Kaston has a small guesthouse in the back that isn't being used."

"I couldn't intrude on your happiness, Lux. It isn't in me."

"Why do you have this warped idea that because I'm with Kaston I can't have you? You're my family, Delta, and a person can't be truly happy without all their family, as in the whole thing, not just part. That means you're also Kaston's family. We've talked. You're not an intrusion, and you never will be."

"I don't know that I can be a mother. I can barely take care of myself."

"You can. If you want to be. And I'm certain you'll do it better than the one you call Mom. Just because we had shitty a mother doesn't mean we have to be one."

"You really would have been a great mother. I remember how peaceful she looked in your arms that day."

Lux squeezes my hand. Her eyes give off the slightest glare, as if she's working to keep her tears at bay. I wish she'd talk about her.

Just once I wish she would let it all out so that she can cleanse her soul instead of keeping it all bottled up. She takes a deep breath, as if giving up. "She would have had a hard life. A baby can't raise another baby. She was too perfect and good to be raised up with a drug dealer as a father. Everything I do is for her. To better myself. To prove to her that she didn't die in vain."

She swipes a tear under her eye. "I dream about her sometimes. She's up there dancing on clouds with a woman I don't recognize in a little white dress, her dirty blonde hair bouncing on her shoulders with a halo made of wild flowers. She has the sweetest laugh and my blue eyes. She's happy. And she's my only. That's how I make peace with it."

My lips are trembling. "Lux . . ." I whisper.

"Delta Rohr."

Lux slides her mask back into place and stands as the girl in scrubs waits for us at the door. "We have to do this. The fire is too hot to pull someone else into this Hell. One of us needs to fight to keep it, and mine gained her wings long before my heart was ready."

CHAPTER TWENTY-ONE

Detta

I stare at the small ultrasound photo from the edge of our bed, my eyes glued to the tiny peanut-looking creature in the middle. Six weeks. That's how far along I am. Which is further than I thought. Far enough I saw the tiny flicker in the middle they said was the heartbeat. It's old enough to have a beating heart. To have large eye sockets that remind me of an alien. To have a body even though it looks more like a fish with a tail than a person. We created a human. Kross and I. We have a baby floating around inside of me.

It's hard to wrap my mind around.

It's not yet big enough to make itself known, but it's there, living in me; its mother. *Take care of it,* the doctor said. It's depending on me. It can't survive without my help. And as crazy as it seems, I love it already. Our baby. Boy or girl? Will it look like Kross or me? Will it be healthy? What will it be like to have a baby? Will I be a good mom? Will he help me?

All questions swarming around in my mind. None of which I have an answer to. All I can do is stare. Stare at the one thing I didn't mean to happen. The thing that I never thought I'd have. The thing I've always been the most careful to avoid. The thing I also want desperately. The one thing I will sacrifice everything else to keep . . . even Kross.

"Delta!" he calls out, close to the door. I quickly shove the photo under the mattress, not ready to tell him. I'm not sure how. And until I do—know how that is—I'll keep it to myself.

The door swings open. My mouth parts at what exists on the other side. I close it before drool has a chance to exit. Athletic shorts hung low on the hips, sneakers, and no shirt with a straight bill hat tipped to the side of his forehead. Sweat glistening, making his tattoos stand out even more. Why the fuck is he not wearing a shirt?

His abs contract with every breath. How is it fair for any man to look that yummy? Furthermore, how the hell did I end up having sex with that? I can't ever remember a time I've been with a man that physically attractive. "You're back?"

The paranoia hits. "Yes. You're sweaty. Where have you been?"

"Gym."

"Is that where you were when you left before we went to Chicago?"

"Yes."

"Do you go often?"

"Almost daily."

It feels stupid asking these questions, considering we live together and are with each other more times than not. But I always try not to question him too much. "When?"

"While you sleep."

"Oh."

"What are you looking at?"

"Seriously? Do you not know how hot you are?"

He raises a brow. "Can't say that I do."

I fall back against the mattress, arms splaying to my sides. "Of course you don't. You're the one asshole that's an asshole for totally different reasons than the rest."

The next thing I know he's leaning over me, staring down into my eyes. Deodorant, manly musk of sweat and soap, and hints of faded cologne. All scents attacking me in ways they never have. I close my eyes. "Fuck, even your sweat smells good," I whine.

A gush of wetness fills my panties as his lips touch down on my neck, his tongue swiping out halfway through his descent to my breast. He stops at the neckline of my V-neck shirt, not far from my nipple with a small tug of the fabric. My eyes open, one peek at a time, when I can no longer feel him. "Why are you stopping?"

He laughs. To the point that it's contagious. "I'm guessing you missed me."

"Maybe . . ."

"Want to go downstairs and practice?"

It's become my favorite thing to do with him. And since the day he showed me the studio downstairs he's kept his promise. We usually practice three to four times a week, but with the news so fresh there is no way I can concentrate on that right now. "Are you in the giving mood?"

"Maybe," he copies from earlier.

"Then I have a better idea."

"And what's that?"

I take a deep breath, preparing for the response I intend to get, but watching Kaston and Lux prepare for the holidays has rubbed off on me. "Can we put up a Christmas tree? I have one in storage. It's only tabletop height. It's not much, but it's something. I usually have it up by the first of December."

"I've never had a Christmas tree."

I frown. "That makes me sad."

He shrugs. "No big deal. Can't miss what you've never had."

"It's a big deal to me. Please."

"If you'll pick out all the shit, then yes. I just need to get a shower and we'll go."

"I didn't mean you had to buy one. We can use mine."

He kisses me, a smirk slowly growing. "No offense, but if we're going to 'put up' a Christmas tree, then it might as well be a normal sized tree that you actually have to 'put up' or 'put together'. You can put your Charlie Brown tree on the side table in the lobby at the shop. Cassie would probably love it."

I smile, growing more excited with the thought of us shopping together for our very own tree. "What happened to that whole phrase, 'size isn't everything'?"

"Every man knows that was made up bullshit by a woman trying to justify being stuck with a little dick for whatever reason. No one ever chooses little anything when given the choice."

"I guess it's good for me that size was on your side then, because there is nothing little about you."

He snatches the waistband of my yoga pants and rips them down my legs, before taking stance on the bed with his hands on the insides of my thighs. "I thought we were getting ready to leave."

"I've got to take care of something first."

His mouth then touches down on my lips, legs wide. His tongue spreads me open, my bottom already jerking forward. "Shit. You're so good at that."

He grunts against me, leaving no time for words before everything blurs except the feeling of his tongue wading through my folds, the tip striking against my clit in a repetitive, quick motion. And I'll be damned if this doesn't feel better than any time before.

CHAPTER TWENTY-TWO

I glance at the large nine foot Christmas tree I put together about an hour ago standing tall in the corner of the room from my recliner. I wasn't expecting this to take so long. "What exactly are you doing?"

She straightens from the bent over position she's in, eliminating the view I had of her ass. "You can't just go hanging ornaments on the grouped branches. You have to fluff. There is an art to this."

"Says the person that had a tabletop tree?"

She rolls her eyes. "You're such a cynical person. I haven't always had a tabletop tree. My mother actually did like Christmas. Decorating the tree was the one thing she did with me every year. For a few hours she pretended to like me." She scratches at her chin, a thoughtful expression. "Could have been the spiked eggnog.

Even with the horrible Merry fucking Christmas music in the background that makes me feel like I want to slit my throat, I can't imagine someone not liking Delta, yet she says it so often, so freely, like it doesn't bother her at all. "I'd likely kill your mother if I ever met her."

She laughs, as if I'm joking. "I'm sure I've had the thought a time or two."

"It's not a thought. It's a fact."

Her playful mood ceases. "She's not worth getting put in jail over, Kross. Someone would report her stupid ass missing. She's too social and fake to everyone that doesn't know her personally. She has a likable personality. And, well, she is my mother."

I spin the blade of the knife between my fingers, trying to keep them occupied. I don't do well with sitting for long periods of time if I'm not tattooing. I need to be doing something to keep my head clear. Oddly, she helps. "What makes you think I'd get caught?"

"You know, that thing called forensics and all."

"Has to be a body."

"I'm not sure I want to know, but how many people have you . . ."

"Killed?"

"Yes."

I drag the blade against my stubble, lightly scratching my face. "No clue. Enough to know I liked it too much to keep going the way I was. I had to tone it down to killing out of necessity instead of letting my temper control me."

She stares at me, wide-eyed. "Well, pretending I didn't hear that . . . and like I said, she is my mother, so . . ."

"I don't know much about parenting and never will, but I would think that genetics doesn't entitle you to treat someone like shit."

She flinches as if I slapped her. Something is going on. I'm not sure what. She walks toward me, straddling my lap. My hands go to her hips, pulling her closer. Her hands encircle my neck. "You said your mother abandoned you? Do you remember her?"

"No."

"Anything? Other than the neon."

"Leave it."

Her green eyes deepen in color. And then she says something that stabs me in the chest harder than a serrated edged blade. "I thought you trusted me."

"I have dreams sometimes. They aren't attached to a memory. They just exist in my mind. I don't remember them actually happening."

"Do you ever dream about her?"

"I don't know. I dream about a woman, but she was young. I'm not sure who she is. She couldn't have been more than twenty-one, give or take."

My body feels weighted, paralyzed to this goddamned chair.

"Do you know anything about her?"

"Her name is Rachel."

She places her palm over my pounding heart. I try to blink away the flickers fighting to come back. I've never said that name aloud to anyone else. Her lips touch down on mine and everything disappears, leaving me in peace once again. "I'm sorry. No more today."

She stands, tugging on my hands. "Come on. Enough of all this serious talk. We have a tree to decorate."

For once, I welcome something normal, because those demons are never welcome, yet they haunt me every chance they get.

CHAPTER TWENTY-THREE

Detta

I grab a handful of toilet paper to wipe my mouth, my throat burning and eyes watering from emptying my stomach. I watch as the water in the toilet swirls around, ridding of the evidence. Another wave of nausea hits, sending me into a folded over position once again. I groan when it's over, falling against the wall of the guest bathroom, my abs hurting from constricting so many times. "No need in writing this Christmas Eve down in the books. I won't forget this."

"What are you hiding from me?" I jump, my feet almost leaving the floor. Kross is leaning through the doorway, arms clenched so tight around the top of the frame his muscles are strained. He does not look happy.

I take a deep breath, warding off the nausea that's still lingering. It wasn't my intention to keep it from him this long, but after he said he'd never be a parent I got scared. I know there is a very real possibility I could lose him after this, and I think I've been trying to bide more time. But the truth is, I'm tired of keeping it a secret. Honestly, it's a lot of work.

I stare into his eyes, trying to will my lips to say the words. *Don't leave me,* my brain chants instead. He straightens. "I'm pregnant," I blurt out.

"Jesus Christ, Delta! How?"

His anger is evident. It's written all over his face. My nerves take a turn for the worst. "What do you mean how? You haven't worn a condom, ever. And I don't recall a single time you've pulled out."

A look I've been dreading falls over him. His voice is accusing, raw, and angry. "And birth control?"

"I haven't been on it in a couple of years. I got off of it when I *stopped* having sex. You never asked. I never told. I just took Plan B every time we had sex. Well, every time that I can remember. I ran out before we left for Chicago and never had the option to stop at a pharmacy. It's not exactly easy to get away, Kross."

"Do you think I would have still nut in you had you told me you weren't on birth control?"

"We never discussed birth control! Not even the first time when you plowed into me in the dressing room of the club."

"Well I assumed if you were whoring around at a strip club you were protecting yourself from a bastard like me."

My mouth shuts, taken aback. My skin is tingling as if a slap lingers, even though the action never ensued. I breathe heavily, my anger raging through my body, masking the hurt I feel in my heart. "You gonna pin this on me?"

"You should have told me."

"Like you should have asked if you could fuck me without a

condom the first time, or fuck me for that matter! It's done. There is no sense in arguing on should haves."

He scrubs his face in his palms, agitated. "How long have you known?"

"I'm eight weeks now. I was six at the ultrasound."

He looks at me in a way he never has. Guilt settles within my veins. "You've lied to me for that long? You went to a doctor without even telling me? What else have you lied about? Is it even mine?" he spits.

I narrow my eyes at him, insulted. "You know what? Fuck you!" I surge forward, angry, trying to blow past him. I don't get past a hard chest blocking the door. "Move, Kross."

His jaw works back and forth. He comes at me full force, lifting me and shoving me against the bathroom door. Pants drop. Panties tear. I'm filled to the brim with hot, hard muscle. My head slams against the wood, taking every beating of his balls against my center as he pounds himself inside of me, over and over, no remorse for taking what he wants without asking. I moan; my arms wrapped around his neck.

He thrusts inside and stops, before taking my hips and forcing them to move in a constant circle as our bodies grind against each other. I rock against him, my orgasm already building. I explode, everything tensing and tightening around him. He clenches my hips and finishes inside of me, his fingers digging into my skin as his head goes to the crook of my neck. "I love you," I say, unable to stop the words from spilling.

He pulls out of me and sets me back on my feet, repositioning his gray sweatpants, a mask already in place. "Get rid of it, Delta. Who I am won't change—not for anyone—and there is no place for a kid in the equation. It's a parasite. I told you to run. You chose to stay. I had you first, and I won't share." My eyes well up. I don't even recognize the eyes staring back at me. They're void, lifeless, and soulless. He rubs his thumb along my bottom lip, before his lips press against mine, but only for a moment. "I told you I was a bad man. Figure out the cost and I'll pay it."

Then he walks away, leaving me completely alone, and with the sound of the front door slamming shut, I break. My back presses against the wall. The air rushes from my lungs as if I've been holding it in for many minutes. I slide down the sheetrock. The tears run down my face with no direction of where they're going. A wail tears from my throat in a sound I don't recognize.

He doesn't want it.

He called our baby a parasite.

He asked me to kill our child.

I knew I could lose him, but I never imagined he would keep me and make me get rid of it like it's a pest. My hands go to my belly, instinctively trying to protect the tiny baby growing inside of me. Then it hits me. I have a choice. It's my body. The only way this baby is going is if I go. He wants to kill it then he'll have to kill me too.

The answer becomes obvious. I have to leave. I have to find my own way. I have to do this alone, even if that means sacrificing every dream I have to make it. I have to fight for my baby. I have to do right by it. It may not have the world, but it will be loved. It will know that someone wanted it. It will know that it's worth everything, even the man I've fallen completely in love with, despite who is he. This baby will know its life meant something.

I've walked away from everything before; I can do it again. Even if it destroys me this time. Somehow I will pull myself out of it, because when I hold my baby and know that I created it, brought it into this world, it'll all be worth it.

I walk toward the front door now decorated with a wreath and anchored by two lit up potted trees. I take a deep breath, my fist pausing a few inches from the door. Finally, I knock, and wait for it to open.

Kaston stands on the other side, studying my tear-stained face and then his eyes trail to the suitcase behind me. "He knows?"

I nod, unable to speak. My voice is gone and my heart is butchered inside my chest. I've cried until I feel like there is nothing left. I love him, and I don't want to leave. Deep down I think Kross just needs someone to love him. I think he needs someone to remind him daily that he's worth more than his scars. I truly believe that if he experienced life with someone that treated him like he's irreplaceable he'd learn to love another. The broken man lies beneath layers upon layers of armor, in need of healing, of forgiveness, and to know that he's good, regardless of what anyone has ever told him.

I wanted that person to be me. I wanted us to work this out somehow. I wanted him to be my forever. Neither of us knows what the hell we're doing, but my hopes were that we would figure it out together. But sometimes in life we have to lose one thing to gain another. If anyone knows this it's me. I left Chuck to find myself. I walked away from my mother for freedom.

Freedom to love without restriction. Freedom from the chains I was in seeking her love. Freedom from a life of being taken for granted. One day I woke up and realized life is too short for misery.

That I was worth more. I am *more*. We all just want to love someone in the end. And even more, we want to be loved. I'm tired of giving love and not getting it in return. This is me *believing* that I'm more. I made a choice. I chose my baby, because everyone deserves to be wanted.

Kaston opens the door all the way and walks outside, lifting my large duffel bag off the walkway, and pulls me into a side embrace, before leading me toward the door. "Give him time, Delta. Kross is slow to open but when he does he never lets go. People like that are lifers. He'll come around. You can stay here as long as it takes."

"I wish I could believe you, but in this case, I don't think he will."

We walk inside the door and he shuts it behind us. "Kross doesn't do well with change. He thrives on routine. The way he adapts is very different from the rest of us, and I'm sure he has underlying reasons that even I haven't figured out yet, but for any guy fatherhood is scary as hell. And Kross is nothing like the rest. Remember, I warned you. He will adjust in his own way."

"What about you? You didn't look scared when you thought it was Lux."

His hands go into his pants pockets after sitting my bag down. "That's not true. Only two things scare me: the thought of losing Lux and the idea of being a father, but I found my girl. Settling down is something I've thought about for years off and on. Unlike the rest of you three, I had a father that gave a damn, and one that believed in the sanctity of marriage for love, so it would only make sense that I'm more prepared."

"Delta?"

I glance up at Lux standing at the top of the stairs. I shrug at her. She comes running and embraces me. Unable to stop them, the waterworks start again. "You'll get through this. I'll be by your side the whole way."

Here we are again—her and me against the world, facing the shit thrown at us full force. I close my eyes, letting the Deja vu take over, only this time . . . in reverse.

THEIR STORY CONTINUES IN LOVE AND WAR: VOLUME TWO

Available Now!

ALSO BY CHARISSE SPIERS

Do I have any music lovers here? Do you want access to my "Love and War" Spotify playlist? Here's the link below (click playlist) . . .

Love and War Playlist

P.S. I feel I should explain my book playlists first before you go "what? 130 something songs." lol. Mine are not traditional book playlists at 12 or so songs. These are my "writing playlists" so the more songs the better since I listen as I write. When I hear a song, if a certain couple starts playing out scenes in my head, that song goes onto their playlist. Not EVERY word of EVERY song will be accurate to the plot, but the feel, the emotions behind the song, the mood, the lyrics, and the vibe in general—all that goes into the development of my stories, so if you want to listen, there it is. Free accounts can listen in shuffle mode with the occasional commercial.

xoxo,

Charisse

If you liked the men of *Inked aKross the Skin,* there will be a spin-off series with Kross, Delta, their life in tattoo, and the characters in the shop (at some point). I'm already getting requests for Johnny's book, Wesson's, and Remington's. The stories are talking, if I can just find the time to write them.

A NOTE FROM THE AUTHOR

Thank you for taking the time to read Love and War: Volume One. Volume Two is currently available to finish their story. I hope you liked reading it as much as I did writing it. I know you have to keep an open mind, but there were things I did not want to omit in fear you would not get the most accurate feel for Kross and who he is. Yes, it ended on a cliffhanger and I don't do them often, but I hope you will give the rest a chance. Volume Two, I feel, is the best part. I had to do it this way to keep it from being too long, and to give you an emotional break. I hope part one was fun and gave you a few laughs. You will need it to go into part two, because the darkest part is to come. The rest of their story is not for the faint of heart. The dark themes may contain emotional triggers for some. Please read with caution.

Kross and Delta are a very different couple for me. They have a special place in my heart and they have been demanding an out for quite some time. I had to be in the right frame of mind to write their story. Kross is much darker than any character I've ever written, but I think his story is the most worthwhile. I know a lot of you have been waiting on it for a long time, and finally, it is here. Thank you for your patience to this point, and I hope that you will find it was worth it.

Please, if you love the stories that we put our blood and sweat into, consider leaving a review on the retailer of your choice.

XOXO,
Charisse

ACKNOWLEDGMENTS

As I embark on my fourth year publishing anniversary, I want to say how truly blessed I am to be a part of this community. I don't always frequent social media if you're a loyal follower, because I use it as a business platform and not a personal tool, but I am there. I do get on and check notifications, answer messages, comments, and tags as long as I see it. I participate as time allows. Usually Instagram is where I post the most. Between a full time job, being a wife, a mother, and trying to give time to my writing life and attention to my characters, sometimes it's not often.

This community has pulled me through some dark times, and it gave me a life I never even dreamed of. That is why my biography will always be in first person, giving you a small personal look into what makes me, me, and to show how much books impacted my life, not only as an author, but first a reader. I still sit on the other side of books, allowing myself to get lost in the characters as merely a reader, letting all the feels consume me as I experience someone else's story. It is something I'll never give up completely, no matter how busy I become with my own books.

Writing, on the other hand, is also something I need. It's an outlet for me. Did I sit as I child and envision myself as being a writer like so many did—no. But now that I'm here, I think, how did I ever get along without it? In that sense it's like being a mother. You don't know what you're missing until it becomes a part of you, and then, you know you can't live without it. Fiction is a happy place for me. The stories are my literary babies—something I pour my heart and soul into—and the reader gives them the magic to come to life through reading, loving, recommending, making teasers and leaving reviews.

If you're still reading, I want to thank the readers for continuing to support my writing. I know I don't always write in the order you may want, but know that every book will come out when it's supposed to. It has not been forgotten, not even Fate series. For me, the characters choose who is written next, and some of them are stronger than others. The ones that follow on social media do not go unnoticed. Your comments make me smile. Even the readers that remain publicly silent, but continue to purchase book after book, thank you. You all make the hard work worthwhile and keep the stories flowing. You guys are my motivation to continue day after day, year after year.

Thank you to my cover designer, Clarise Tan with CT Cover Creations, on such a beautiful cover. You, girl, are my Rockstar. Every design scheme in my head you execute better than I imagined.

Thank you to Darren Birks with Darren Birks photography for a kickass Delta, also known as Isabella "Bella" Frayne, and to Golden Czermak with Furious Fotog for the only Kross that ever fit, Andrew England. Both of these photographers put in so much time and effort to find and bring us authors models that make our characters that much more real. If you visit their website or social media pages, give them a shout out for their awesome hard work and tell them I sent you.

If you would like to be the first to know about my releases, giveaways, or excerpts, you are welcome to sign up for my newsletter. I promise I won't spam your inbox.

Elizabeth Thiele, my assistant, thank you for all the hard work you put in year after year that we've been together, even having a family of your own. Had you not come to me all those years ago after reading one of my books, I would have missed out on a beautiful friendship. I hope you will be there alongside me for many years to come.

Thank you to my beta readers; those I gladly call friends— Tammy Huckabee, Susan Walker, and Innergoddess booklover (for her privacy)

Last but not least, thank you to one of my very best friends, Nancy Henderson, writing under N. E. Henderson—my partner in crime, author buddy, signing co-author, print formatter and editor. Not only are you my best friend day in and day out, but also the person that helps me make my books better, my personal motivator, and the only one that truly understands what it's like to have characters screaming stories at you. We talk fiction as if they're real, for hours on end. I don't know what it'd be like to go a day without talking to you. You, and your never-ending love for Kross is probably why he's here now. If you haven't read her books, check them out. I know, personally, that you'll love them too. Visit her website here

Here's a toast to another year. I love you all.

XOXO,

Charisse

ABOUT THE AUTHOR

I found books when I was going through a hard time in life. They became my means of escape when things got bad. I realized quickly how much I loved to take a backseat to someone else's life and watch the journey unfold. That began my journey with books in November of 2012. I constantly had a book open on my Kindle app. Never in a million years would I have imagined myself as a writer, because I never thought I was creative enough. I'm living proof that things will fall into place when they're meant to be. People will make their way into our lives when we don't expect it, setting the path for what we are meant to do. Never give up on people. Never stop taking a chance on others. Someone took a chance on trusting me with her work when she didn't know me from a stranger on the street and gave me the opportunity of a lifetime as our relationship progressed, which led me to editing and writing as well. This is my dream I never knew I had. As soon as I sat down and gave writing a shot, it was like the floodgates opened. Now, I am lost in a world of fiction in my head, new characters constantly screaming for their stories to be told. Continue to dream and to go for them. No one ever found happiness by sitting on the sidelines. Sometimes we have to take risks and put ourselves out there. Thank you for all of your support, and may there be many books to come. XOXO- C

Stay up to date on release info
www.charissespiers.com
charissespiersbooks@gmail.com

Printed in Great Britain
by Amazon

76119961R00179